... examines them with greater acuity and forgiveness, than she does' Michael Chabon

'Karen Joy Fowler has written the book she's always had in her to write' Ursula K. Le Guin

'One of the greatest pleasures I take in reading is being able to hand over the books that thrill me, which this summer would be Karen Joy Fowler's *We Are All Completely Beside Ourselves*' Ann Patchett, *Wall Street Journal*

'A gripping and surreptitiously intelligent book about a family's falling apart after a young daughter is sent away ... The book is far deeper and more ambitious, however, than its central conceit would lead one to think' Khaled Hosseini

'Intelligent and forces the reader to question what we owe our fellow creatures' Elizabeth George

'[An] achingly funny, deeply serious heartbreaker ... This is a moral comedy to shout about from the treetops' Liz Jensen, *Guardian*

'There have been many books written about sibling love and rivalry but few, I'm sure, can rend the heart and bore beneath the skin quite like this one ... prepare to be charmed and traumatised' Carol Midgley, *The Times*

'Karen Joy Fowler's smart, witty take on what constitutes a family, and the part the individual ingredients play in the whole, is a beautifully skewed look at domestic relationships' John Harding, *Daily Mail*

'Utterly beguiling ... combines a precise Austenian sensitivity to emotional nuance with the discomforted perception of a narrator who feels herself an alien ... has an unforgettable, tender ferocity' Jane Shilling, *New Statesman*

'Anyone with an interest in animals – human or otherwise – will love this book' Henry Nicholls, *Guardian*

'A novel that is both one giant moral compass and a harrowing depiction of a family's implosion, the prose of which zings on the pages ... deserves to be acclaimed for the right reasons' Lucy Scholes, *Observer*

'Delivers an unforgettable "I didn't see that coming!" moment ... Asks the important questions, about how and why we love one another, what happens when that love is taken away, and what responsibility we have once we instil and respond to love ... an irresistible, if often distressing, read' Lesley McDowell, *Independent on Sunday*

'A heartbreaking, heartening read, asking complex, disturbing questions with a witty elegance' Eithne Farry, *Sunday Express*

'An unsentimental but profoundly compassionate and deeply moral look at what it means to be human and how people treat creatures who are different to them ... If ever there was a popular novel – or at least, one that deserves to be – that blends comedy and tragedy, this is it' Tina Jackson, *Metro*

'An unsettling, emotionally complex story that plumbs the mystery of our strange relationship with the animal kingdom – relatives included' Ron Charles, *Washington Post*

'One of the best twists in years makes this novel unique, captivating and so moving it will stay with you for a long time' *Stylist*

'*We Are All Completely Beside Ourselves* is that rare thing, a comic novel that wrestles seriously with serious moral questions' *Salon*

'Smart, funny, moving' *Marie Claire*

'Very good indeed ... nothing less than a full-on exploration of what makes human beings human' *Reader's Digest*

'Rosemary's voice hooked me in, making it impossible to put down this thought-provoking, moving and entertaining novel' *Woman & Home*

'This novel is weighty, yet written with a lightness of touch ... It charts a profound philosophic journey, mixing wit with scientific rigour. The result might be Fowler's most important work yet' *Sydney Morning Herald*

'A masterful novel, painful and memorable, and, like all the best novels, it will stay with you long afterwards' *Psychologies*

'A beautifully written, compelling story, peopled with quirky, memorable characters, an engaging and moving tale recounted by a wonderful, original, witty narrator' Justine Carbery, *Sunday Independent* (Ireland)

'Fowler has given us the gift of a splendid novel. Not only is the story fascinating, moving and beautifully written, but also it ripples with humour' *Boston Globe*

WE
ARE ALL
Completely
BESIDE
OURSELVES

KAREN JOY FOWLER

A complete catalogue record for this book can be obtained from the British Library on request

First published in the USA in 2013 as a Marian Wood Book by G.P Putnam's Sons, New York

This paperback edition published in 2021
First published in the UK in 2014 by Serpent's Tail,
an imprint of Profile Books Ltd
29 Cloth Fair
London EC1A 7JQ
www.serpentstail.com

The passages from Franz Kafka's 'A Report for an Academy' are quoted
from a translation prepared by Ian Johnston of Malaspina University-College
(now Vancouver Island University), Nanaimo, British Columbia, Canada.

The poem by Issa is quoted from a translation that appeared
on Yoshi Mikami's Issa's Haiku home page.

Lyrics are quoted from 'The Hukilau Song' by Jack Owens, and
'Love Potion No. 9' by Jerry Leiber and Mike Stoller.

'On Apes in the Wild' © Copyright by Richard Wrangham 2014

ISBN 978 1 78816 710 9
eISBN 978 1 78283 020 7

Printed and bound in Great Britain by
CPI Group (UK) Ltd, Croydon CR0 4YY

1098765432

... Your experience as apes, gentlemen—to the extent that you have something of that sort behind you—cannot be more distant from you than mine is from me. But it tickles at the heels of everyone who walks here on earth, the small chimpanzee as well as the great Achilles.

—FRANZ KAFKA, "A Report for an Academy"

PROLOGUE

THOSE WHO KNOW ME NOW will be surprised to learn that I was a great talker as a child. We have a home movie taken when I was two years old, the old-fashioned kind with no sound track, and by now the colors have bled out—a white sky, my red sneakers a ghostly pink—but you can still see how much I used to talk.

I'm doing a bit of landscaping, picking up one stone at a time from our gravel driveway, carrying it to a large tin washtub, dropping it in, and going back for the next. I'm working hard, but showily. I widen my eyes like a silent film star. I hold up a clear piece of quartz to be admired, put it in my mouth, stuff it into one cheek.

My mother appears and removes it. She steps back then, out of the frame, but I'm speaking emphatically now—you can see this in my gestures—and she returns, drops the stone into the tub. The whole thing lasts about five minutes and I never stop talking.

A few years later, Mom read us that old fairy tale in which one sister (the older) speaks in toads and snakes and the other (the younger) in flowers and jewels, and this is the image it conjured for me, this scene from this movie, where my mother puts her hand into my mouth and pulls out a diamond.

I was towheaded back then, prettier as a child than I've turned out, and dolled up for the camera. My flyaway bangs are pasted down with water and held on one side by a rhinestone barrette shaped like a bow. Whenever I turn my head, the barrette blinks in the sunlight. My little hand sweeps over my tub of rocks. All this, I could be saying, all this will be yours someday.

Or something else entirely. The point of the movie isn't the words themselves. What my parents valued was their extravagant abundance, their inexhaustible flow.

Still, there were occasions on which I had to be stopped. When you think of two things to say, pick your favorite and only say that, my mother suggested once, as a tip to polite social behavior, and the rule was later modified to one in three. My father would come to my bedroom door each night to wish me happy dreams and I would speak without taking a breath, trying desperately to keep him in my room with only my voice. I would see his hand on the doorknob, the door beginning to swing shut. I have something to say! I'd tell him, and the door would stop midway.

Start in the middle then, he'd answer, a shadow with the hall light behind him, and tired in the evenings the way grown-ups are. The light would reflect in my bedroom window like a star you could wish on.

Skip the beginning. Start in the middle.

PART ONE

❋

The storm which blew me out of my past eased off.

—Franz Kafka, "A Report for an Academy"

I

So the middle of my story comes in the winter of 1996. By then, we'd long since dwindled to the family that old home movie foreshadowed—me, my mother, and, unseen but evident behind the camera, my father. In 1996, ten years had passed since I'd last seen my brother, seventeen since my sister disappeared. The middle of my story is all about their absence, though if I hadn't told you that, you might not have known. By 1996, whole days went by in which I hardly thought of either one.

1996. Leap year. Year of the Fire Rat. President Clinton had just been reelected; this would all end in tears. Kabul had fallen to the Taliban. The Siege of Sarajevo had ended. Charles had recently divorced Diana.

Hale-Bopp came swinging into our sky. Claims of a Saturn-like object in the comet's wake first surfaced that November. Dolly, the cloned sheep, and Deep Blue, the chess-playing computer program, were superstars. There was evidence of life on Mars. The Saturn-like object in Hale-Bopp's tail was maybe an alien spaceship. In May of '97, thirty-nine people would kill themselves as a prerequisite to climbing aboard.

Against this backdrop, how ordinary I look. In 1996, I was

twenty-two years old, meandering through my fifth year at the University of California, Davis, and still maybe only a junior or maybe a senior, but so thoroughly uninterested in the niceties of units or requirements or degrees that I wouldn't be graduating anytime soon. My education, my father liked to point out, was wider than it was deep. He said this often.

But I saw no reason to hurry. I'd no particular ambitions beyond being either widely admired or stealthily influential—I was torn between the two. It hardly mattered, as no major seemed to lead reliably to either.

My parents, who were still paying my expenses, found me aggravating. My mother was often aggravated those days. It was something new for her, analeptic doses of righteous aggravation. She was rejuvenated by it. She'd recently announced that she was through being a translator and go-between for me and my father; he and I had hardly spoken since. I don't remember minding. My father was himself a college professor and a pedant to the bone. Every exchange contained a lesson, like the pit in a cherry. To this day, the Socratic method makes me want to bite someone.

Autumn came suddenly that year, like a door opening. One morning I was bicycling to class when a large flock of Canada geese passed overhead. I couldn't see them, or much of anything else, but I heard the jazzy honking above me. There was a tule fog off the fields and I was wrapped inside it, pedaling through clouds. Tule fogs are not like other fogs, not spotty or drifting, but fixed and substantial. Probably anyone would have felt the risk of moving quickly through an unseen world, but I have—or had as a child—a particular penchant for slapstick and mishap, so I took the full thrill from it.

I felt polished by the wet air and maybe just a little migratory myself, just a little wild. This meant I might flirt a bit in the library if I sat next to anyone flirtable or I might daydream in class. I often felt wild back then; I enjoyed the feeling, but nothing had ever come of it.

At lunchtime I grabbed something, probably grilled cheese, let's say it was grilled cheese, in the school cafeteria. I was in the habit of leaving my books on the chair next to me, where they could be quickly moved if someone interesting came by but would discourage the uninteresting. At twenty-two, I had the callowest possible definition of interesting and, by the measure of my own calipers, was far from interesting myself.

A couple was sitting at a table near me and the girl's voice gradually rose to the point where I was forced to pay attention. "You want some fucking space?" she said. She was wearing a short blue T-shirt and a necklace with a glass pendant of an angelfish. Long, dark hair fell in a messy braid down her back. She stood and cleared the table with one motion of her arm. She had beautiful biceps; I remember wishing I had arms like hers.

Dishes fell to the floor and shattered; catsup and cola spilled and mixed in the breakage. There must have been music in the background, because there's always music in the background now, our whole lives sound-tracked (and most of it too ironic to be random. I'm just saying), but honestly I don't remember. Maybe there was only a sweet silence and the spit of grease on the grill.

"How's that?" the girl asked. "Don't tell me to be quiet. I'm just making more space for you." She pushed the table itself over, swung it to one side, dropped it. "Better?" She raised her voice. "Can everyone please leave the room so my boyfriend has more space? He needs a fucking lot of space." She slammed her chair down onto the pile of catsup and dishes. More sounds of breakage and a sudden waft of coffee.

The rest of us were frozen—forks halfway to our mouths, spoons dipped in our soups, the way people were found after the eruption of Vesuvius.

"Don't do this, baby," her boyfriend said once, but she was doing it and he didn't bother to repeat himself. She moved to another table, empty except for a tray with dirty dishes. There, she methodically broke everything that could be broken, threw everything that could be thrown. A saltshaker spun across the floor to my foot.

A young man rose from his seat, telling her, with a slight stutter, to take a chill pill. She threw a spoon that bounced audibly off his forehead. "Don't side with assholes," she said. Her voice was very not chill.

He sank back, eyes wide. "I'm okay," he assured the room at large, but he sounded unconvinced. And then surprised. "Holy shit! I've been assaulted."

"This is just the shit I can't take," the boyfriend said. He was a big guy, with a thin face, loose jeans, and a long coat. Nose like a knife. "You go ahead and tear it up, you psycho bitch. Just give me back the key to my place first."

She swung another chair, missing my head by maybe four feet—I'm being charitable; it seemed like a lot less—striking my table and upsetting it. I grabbed my glass and plate. My books hit the floor with a loud slap. "Come and get it," she told him.

It struck me funny, a cook's invitation over a pile of broken plates, and I laughed once, convulsively, a strange duck-like hoot that made everyone turn. And then I stopped laughing, because it was no laughing matter, and everyone turned back. Through the glass walls I could see some people on the quad who'd noticed the commotion and were watching. A threesome on their way in for lunch stopped short at the door.

"Don't think I won't." He took a few steps in her direction. She scooped up a handful of catsup-stained sugar cubes and threw them.

"I'm finished," he said. "We're finished. I'm putting your shit in the hallway and I'm changing the locks." He turned and she threw a glass, which bounced off his ear. He missed a step, staggered, touched the spot with one hand, checked his fingers for blood. "You owe me for gas," he said without looking back. "Mail it." And he was gone.

There was a moment's pause as the door closed. Then the girl turned on the rest of us. "What are you losers looking at?" She picked up one of the chairs and I couldn't tell if she was going to put it back or throw it. I don't think she'd decided.

A campus policeman arrived. He approached me cautiously, hand on his holster. Me! Standing above my toppled table and chair, still holding my harmless glass of milk and my plate with the harmless half-eaten grilled cheese sandwich. "Just put it down, honey," he said, "and sit for a minute." Put it down where? Sit where? Nothing in my vicinity was upright but me. "We can talk about this. You can tell me what's going on. You're not in any trouble yet."

"Not her," the woman behind the counter told him. She was a large woman, and old—forty or more—with a beauty mark on her upper lip and eyeliner collecting in the corners of her eyes. You all act like you own the place, she'd said to me once, on another occasion, when I sent back a burger for more cooking. But you just come and go. You don't even think how I'm the one who stays.

"The tall one," she told the cop. She pointed, but he was paying no attention, so intent on me and whatever my next move would be.

"Calm down," he said again, soft and friendly. "You're not in any trouble yet." He stepped forward, passing right by the girl with the braid and the chair. I saw her eyes behind his shoulder.

"Never a policeman when you need one," she said to me. She smiled and it was a nice smile. Big white teeth. "No rest for the wicked." She hoisted the chair over her head. "No soup for you." She launched it away from me and the cop, toward the door. It landed on its back.

When the policeman turned to look, I dropped my plate and my fork. I honestly didn't mean to. The fingers of my left hand just unclenched all of a sudden. The noise spun the cop back to me.

I was still holding my glass, half full of milk. I raised it a little, as if proposing a toast. "Don't do it," he said, a whole lot less friendly now. "I'm not playing around here. Don't you fucking test me."

And I threw the glass onto the floor. It broke and splashed milk over one of my shoes and up into my sock. I didn't just let it go. I threw that glass down as hard as I could.

2

FORTY MINUTES LATER, the psycho bitch and I were tucked like ticks into the back of a Yolo County police car, the matter now being way too big for the guileless campus cops. Handcuffed, too, which hurt my wrists a great deal more than I'd ever imagined it would.

Being arrested had seriously improved the woman's mood. "I *told* him I wasn't fucking around," she said, which was almost exactly what the campus cop had also said to me, only more in sorrow than in triumph. "So glad you decided to come with. I'm Harlow Fielding. Drama department."

No shit.

"I never met a Harlow before," I said. I meant a first name Harlow. I'd met a last name Harlow.

"Named after my mother, who was named after Jean Harlow. Because Jean Harlow had beauty *and* brains and *not* because Gramps was a dirty old man. Not even. But what good did beauty and brains do her? I ask you. Like she's this great role model?"

I knew nothing about Jean Harlow except that she was maybe in *Gone With the Wind*, which I'd never seen nor ever wanted to see. That war is over. Get over it. "I'm Rosemary Cooke."

"Rosemary for remembrance," Harlow said. "Awesome. Totally, totally charmed." She slid her arms under her butt and then under her legs so her cuffed wrists ended up twisted in front of her. If I'd been able to do the same, we could have shaken hands, as seemed to be her intention, but I couldn't.

We were taken then to the county jail, where this same maneuver created a sensation. A number of policemen were called to watch as Harlow obligingly squatted and stepped over her cuffed hands and back again several times. She deflected their enthusiasm with a winning modesty. "I have very long arms," she said. "I can never find sleeves that fit."

Our arresting officer's name was Arnie Haddick. When Officer Haddick took off his hat, his hair was receding from his forehead in a clean, round curve that left his features nicely uncluttered, like a happy face.

He removed our cuffs and turned us over to the county for processing. "As if we were cheese," Harlow noted. She gave every indication of being an old pro at this.

I was not. The wildness I'd felt that morning had long since vanished and left something squeezed into its place, something like grief or maybe homesickness. What had I done? Why in the world had I done it? Fluorescent lights buzzed like flies above us, picking up the shadows under everyone's eyes, turning us all old, desperate, and a little green.

"Excuse me? How long will this take?" I asked. I was polite as could be. It occurred to me that I was going to miss my afternoon class. European Medieval History. Iron maidens and oubliettes and burned at the stake.

"It takes as long as it takes." The woman from the county gave me a nasty, green look. "Be faster if you don't irritate me with questions."

Too late for that. In the next breath, she sent me to a cell so I'd be out of her hair while she did the paperwork on Harlow. "Don't worry, boss," Harlow told me. "I'll be right along."

"Boss?" the woman from the county repeated.

Harlow shrugged. "Boss. Leader. Mastermind." She gave me that flaming-Zamboni smile. "El Capitán."

The day may come when policemen and college students aren't natural enemies, but I sure don't expect to live to see it. I was made to remove my watch, shoes, and belt, and taken barefoot into a cage with bars and a sticky floor. The woman who collected my things was as mean as she could be. There was an odor in the air, a strong amalgamation of beer, cafeteria lasagna, bug spray, and piss.

The bars went all the way to the top of the cell. I checked to be sure; I'm a pretty good climber, for a girl. More fluorescents in the ceiling, louder buzzing, and one of the lights was blinking, so the scene in the cell dimmed and brightened as if whole days were rapidly passing. Good morning, good night, good morning, good night. It would have been nice to be wearing shoes.

Two women were already in residence. One sat on the single naked mattress. She was young and fragile, black and drunk. "I need a doctor," she said to me. She held out her elbow; blood was slowly oozing from a narrow gash, its color changing from red to purple in the blinking light. She screamed so suddenly I flinched. "I need help here! Why won't anyone help me?" No one, myself included, responded and she didn't speak again.

The other woman was middle-aged, white, nervous, and thin as a needle. She had stiff, bleached hair and a salmon-colored suit that was dressy, considering the occasion. She'd just rear-ended a cop car and she said that only the week before she'd been arrested shoplifting tortillas and salsa for a Sunday afternoon football party at her house. "This is so not good," she told me. "Honestly, I have the worst luck."

Eventually I was processed. I can't tell you how many hours had passed, as I had no watch, but it was considerably after I'd given up all hope. Harlow was still in the office, shifting about on a rocky chair, making the leg thump while she fine-tuned her statement. She'd been charged with destruction of property and creating a public nuisance. They were garbage charges, she told me. They didn't concern her; they shouldn't concern me. She made a phone call to her boyfriend, the guy from the cafeteria. He drove right over and she was gone before they finished my paperwork.

I saw how useful it could be to have a boyfriend. Not for the first time.

I faced the same charges, but with one important addition—I was also accused of assaulting an officer and no one suggested this charge was garbage.

By now I'd convinced myself I'd done absolutely nothing but be in the wrong place at the wrong time. I called my parents, because who else was I going to call? I hoped my mother would answer, as she usually did, but she was out playing bridge. She's an infamous bridge hustler—I'm amazed there are still people who'll play with her, but that's how desperate for bridge some people get; it's like a drug. She'd be home in an hour or two with her ill-gotten winnings rattling in a silver catch purse, happier than usual.

Until my father told her my news. "What the hell did you do?" My father's voice was exasperated, as if I'd interrupted him in the midst of something more important, but it was just as he'd expected.

"Nothing. Called out a campus cop." I felt my worries slipping from me like skin from a snake. My father often had this effect on me. The more irritated he was, the more I became smooth and amused, which, of course, irritated him all the more. It would anyone, let's be fair.

"The littler the job, the bigger the chip on the shoulder," my father said; that's how quickly my arrest became a teaching moment. "I always thought your brother would be the one to call from jail," he added. It startled me, this rare mention of my brother. My father was usually more circumspect, especially on the home phone, which he believed was bugged.

Nor did I respond with the obvious, that my brother might very well go to jail, probably would someday, but he would never ever call.

Three words were scratched in ballpoint blue on the wall above the phone. *Think a head*. I thought how that was good advice, but maybe a bit late for anyone using that phone. I thought how it would be a good name for a beauty salon.

"I don't have a clue what to do next here," my father said. "You're going to have to talk me through it."

"It's my first time, too, Dad."

"You're in no position to be cute."

And then, all of a sudden, I was crying so hard I couldn't speak. I took several runny breaths and made several tries, but no words came out.

Dad's tone changed. "I suppose someone put you up to it," he said. "You've always been a follower. Well, sit tight there"—as if I had a choice—"and I'll see what I can do."

The bleached blonde was the next to make a call. "You'll never guess where I am!" she said. Her tone was bright and breathy, and it turned out she'd dialed the wrong number.

Because of who he was, a professional man used to having his own way, my father managed to get the arresting officer on the phone. Officer Haddick had children of his own: he treated my father with all the sympathy my father felt he deserved. Soon they were calling each other Vince and Arnie, and the assault charge had been reduced to interfering with a police officer in the performance of his duty and soon after that it was dropped altogether. I was left with destruction of property and creating a public nuisance. And then these charges were dropped, too, because the eyeliner woman at the cafeteria came down and spoke for me. She insisted that I was an innocent bystander and had clearly not meant to break my glass. "We were all in shock," she said. "It was such a scene, you can't imagine." But by then I'd been forced to promise my dad that I would come home for the whole of Thanksgiving so the matter could be properly discussed over four days and face-to-face. It was a heavy price to pay for spilling my milk. Not even counting time served.

3

THE IDEA THAT we would spend the holiday talking about anything as potentially explosive as my arrest was a fiction, and we all knew this even as I was being made to promise to do so. My parents persisted in pretending we were a close-knit family, a family who enjoyed a good heart-to-heart, a family who turned to each other in times of trial. In light of my two missing siblings, this was an astonishing triumph of wishful thinking; I could almost admire it. At the same time, I am very clear in my own mind. We were *never* that family.

Random example: sex. My parents believed in themselves as scientists, dealers in the hard facts of life, and also as children of the openly orgasmic sixties. Yet whatever it is I think I know, I learned mostly from PBS's wildlife and nature programming, novels whose authors were probably no experts, and the occasional cold-blooded experiment in which more questions are raised than answers found. One day, a package of junior-sized tampons was left on my bed along with a pamphlet that looked technical and boring, so I didn't read it. Nothing was ever said to me about the tampons. It was just blind luck I didn't smoke them.

I grew up in Bloomington, Indiana, which is where my parents still lived in 1996, so it wasn't easy to get back for a weekend and I didn't manage the four days I'd promised. Already the cheap seats were gone on Wednesday and Sunday, so I arrived in Indianapolis on Thursday morning and flew back Saturday night.

Except for Thanksgiving dinner, I hardly saw my father. He had a grant from the NIH and was happily sidelined by inspiration. He spent most of my visit in his study, filling his personal blackboard with equations like $\_o' = [o\ o\ 1]$ and $P(S1n+1) = (P(S1n)(1-e)q + P(S2n)(1-s) + P(S0n)cq$. He barely ate. I'm not sure he slept. He didn't shave, and he usually shaved twice a day; he had an exuberant beard. Grandma Donna used to say his four-o'clock shadow was just like Nixon's, pretending that was a compliment but knowing it irritated the hell out of him. He emerged only for coffee or to take his fly-fishing rod out to the front yard. Mom and I would stand at the kitchen window, washing and drying the dishes, watching him lay out his line, the fly flicking over the icy borders of the lawn. This was the meditative activity he favored and there were too many trees in the back. The neighbors were still getting used to it.

When he worked like this, he didn't drink, which we all appreciated. He'd been diagnosed with diabetes a few years back and shouldn't have been drinking at any time. Instead he'd become a secret drinker. It kept Mom on high alert and I worried sometimes that their marriage had become the sort Inspector Javert might have had with Jean Valjean.

It was my grandma Donna's turn to have us for Thanksgiving, along with my uncle Bob, his wife, and my two younger cousins. We alternated between grandparents on holidays, because fair is fair and why should one side of the family have all the delight? Grandma Donna is my mother's mother, Grandma Fredericka my father's.

At Grandma Fredericka's, the food had a moist carbohydrate heft. A little went a long way, and there was never only a little. Her house was strewn with cheap Asian tchotchkes—painted fans, jade figurines, lacquered chopsticks. There was a pair of matching lamps—red silk shades and stone bases carved into the shapes of two old sages. The men had long, skinny beards and real human fingernails inset creepily into their stony hands. A few years ago, Grandma Fredericka told me that the third level of the Rock and Roll Hall of Fame was the most beautiful place she had ever seen. It just makes you want to be a better person, she said.

Grandma Fredericka was the sort of hostess who believed that bullying guests into second and third helpings was only being polite. Yet we all ate more at Grandma Donna's, where we were left alone to fill our plates or not, where the piecrusts were flaky and the orange-cranberry muffins light as clouds; where there were silver candles in silver candlesticks, a centerpiece of autumn leaves, and everything was done with unassailable taste.

Grandma Donna passed the oyster stuffing and asked my father straight out what he was working on, it being so obvious his thoughts were not with us. She meant it as a reprimand. He was the only one at the table who didn't know this, or else he was ignoring it. He told her he was running a Markov chain analysis of avoidance conditioning. He cleared his throat. He was going to tell us more.

We moved to close off the opportunity. Wheeled like a school of fish, practiced, synchronized. It was beautiful. It was Pavlovian. It was a goddamn dance of avoidance conditioning.

"Pass the turkey, Mother," my uncle Bob said, sliding smoothly into his traditional rant about the way turkeys are being bred for more white meat and less dark. "The poor birds can hardly walk. Miserable freaks." This, too, was intended as a dig at my father, the enterprise being another of science's excesses, like cloning or whisking up a bunch of genes to make your own animal. Antagonism in my family comes wrapped in layers of code, sideways feints, full deniability.

I believe the same can be said of many families.

Bob helped himself ostentatiously to a slice of dark meat. "They stagger around with these huge ungodly breasts."

My father made a crude joke. He made the same joke or some variation of it every time Bob gave him the opening, which was every other year. If the joke were witty, I'd include it, but it wasn't. You'd think less of him and thinking less of him is my job, not yours.

The silence that followed was filled with pity for my mother, who could have married Will Barker if she hadn't lost her mind and chosen my father, a chain-smoking, hard-drinking, fly-fishing atheist from Indianapolis, instead. The Barker family owned a stationery store downtown and Will was an estate lawyer, which didn't matter nearly so much as what he wasn't. What he wasn't was a psychologist like my father.

In Bloomington, to someone my grandma's age, the word *psychologist* evoked Kinsey and his prurient studies, Skinner and his preposterous baby boxes. Psychologists didn't leave their work at the office. They brought it home. They conducted experiments around the breakfast table, made freak shows of their own families, and all to answer questions nice people wouldn't even think to ask.

Will Barker thought your mother hung the moon, Grandma Donna used to tell me, and I often wondered if she ever stopped to think that there would be no me if this advantageous marriage had taken place. Did Grandma Donna think the no-me part was a bug or a feature?

I think now that she was one of those women who loved her children so much there was really no room for anyone else. Her grandchildren mattered greatly to her, but only because they mattered so greatly to her children. I don't mean that as a criticism. I'm glad my mother grew up so loved.

Tryptophan: a chemical in turkey meat rumored to make you sleepy and careless. One of the many minefields in the landscape of the family Thanksgiving.

Minefield #2: the good china. When I was five, I bit a tooth-sized chunk out of one of Grandma Donna's Waterford goblets for no other reason than to see if I could. Ever since, I'd been served my milk in a plastic tumbler with Ronald McDonald (though less and less of him each year) imprinted on it. By 1996 I was old enough for wine, but the tumbler was the same, it being the sort of joke that never gets old.

I don't remember most of what we talked about that year. But I can, with confidence, provide a partial list of things not talked about:

Missing family members. Gone was gone.

Clinton's reelection. Two years back, the day had been ruined by my father's reaction to my uncle Bob's assertion that Clinton had raped a woman or probably several women in Arkansas. My uncle Bob sees the whole world in a fun-house mirror, TRUST NO ONE lipsticked luridly across its bowed face. No more politics, Grandma Donna had said as a permanent new rule, since we wouldn't agree to disagree and all of us had access to cutlery.

My own legal troubles, about which no one but my mother and father knew. My relatives had been waiting a long time to see me come to no good; it did them no harm to keep waiting. In fact, it kept them in fighting trim.

My cousin Peter's tragic SAT scores, about which we all knew but were pretending we didn't. 1996 was the year Peter turned eighteen, but the day he was born he was more of a grown-up than I'll ever be. His mother, my aunt Vivi, fit into our family about as well as my father—we're a hard club to join, it seems. Vivi has mysterious flutters, weeps, and frets, so by the time Peter was ten, he could come home from school, look in the refrigerator, and cook a dinner for four from whatever he found there. He could make a white sauce when he was six years old, a fact often impressed upon me by one adult or another, with an obvious and iniquitous agenda.

Peter was also probably the only all-city cellist in the history of the world to be voted Best-Looking at his high school. He had brown hair and the shadows of freckles dusted like snow over his cheekbones, an old scar curving across the bridge of his nose and ending way too close to his eye.

Everyone loved Peter. My dad loved him because they were fishing buddies and often escaped to Lake Lemon to menace the bass there. My mom loved him because he loved my dad when no one else in her family could manage it.

I loved him because of the way he treated his sister. In 1996, Janice was fourteen, sullen, peppered with zits, and no weirder than anyone else (which is to say, weird on stilts). But Peter drove her to school every morning and picked her up every afternoon that he didn't have orchestra. When she made a joke, he laughed. When she was unhappy, he listened. He bought her jewelry or perfume for her birthdays, defended her from their parents or her classmates, as needed. He was so nice, it hurt to watch.

He saw something in her, and who knows you better than your own brother? If your brother loves you, I say it counts for something.

Just before dessert, Vivi asked my father what he thought of standardized testing. He didn't answer. He was staring into his yams, his fork making little circles and stabs as if he were writing in the air.

"Vince!" my mother said. She gave him a prompt. "Standardized tests."

"Very imprecise."

Which was just the answer Vivi wanted. Peter had such excellent grades. He worked so hard. His SAT scores were a terrible injustice. There was a moment of congenial conspiracy and the end of Grandma Donna's wonderful dinner. Pie was served—pumpkin, apple, and pecan.

Then my dad spoiled things. "Rosie had such good SATs," he said, as if we weren't all carefully *not* talking about the SATs, as if Peter wanted to hear how well I had done. My dad had his pie shoved politely out of the way in one cheek, smiling at me proudly, visions of Markov avoidance chains banging together like trash-can lids in his head. "She wouldn't open the envelope for two whole days and then she'd aced them. Especially the verbal." A little bow in my direction. "Of course."

Uncle Bob's fork came down on the edge of his plate with a click.

"It comes of being tested so often when she was little." My mother spoke directly to Bob. "She's a good test-taker. She learned how to take a test, is all." And then, turning to me, as if I wouldn't have heard the other, "We're so proud of you, honey."

"We expected great things," my father said.

"Expect!" My mother's smile never faltered; her tone was desperately gay. "We expect great things!" Her eyes went from me to Peter to Janice. "From all of you!"

Aunt Vivi's mouth was hidden behind her napkin. Uncle Bob stared over the table at a still life on the wall—piles of shiny fruit and one limp pheasant. Breast unmodified, just as God intended. Dead, but then that's also part of God's plan.

"Do you remember," my father said, "how her class spent a rainy recess playing hangman and when it was her turn the word she chose was *refulgent*? Seven years old. She came home crying because the teacher said she'd cheated by inventing a word."

(My father had misremembered this; no teacher at my grammar school would have ever said that. What my teacher had said was that she was sure I hadn't *meant* to cheat. Her tone generous, her face beatific.)

"I remember Rose's scores." Peter whistled appreciatively. "I didn't know how impressed I should have been. That's a hard test, or at least I thought so." Such a sweetheart. But don't get attached to him; he's not really part of this story.

MOM CAME INTO my room on Friday, my last night at home. I was outlining a chapter in my text on medieval economies. This was pure Kabuki—look how hard I'm working! Everyone on holiday but me—until I'd gotten distracted by a cardinal outside the window. He was squabbling with a twig, hankering after something I hadn't yet figured out. There are no red birds in California, and the state is the poorer for it.

The sound of my mother at the door made my pencil hop to. *Mercantilism. Guild monopolies. Thomas More's* Utopia. "Did you know," I asked her, "that there's still war in Utopia? And slaves?"

She did not.

She floated about for a bit, straightening the bedding, picking up some of the stones on the dresser, geodes mostly, split open to their crystal innards like Fabergé eggs.

Those rocks are mine. I found them on childhood trips to the quarries or the woods, and I broke them open with hammers or by dropping them onto the driveway from a second-story window, but this isn't the house I grew up in and this room isn't my room. We've moved three times since I was born, and my parents landed here only after I took off for college. The empty rooms in our old house, my mother said, made her sad. No looking back. Our houses, like our family, grow smaller; each successive one would fit inside the last.

Our first house was outside of town—a large farmhouse with twenty acres of dogwood, sumac, goldenrod, and poison ivy; with frogs and fireflies and a feral cat with moon-colored eyes. I don't remember the house so well as the barn, and remember the barn less than the creek, and the creek less than an apple tree my brother and sister would climb to get into or out of their bedrooms. I couldn't climb up, because I couldn't reach the first branch from the bottom, so about the time I turned four, I went upstairs and climbed down the tree instead. I broke my collarbone and you could have killed yourself, my mother said, which would have been true if I'd fallen from the upstairs. But I made it almost the whole way down, which no one seemed to notice. What have you learned? my father asked, and I didn't have the words then, but, in retrospect, the lesson seemed to be that what you accomplish will never matter so much as where you fail.

About this same time, I made up a friend for myself. I gave her the half of my name I wasn't using, the Mary part, and various bits of my personality I also didn't immediately need. We spent a lot of time together, Mary and I, until the day I went off to school and

Mother told me Mary couldn't go. This was alarming. I felt I was being told I mustn't be myself at school, not my whole self.

Fair warning, as it turned out—kindergarten is all about learning which parts of you are welcome at school and which are not. In kindergarten, to give you one example out of many, you are expected to spend much, much more of the day being quiet than talking, even if what you have to say is more interesting to everyone than anything your teacher is saying.

"Mary can stay here with me," my mother offered.

Even more alarming and unexpectedly cunning of Mary. My mother didn't like Mary much and that not-liking was a critical component of Mary's appeal. Suddenly I saw that Mom's opinion of Mary could improve, that it could all end with Mom liking Mary better than me. So Mary spent the time when I was at school sleeping in a culvert by our house, charming no one, until one day she simply didn't come home and, in the family tradition, was never spoken of again.

We left that farmhouse the summer after I turned five. Eventually the town swept over it, carried it away in a tide of development so it's all culs-de-sac now, with new houses and no fields or barns or orchards. Long before that, we were living in a saltbox by the university, ostensibly so that my father could walk to work. That's the house I think of when I think of home, though for my brother it's the earlier one; he pitched a fit when we moved.

The saltbox had a steep roof I was not allowed up on, a small backyard, and a shortage of extra rooms. My bedroom was a girly pink with gingham curtains that came from Sears until one day Grandpa Joe, my father's father, painted it blue while I was at school, without even asking. *When your room's pink, you don't sleep a wink. When your room's blue, you sleep the night through,* he told me when I protested, apparently under the misapprehension that I could be silenced with rhyme.

And now we were in this third house, all stone floors, high windows, recessed lights, and glass cabinets—an airy, geometric minimalism, with no bright colors, only oatmeal, sand, and ivory. And still, three years after the move, oddly bare, as if no one planned to be here long.

I recognized my rocks, but not the dresser beneath them, nor the bedspread, which was a quilted velvet-gray, nor the painting on the wall—something murky in blues and black—lilies and swans, or maybe seaweed and fish, or maybe planets and comets. The geodes did not look as if they belonged here and I wondered if they'd been brought out for my visit and would be boxed up as soon as I left. I had a momentary suspicion that the whole thing was an intricate charade. When I left, my parents would go back to their real house, the one with no room for me in it.

Mom sat on the bed and I put down my pencil. Surely there was preliminary, throat-clearing conversation, but I don't remember. Probably, "It hurts your father when you don't talk to him. You think he doesn't notice, but he does." This is a holiday classic—like *It's a Wonderful Life*, we rarely get through the season without it.

Eventually she got to her point. "Dad and I have been talking about my old journals," she said, "and what I ought to do with them. I still feel they're sort of private, but your father thinks they should go to a library. Maybe one of those collections that can't be opened until fifty years after your death, though I hear that libraries don't really like that. Maybe we could make an exception for family."

I'd been taken by surprise. My mother was almost, but not quite, talking about things we absolutely, resolutely did not talk about. The past. Heart clicking loudly, I answered by rote. "You should do whatever you want, Mom," I said. "What Dad wants isn't relevant."

She gave me a quick, unhappy look. "I'm not asking for your advice, dear. I've decided to give them to you. Your dad is probably right that some library would take them, though I think he remembers them as more scientific than they are.

"Anyway. The choice is yours. Maybe you don't want them. Maybe you're still not ready. Toss them if you like, make paper hats. I promise never to ask."

I struggled to say something to her, something that would acknowledge the gesture without opening the subject. Even now, even with years of forewarning, I can't think just how I might have done that. I hope I said something graceful, something generous, but it doesn't seem likely.

What I remember next is my father joining us in the guest room with a present, a fortune he'd gotten in a cookie months ago and saved in his wallet, because he said it was obviously for me. *Don't forget, you are always on our minds.*

There are moments when history and memory seem like a mist, as if what really happened matters less than what should have happened. The mist lifts and suddenly there we are, my good parents and their good children, their grateful children who phone for no reason but to talk, say their good-nights with a kiss, and look forward to home on the holidays. I see how, in a family like mine, love doesn't have to be earned and it can't be lost. Just for a moment, I see us that way; I see us all. Restored and repaired. Reunited. Refulgent.

4

TOUCHED AS I WAS, there was nothing I wanted less than my mother's journals. What's the point of never talking about the past if you wrote it all down and you know where those pages are?

Mom's journals were large, the size of sketch pads but thicker, and there were two of them, tied together with old green Christmas ribbon. I had to empty my suitcase and repack, sit on it to zip it closed again.

At some point, perhaps when I changed planes in Chicago, the suitcase waltzed off on its own adventures. I arrived in Sacramento, waited an hour at the luggage carousel, talked for another hour to a bunch of people with clear consciences and bad attitudes. I caught the last bus to Davis, empty-handed.

I felt guilty because I'd owned the journals less than a day and already lost them. I felt happy because just this once, the airlines had used their incompetence for good instead of evil and maybe, through no fault of my own beyond an excessive trust in everyone's ability to do their job, I'd never see those notebooks again. I felt lucky not to have checked my textbooks.

Mostly I felt tired. The minute I stepped out of the elevator onto my floor, I could hear Joan Osborne's "One of Us" and the music grew louder the closer I got to my own apartment. This surprised me, because I'd thought Todd (my roommate) wasn't getting back until Sunday and I thought Todd was standing alone against the world in not liking "One of Us."

I hoped he wouldn't want to talk. Last time he'd gone to visit his father, they'd had a long conversation about everything they believed and wanted and were. It had all been so glorious that Todd had gone back downstairs after the good-nights to say how close to his father he now felt. From the doorway, he'd overheard Dad talking to the new wife. "Jeebus," his dad was saying. "What an eejit. I've always wondered if he's really mine." If Todd had come home early, it was not for anything small.

I opened the door and Harlow was on my couch. She was wrapped in the crocheted shawl Grandma Fredericka had made for me when I had the measles, and she was drinking one of my diet sodas. She sprang up to turn the music down. Her dark hair was twisted onto her head and had a pencil stuck through it. I could see I gave her quite a start.

ONCE, at a parent-teacher conference, my kindergarten teacher had said that I had boundary issues. I must learn to keep my hands to myself, she'd said. I remember the mortification of being told this. I'd truly had no idea that other people weren't to be touched; in fact, I'd thought quite the opposite. But I was always making mistakes like that.

So you'll have to tell me what the normal reaction to coming home and finding someone you hardly know in your house would be. I was already tired and wired. My response was to gape silently, like a goldfish.

"You scared me!" Harlow said.

More dim-witted gaping.

She waited a moment. "God, I hope you don't mind?" As if it had only just occurred to her I might. Notes of sincerity, contrition. She began talking faster. "Reg kicked me out because he thinks I have no money and nowhere to go. He thought I'd walk around for a couple of hours and then have to crawl home and beg him to let me back in. He pisses the hell out of me." Sisterhood! "So I came here. I thought you wouldn't be back until tomorrow." Reason. Composure. "Look, I can see you're tired." Compassion. "I'll get right out of your hair." Commitment.

She was trying so hard to get a read on me, but there was nothing to read. All I felt was exhausted, to the marrow of my heavy bones, to the roots of my stolid hair.

Well, and maybe curious. Just the tiniest bit. "How did you know where I live?" I asked.

"I got it off your police report."

"How did you get in?"

She pulled the pencil, and her hair dropped silkily to her shoulders. "I gave your apartment manager a pretty face and a sad story. I'm afraid he can't really be trusted." Her tone now was one of great concern.

I MUST HAVE gotten angry while I slept, because that's how I woke up. The phone was ringing and it was the airline, saying they had my bag and would deliver it in the afternoon. They hoped I'd think of them the next time I flew.

I went to use the toilet and it overflowed. After several futile attempts to flush, I called the apartment manager, embarrassed to have him in my bathroom dealing so openly with my piss, but grateful it was nothing more.

Though he was eager. He came at a run, in a clean shirt rolled to show his upper arms, his plunger brandished like a rapier. He looked about for Harlow, but it was a tiny place, no way to miss her unless she was gone. "Where's your friend?" he asked. His name was Ezra Metzger, a name of considerable poetry. Obviously, his parents had had hopes.

"Home with her boyfriend." I was in no mood to soften this news. Besides, I'd been good to Ezra on other occasions. One time, two nondescript men had come to my door and asked questions about him. They said he'd applied for a job in the CIA, which struck me as a terrible idea no matter how you looked at it, and I still gave him the best recommendation I could make up on the spot. "I never see the guy," I said, "unless he wants to be seen."

"The boyfriend. She told me about him." Ezra looked at me. He had a habit of sucking on his teeth so his mustache furled and un-furled. I expect he did that for a while. Then he said, "Bad news there. You shouldn't have let her go back."

"You shouldn't have let her in. Without anyone here? Is that even legal?"

Ezra had told me once that he didn't think of himself as the man-ager of the apartment house so much as its beating heart. Life was a jungle, Ezra said, and there were those who'd like to bring him down. A cabal on the third floor. He knew them, but they didn't know him, didn't know who the fuck they were dealing with. They'd find out. Ezra saw conspiracies. He lived his life camped out on the grassy knoll.

He also talked a lot about honor. Now I saw his mustache in full anguished quiver; if he could have committed seppuku with the plunger on the spot, he'd have done it. Mere moments later, he saw how he'd done nothing wrong. Anguish became outrage. "You know how many women are killed every year by their boyfriends?" he asked. "Pardon the shit out of me for trying to save your friend's life."

We settled on a wintry silence. Fifteen minutes passed before he reeled in a tampon. It wasn't mine.

I tried to go back to bed, but there were long, dark hairs on my pillowcase and the smell of vanilla cologne on my sheets. I found Pixy Stix straws in the trash and fresh scratches in the gold-specked Formica where she'd cut something without a cutting board. Harlow was not a person who lived lightly on the land. The blueberry yogurt I'd planned for lunch was gone. Todd came slamming in, bad mood walking, made worse by the news that we'd been squatted on.

Todd had a third-generation Irish-American father and a second-generation Japanese-American mother, who hated each other. As a kid, he'd spent summers with his dad, coming home with itemized lists of unexpected expenses his mother was expected to cover. Replacement of ripped *Star Wars* T-shirt—$17.60. New shoelaces—$1.95. It must be so great, Todd used to tell me, having a normal family like you.

Once, he'd dreamed of experimental fusions, that he would be the one to merge folk harps with anime. Now he saw the incommensurability. In his own words: matter and antimatter. The end of the world.

Ever since the Great Eejit Incident, Todd had reached into his Japanese heritage when he needed an insult. *Baka* (idiot). *O-baka-san* (honorable idiot). *Kisama* (jackass). "What kind of *kisama* does something like that?" he asked now. "Do we have to change the locks? Do you know how fucking much that's going to cost?" He went to his bedroom to count his CDs and then went out again. I would have left myself, gotten a coffee downtown, but I needed to be home for the suitcase.

No sign of it. At five of five, I called the airline number—800-FUCK-YOU—and was told I had to speak directly to lost luggage at the Sacramento Airport. No one answered in Sacramento, though my call was important to them.

About seven p.m., the phone rang, but it was my mother checking to see I'd gotten home all right. "I know I said I'd never mention it," she told me. "But I feel so good about giving you those journals. Like a weight's been lifted. There. That's the last thing I'll say about them."

Todd came back around nine, with a pizza of apology from the Symposium Restaurant. His girlfriend, Kimmy Uchida, joined us and we all ate in front of *Married . . . with Children* and then the couch got a little busy, since it had been four whole days since Kimmy and Todd last saw each other. I went to my room and read for a while. I think I was reading *The Mosquito Coast* then. There seemed to be no end to the insane things fathers did to their families.

5

NEXT MORNING THE PHONE woke me up. It was the airline saying they had my suitcase and would deliver it in the afternoon. Since I had a class, they promised to leave it with my apartment manager.

Three nights passed then before I managed to find Ezra again. On one of those, I'd gone out with Harlow. She'd come to my door, wearing a jeans jacket and tiny hoop earrings. Gold glitter frosted her hair because, she said, brushing it away with her fingers, she'd walked through a party on her way to my place. A golden wedding anniversary. "Like having just one husband in your whole life is something to brag about," she said. And then, "Look. I know you're mad. That was totally wack, crashing at your place without asking. I get it."

"I'm over it," I told her, and she said in that case, even though it was only Tuesday and too early for the traditional weekend bacchanal (in 1996, I believe, that still started on Thursday; I'm told it's Wednesday now), I should let her buy me a beer. We walked downtown, past Sweet Briar Books and the big tomato sculpture at the food co-op, past the Jack in the Box and Valley Wine to the corner opposite the train station where the Paragon bar was. The sun was down, but the horizon still a scarlet slash. Crows were rioting in the trees.

I hadn't always loved the big sky here, or the flat, fenced yards, or the year-round summery smell of cow shit. But I'd submitted to the fences, stopped noticing the smell, and was a convert to the sky. The sunset you see is always better than the one you don't. More stars are always better than less. I feel the same about crows, though I know there are some who don't. Their loss.

I'd rarely been to the Paragon; the college crowd goes elsewhere. It's about as close as Davis gets to rough, which means that the drinkers there are serious, they *show up*, an army of the mutant undead who mostly once went to Davis High School, where they lived high old lives of football or skateboarding or keggers. There was a game on the television, volume up—Knicks versus Lakers—plus a lot of zombified nostalgia in the room. It added up to an intermittent din.

Everyone seemed to know Harlow. The bartender brought our drinks himself. Every time I ate a few peanuts, he came and refilled the bowl. Every time we finished our beers, new ones arrived, courtesy of one guy or another, who'd then come to the table only to have Harlow send him away. "I'm so sorry," she'd say with a sugar-sparkle smile. "But we are just *right* in the middle of something here."

I asked her: where she was from (Fresno), how long she'd been in Davis (three years), and what she planned after college. Her dream was to live in Ashland, Oregon, and design sets and lighting for the Shakespeare Company there.

She asked me: would I rather be deaf or blind, smart or beautiful? Would I marry a man I hated to save his soul? Had I ever had a vaginal orgasm? Who was my favorite superhero? Which politicians would I go down on?

I have never been so thoroughly drawn out.

Whom did I love best, my mother or my father?

Now we were inching into dangerous territory. Sometimes you best avoid talking by being quiet, but sometimes you best avoid talking by talking. I can still talk when I need to. I haven't forgotten how to talk.

So I told Harlow about a summer when I was little, the summer we moved from the farmhouse. It's a story I've told often, my go-to story when I'm being asked about my family. It's meant to look intimate, meant to look like me opening up and digging deep. It works less well when bits have to be shouted top-volume in a rampageous bar.

It starts in the middle, with me being shipped off to my Grandpa Joe and Grandma Fredericka's. There was no warning of this and I couldn't now remember what my parents had told me as to why—whatever it was, I wasn't buying. I knew the winds of doom when they blew. I believed I'd done something so bad, I'd been given away.

MY COOKE GRANDPARENTS lived in Indianapolis. They had this hot, airless house with a smell that was almost nice but not quite, sort of like stale cookies. There was a painting of a man and woman in harlequin masks in my bedroom and all that faux Asian stuff in the living room. Really faux. Faux faux. Remember those disturbing sages with their real human fingernails? Now imagine trying to sleep in that house.

The few other kids on the street were a lot older. I would stand behind the front-door screen and watch them, wishing they'd ask me something I knew the answer to, but they didn't. Sometimes I would go out back, but Grandpa Joe had put in concrete so as to not have the yard work, and it was even hotter than in the house. I'd bounce a ball or watch ants in the flower beds for a while, and then I'd go back in and whine for a popsicle.

My grandparents mostly watched TV or slept in their chairs in front of it. I got to see cartoons every Saturday, which wasn't allowed at home, and I saw at least three episodes of *Super Friends*, so I must have been there at least three weeks. Most afternoons, there was a soap opera we all watched together. There was this guy named Larry and his wife, Karen. Larry was head of a hospital and Karen entertained gentlemen while he was at work, which didn't sound so bad to me, yet clearly was.

"One Life to Live," said Harlow.

"Whatever."

Grandma Fredericka would get annoyed because I talked all through the show even as she complained that it was all sexed up and no good anymore. It used to be about family, she'd say. It used to be something you could watch with your five-year-old grand-baby in the room. But Grandpa Joe said my talking made the show better. He warned me, though, to remember that real people didn't really behave like this, as if I might go home thinking it was okay to switch places with your twin brother so as to fake your own death, or steal another mother's baby if your own had died.

But mostly there was nothing to do. Every day exactly the same, and every night, bad dreams of pinching fingers and harlequin masks. Lots of breakfasts of scrambled eggs with gross little white flecks in them, which I never ate but they kept serving me anyway.

"You'll never be bigger than a minute," Grandma Fredericka would say, scraping my plate sadly into the trash. And—"Can you hush up for just one minute so I can hear myself think?" Something people had been asking me for as long as I could remember. Back then, the answer was no.

Then she met some woman at the beauty shop, who said I could come and play with her kids. We had to drive to get there. Her kids turned out to be two strapping boys—one of them was only six, but he was already enormous. They had a trampoline and I was wearing a skirt that flew up when I jumped and everyone could see my underpants. I don't remember if they were mean about it or I was just humiliated on principle. But that was the end for me; I cracked. When no one was paying attention, I walked out the door and I intended to walk the whole way home. Real home. Bloomington.

I knew I would have to walk a long time. I don't think it ever crossed my mind I might go in the wrong direction. I chose streets with shady lawns and sprinklers. A woman on a porch asked me where my parents were and I said I was visiting my grandparents. She didn't ask anything else. It must have already been very late when I started, because I was only five; I can't have walked too far, whatever it felt like, and soon it was getting dark.

I picked out a house because I liked the color. It was painted bright blue and had a red door. And it was tiny, like a house in a fairy tale. I knocked, and a man in a bathrobe and undershirt answered. He asked me in and gave me a glass of Kool-Aid while we sat at the kitchen table. He was nice. I told him about Larry and Karen, the harlequins, the enormous boys, walking back to Bloomington. He listened very seriously and then pointed out a few flaws in my plan I hadn't noticed. He said if I just knocked on doors and asked for dinner or lunch, I might be fed some foods I didn't like. I might be expected to clean my plate, because that was the rule in some houses, and they might give me Brussels sprouts or liver or whatever it was I hated most. I was ready to be talked out of walking to Bloomington anyway.

So I told him my grandparents were the Cookes, and he called a couple of Cookes in the phone book till he found them. They fetched me and I was sent back home the next day, because, they said, I'd turned out to be a handful and real noisy to boot.

"YOUR MOTHER WASN'T having a baby?" Harlow asked.

"No," I said.

"I just thought—I mean, isn't that the usual reason a kid gets sent off to stay with the grandparents? We're talking the classics here."

My mother wasn't having a baby; she was having a nervous breakdown, but I had no intention of telling Harlow that. The beauty, the utility of this story is in its power to distract. So I said instead, "I haven't told you the weird part yet," and Harlow clapped her hands together with a loud smack. Drinking, like being arrested, made her unnervingly agreeable.

A man wearing a Celtics jersey approached our table, but Harlow waved him away. She did so with a this-hurts-me-more-than-it-hurts-you expression on her face. "We're just getting to the weird part," she explained. He hung around a few minutes, hoping to hear the weird part for himself, but it wasn't for everyone and I waited him out.

"When I was in the little blue house, I asked to use the bathroom," I said, lowering my voice and leaning in so close I could smell the hops on Harlow's breath. "The guy in the bathrobe told me it was the second door on the right, but I was five years old. So I opened the wrong door, a bedroom door. And there on the bed was this woman, lying on her stomach, with her hands and feet all tied up with pantyhose behind her back. Trussed. There was something stuffed in her mouth. Maybe men's socks.

"When I opened the door, she turned her head to look at me. I didn't know what to do. I didn't know what to think. I had this silvery sharp sense of something very very wrong. Then—"

There was a brief cold wind as someone opened the door into the Paragon, came inside, closed the door.

"She winked at me," I said.

A MAN WALKED up behind Harlow and put a hand on the back of her neck. He was wearing a black knit toque with a Canadian maple-leaf on it, and had a sharp nose that swerved slightly left. Surfer-type, but in a minor key. He was a good-looking guy and I'd last seen him in the university cafeteria, dodging Harlow's sugar cubes. "Rose, this is Reg," Harlow said. "Of whom you've heard me speak so lovingly."

Reg didn't acknowledge me. "I thought you said you had to work."

"I thought you were going to the library."

"I thought there was some crisis with the show. All hands on deck."

"I thought you had this big test you had to study for. Your whole future hanging in the balance."

Reg grabbed a chair from a neighboring table and helped himself to Harlow's beer. "You'll thank me later," he said.

"Hold your breath, why don't you?" Harlow suggested sweetly. And then, "Rosemary's favorite superhero is Tarzan."

"No, he's not," Reg said, not missing a beat. "Because Tarzan doesn't have superpowers. He's not a superhero."

"I told her that!"

This was true. I hadn't had a favorite superhero until Harlow asked. And then I'd picked Tarzan on impulse, same as I'd done with her other questions, a freewheeling exercise in free-association. But the more she'd questioned my choice, the more committed I'd become to it. I tend to do that in the face of opposition. Ask my dad.

And now that she'd reopened the argument, I thought it was cowardly of her, pretending to be convinced when she was really just lying low, waiting for backup to arrive.

But outnumbered is not persuaded, at least not in my family. "It's a matter of context," I said. "Ordinary powers in one world are superpowers in another. Take Superman."

But Reg refused to take Superman. "Batman is as far as I'll go," he said. "I can go no farther." Under that sexy cap, he had the brains of a bivalve and I was glad not to be the one sleeping with him.

6

IN FACT, I'd never read Burroughs; it wasn't a book my parents would have wanted in the house. All I knew about Tarzan was whatever was in the tap water. When Reg began to lecture me on the racism of the books, I didn't know if the books were racist, which wouldn't be Tarzan's fault, or if Tarzan himself was racist, which would be more problematic. But I didn't think I could win the argument by admitting ignorance. This left as my only option a quick *God, look at the time* withdrawal.

I walked home alone through the dark grid of downtown streets. A long train thundered past on my right, setting off the lights and bells of the barrier arms. There was a cold wind flipping the leaves on the trees, and outside Woodstock's Pizza, a loose scrum of men I crossed the street to avoid. One of them shouted an invitation to me, but it was uninviting.

Todd was still up and he hadn't read Burroughs, either, but there was a manga version—*New Jungle King Tar-chan*—and he was all over that. Tar-chan had superpowers. Most definitely. Todd tried to describe the series to me (which seemed to be a sprightly mix of cooking and pornography) and offered to bring me some issues next time he went home, but it wasn't clear I wouldn't have to be able to read Japanese.

I couldn't get him focused on the point now—that Reg was an asshole—because he was so busy making his own: that Masaya Tokuhiro was a genius. Anyway, it was becoming less clear to me that Reg had been so egregiously out of line. And why had I been jabbering away about Tarzan in the first place? That was indiscreet. I must have been very drunk.

A NIGHT OR TWO LATER, I finally treed Ezra. He had my suitcase, but I was still being punished; it wasn't convenient just then to turn it over. "You're too busy?" I asked incredulously. How many floors did he think this apartment building had?

"Correctamundo," he told me. "That you don't think so just shows how little you know."

Two more days passed before he unlocked the broom closet— (there's shit in there that could seriously fuck up the wells. You could poison the whole town if you wanted, Ezra had told me. It was his job to keep that shit out of the hands of the sort of terrorists who lived on the third floor)—and pulled the suitcase out. It was hard-shelled and powder-blue.

"Oh, yeah," Ezra said. "I forgot. This guy came by yesterday, said he was your brother Travers. He wanted to wait for you, but I told him he couldn't even imagine the hissy fit you'd throw if I let some friend or family member stay in your place when you weren't there."

I was torn between my disbelief that the visitor had really been my brother, a happy amazement that he'd come for me at last, and a steaming disappointment that Ezra had sent him off, probably never to return. These were complicated things to be feeling simultaneously. My heart flopped in my chest like a hooked fish.

Although my parents continued to get the occasional postcard, the last word I'd personally had from my brother came when I graduated high school. *It's a big world,* he'd written on the back of a picture of Angkor Wat. *Get big.* The postmark was London, which meant he could have been anywhere but there. The fact that my brother's name was not Travers was the most persuasive detail in Ezra's account. My brother would never have used his real name.

"Did he say he'd come back?" I asked.

"Maybe. Maybe he said in a couple of days."

"A couple like two days or a couple like a few days? Did he say a couple or did he say a few?"

But Ezra had had enough. Ezra believed in dispensing information only on a need-to-know basis. He sucked on his teeth and said he couldn't remember for sure. He'd been busy. He had an apartment building to run.

When we were kids, my brother was my favorite person in the whole world. He could be, and often was, awful, but there were other times. He'd spent hours teaching me to play catch and also cards. Casino and I doubt it, gin rummy, go fish, hearts, and spades. He was a good poker player, but under his tutelage, I was better, if only because I was so little no one expected me to be. We made some serious book off his friends. They paid him in cash, but I took my winnings in the more universal currency of Garbage Pail Kids cards. I used to have hundreds of those. Buggy Betty, the little green-fly girl, was my favorite. She had such a nice smile.

One day, Steven Claymore threw a snowball at me with a rock inside, because I'd said he was ineluctable, which he didn't like the sound of but proved true. I came home with a spongy lump on my forehead and some gravel in my knee. The next day my brother showed up at school where he held Steven's arm behind his back until Steven apologized and then my brother took me to Dairy Queen and bought me a chocolate-dipped cone with his own money. There was trouble about this later, both the arm-twisting and the two of us leaving our respective schools without telling anyone, but the family rules of conduct had gotten all vague and convoluted where my brother was concerned and there were no real consequences for either of us.

So I'D HAD several reasons for choosing to come to UC Davis.

First, it was far enough from home that no one would know anything about me.

Second, my mother and father had said okay. We'd visited the campus together and they'd found the town practically midwestern. They were particularly besotted with the spacious bike lanes.

But third, and really, I'd come because of my brother, and my parents must have known and had their own hopes. Ordinarily, my father kept his wallet nailed shut and all the bike lanes in all the midwestern-type towns in the world wouldn't have had him forking over a year of out-of-state tuition when there were perfectly good universities right there in Indiana, one of them merely blocks away.

But the FBI had told us that my brother had been in Davis in the spring of '87, about a year after he took off, and the government can't be wrong about everything; even a stopped clock, etc. They'd never said anywhere else they thought he'd been, only Davis.

And I just didn't think I could do it anymore, this business of being my parents' only child. In my fantasies, my brother would rattle his knuckles on my apartment door and I'd open it, not expecting a thing, thinking maybe it was Ezra coming to borrow Todd's Game Boy or instituting new protocols for the building regarding hazardous trash. I would recognize him instantly. God, I've missed you, my brother would say, pulling me into a hug. Tell me everything that's happened since I left.

The last time I saw him, I was eleven years old and he hated my guts.

THE SUITCASE wasn't mine. That goes without saying.

7

THAT STORY I TOLD HARLOW—that story in which I'm sent to my grandparents in Indianapolis—obviously that story isn't really from the middle of this story. I did tell it to Harlow just when I said, so my telling of it is from the middle, but the happening and the telling are very different things. This doesn't mean that the story isn't true, only that I honestly don't know anymore if I really remember it or only remember how to tell it.

Language does this to our memories—simplifies, solidifies, codifies, mummifies. An oft-told story is like a photograph in a family album; eventually, it replaces the moment it was meant to capture.

And I've reached a point here, now that my brother has arrived, where I don't see how to go further forward without going back— back to the end of that story, back to when I returned to my family from my grandparents' house.

Which also happens to be the exact moment when the part I know how to tell ends and the part I've never told before begins.

PART TWO

❖

. . . a short time perhaps when measured by the calendar, but endlessly long to gallop through, as I have done, at times accompanied by splendid people, advice, applause, and orchestral music, but basically alone . . .

——FRANZ KAFKA, "A Report for an Academy"

I

So now it's 1979. Year of the Goat. The Earth Goat.

Here are some things you might remember. Margaret Thatcher had just been elected prime minister. Idi Amin had fled Uganda. Jimmy Carter would soon be facing the Iran hostage crisis. In the meantime, he was the first and last president ever to be attacked by a swamp rabbit. That man could not catch a break.

Here are some things you maybe didn't notice at the time. The same year Israel and Egypt signed a peace treaty, it snowed for half an hour in the Sahara Desert. The Animal Defense League was formed. Up on the Magdalen Islands, eight crew members from the *Sea Shepherd* sprayed more than a thousand seal pups with a harmless but permanent red dye. This dye was designed to ruin their pelts and save the pups from hunters. The activists were arrested and, in pitch-perfect Orwellian double-speak, charged with violating the Seal Protection Act.

Sister Sledge's "We Are Family" was on the radio, *The Dukes of Hazzard* on the TV. *Breaking Away* was in the theaters and Bloomington, Indiana, was ready for its close-up.

The only part of this I was aware of at the time was the *Breaking Away* part. In 1979, I was five years old, and I had problems of my own. But that's how excited Bloomington was—even the suffering children could not miss the white-hot heat of Hollywood.

MY FATHER WOULD surely want me to point out that, at five, I was still in Jean Piaget's preoperational phase with regard to cognitive thinking and emotional development. He would want you to understand that I am undoubtedly, from my more mature perspective, imposing a logical framework on my understanding of events that didn't exist at the time. Emotions in the preoperational stage are dichotomous and extreme.

Consider it said.

Not that there aren't times when dichotomous and extreme are exactly what's warranted. Let's simplify matters and just agree that, at this point in my story, my whole family, all of us, young and old, was really really really upset.

The day after my cross-capital trek from trampoline to little blue house, my father appeared. My grandparents had called him to come fetch me, but no one told me that part. I still thought I was being given away, only not to my grandparents, who'd turned out not to want me. Where next? Who would love me now? I sobbed in as decorous a manner as possible, because my father didn't like it when I cried and I still had hopes. But no one admired my heroic restraint and my father didn't even seem to notice my tears. He had obviously washed his hands of me.

I was sent out of the room, where a good deal of hushed and ominous talking happened, and even when my bag was packed and I was in the backseat and the car was moving, I still didn't know I was being taken home. Which was just as well, because I wasn't.

As a child, I chose to escape unhappy situations by sleeping through them. I did so now, and when I woke I was in a strange room. In many ways, the strangest things about this room were the bits that weren't strange. My chest of drawers was by the window. The bed I was in was my bed, the quilt over me was my quilt—hand-sewn by Grandma Fredericka back when she'd loved me, appliquéd with sunflowers that stretched from the foot to the pillow. But the drawers were all empty and, under that quilt, the mattress was bare to the buttons.

There was a fort made of boxes by the window, one of them a carry-all for beer cans, and through the handholds I could see the cover of my own *Where the Wild Things Are*, with its egg-shaped stain of smeared Hershey's Kiss. I climbed onto a box to look outside and found no apple tree, no barn, no dusty fields. Instead some stranger's backyard, with a barbecue, a rusted swing-set, and a well-kept vegetable garden—tomatoes reddening, pea pods popping—swam mistily behind the double-paned glass. In the farmhouse where I lived such vegetables would have been picked, eaten, or thrown long before they'd ripened on the vine.

The farmhouse where I lived grumbled and whistled and shrieked; there was always someone pounding on the piano or running the washing machine or jumping on the beds or tub-thumping the pans or shouting for everyone to be quiet because they were trying to talk on the phone. This house lay in an oneiric hush.

I'm not sure what I thought then, perhaps that I was to live here alone now. Whatever it was, it sent me sobbing back to bed and back to sleep. In spite of my best hopes, I woke up in the same place in the same tears, calling despairingly for my mother.

My father came instead, picking me up and holding me. "Shh," he said. "Your mother is sleeping in the next room. Were you scared? I'm sorry. This is our new house. This is your new room."

"Everyone lives here with me?" I asked, still too cautious to be hopeful, and I felt my father flinch as if I'd pinched him.

He put me down. "See how much bigger your new room is? I think we're going to be very happy here. You should look around, kiddo. Explore. Just not into your mother's room," pointing out their door, which was right next to mine.

The floors of our old house were a bruised wood or linoleum, anything that could be cleaned in a hurry with a mop and a bucket of water. This house had a scratchy silver carpet extending from my new bedroom into the hall with no break. I wouldn't be skating in my socks here. I wouldn't be riding my scooter on this rug.

The new upstairs consisted of my bedroom, my parents' bedroom, my father's study with its blackboard already propped against the wall, and one bathroom with a blue tub and no shower curtain. My new room may have been bigger than the bright little nook I'd had in the farmhouse, but I could see that the house itself was smaller. Or maybe I couldn't see that when I was five. Ask Piaget.

Downstairs was a living room with a tiled fireplace, the kitchen with our breakfast table in it, another bathroom, smaller, with a shower but no tub, and next to that my brother's room, only my brother's bed had no blankets, because, I found out later that night, he'd refused to set foot in the new house, and had gone instead to stay with his best friend Marco for as long as they'd have him.

And that right there is the difference between me and my brother—I was always afraid of being made to leave and he was always leaving.

All the rooms had boxes in them and almost none of the boxes had been opened. There was nothing on the walls, nothing on the shelves. A few dishes in the kitchen, but no sign of our blender, toaster, bread-maker.

As I made my way for the first time through the house I would live in until I was eighteen, I began to suspect what had happened. I could find no place where the graduate students would work. I looked and looked, back upstairs and then down again, but could find only three bedrooms. One of them was my brother's. One of them was our mother and father's. One of them was mine. I hadn't been given away.

Someone else had.

As part of leaving Bloomington for college and my brand-new start, I'd made a careful decision to never *ever* tell anyone about my sister, Fern. Back in those college days, I never spoke of her and seldom thought of her. If anyone asked about my family, I admitted to two parents, still married, and one brother, older, who traveled a lot. Not mentioning Fern was first a decision, and later a habit, hard and painful even now to break. Even now, way off in 2012, I can't abide someone else bringing her up. I have to ease into it. I have to choose my moment.

Though I was only five when she disappeared from my life, I do remember her. I remember her sharply—her smell and touch, scattered images of her face, her ears, her chin, her eyes. Her arms, her feet, her fingers. But I don't remember her fully, not the way Lowell does.

Lowell is my brother's real name. Our parents met at the Lowell Observatory in Arizona at a high school summer science camp. "I'd come to see the heavens," our father always said. "But the stars were in her eyes," a line that used to please and embarrass me in equal measure. Young geeks in love.

I would think better of myself now if, like Lowell, I'd been angry about Fern's disappearance, but it seemed too dangerous just then to be mad at our parents and I was frightened instead. There was also a part of me relieved, and powerfully, shamefully so, to be the one kept and not the one given away. Whenever I remember this, I try to also remember that I was only five years old. I'd like to be fair here, even to myself. It would be nice to get all the way to forgiveness, though I haven't managed it yet and don't know that I ever will. Or ever should.

Those weeks I spent with our grandparents in Indianapolis still serve as the most extreme demarcation in my life, my personal Rubicon. Before, I had a sister. After, none.

Before, the more I talked the happier our parents seemed. After, they joined the rest of the world in asking me to be quiet. I finally became so. (But not for quite some time and not because I was asked.)

Before, my brother was part of the family. After, he was just killing time until he could be shed of us.

Before, many things that happened are missing in my memory or else stripped down, condensed to their essentials like fairy tales. Once upon a time there was a house with an apple tree in the yard and a creek and a moon-eyed cat. After, for a period of several months, I seem to remember a lot and much of it with a suspiciously well-lit clarity. Take any memory from my early childhood and I can tell you instantly whether it happened while we still had Fern or after she'd gone. I can do this because I remember which me was there. The me with Fern or the me without? Two entirely different people.

Still, there are reasons for suspicion. I was only five. How is it possible that I remember, as I seem to, a handful of conversations word for word, the exact song on the radio, the particular clothes I was wearing? Why are there so many scenes I remember from impossible vantage points, so many things I picture from above, as if I'd climbed the curtains and was looking down on my family? And why is there one thing that I remember distinctly, living color and surround-sound, but believe with all my heart never occurred? Bookmark that thought. We'll come back to it later.

I remember often being told to be quiet, but I seldom remember what I was saying at the time. As I recount things, this lacuna may give you the erroneous impression that I already wasn't talking much. Please assume that I am talking continuously in all the scenes that follow until I tell you that I'm not.

Our parents, on the other hand, had shut their mouths and the rest of my childhood took place in that odd silence. They never reminisced about the time they had to drive halfway back to Indianapolis because I'd left Dexter Poindexter, my terry-cloth penguin (threadbare, ravaged by love—as who amongst us is not) in a gas station restroom, although they often talk about the time our friend Marjorie Weaver left her mother-in-law in the exact same place. Better story, I grant you.

I know from Grandma Fredericka, and not our parents, that I once went missing for long enough that the police were called, and it turned out I'd tailed Santa Claus out of a department store and into a tobacco shop where he was buying cigars, and he gave me the ring off one, so the police being called was just an added bonus on what must have already been a pretty good day.

I know from Grandma Donna, and not our parents, that I once buried a dime in some cake batter as a surprise, and one of the graduate students chipped her tooth on it, and everybody thought Fern had done it, until I spoke up, so brave and honest. Not to mention generous, since the dime had been my own.

So who knows what revelries, what romps my memories have taken with so little corroboration to restrain them? If you don't count the taunting at school, then the only people who talked much about Fern were my grandma Donna, until Mom made her stop, and my brother Lowell, until he left us. Each had too obvious an agenda to be reliable: Grandma Donna wishing to shield our mother from any share of blame, Lowell stropping his stories into knives.

Once upon a time, there was a family with two daughters, and a mother and father who'd promised to love them both exactly the same.

2

IN MOST FAMILIES, there is a favorite child. Parents deny it and maybe they truly don't see it, but it's obvious to the children. Unfairness bothers children greatly. It's hard to always come in second.

It's also hard to be the favorite. Earned or unearned, the favorite is a burdensome thing to be.

I was our mother's favorite child. Lowell was our father's. I loved our father as much as our mother, but I loved Lowell best of all. Fern loved our mother best. Lowell loved Fern more than he loved me.

When I lay out these facts, they seem essentially benign. Something here for everyone. More than enough to go around.

3

THE MONTHS AFTER my return from Indianapolis were the most harrowing time of my life. Our mother was vaporous. She emerged from her bedroom only at night and always in her nightgown, a sheath of flowered flannel with a disturbingly childlike bow at the neck. She'd stopped combing her hair so that it twisted about her face, chaotic as smoke, and her eyes were so sunken they looked bruised. She would start to speak, her hands lifting, and then be suddenly silenced by the sight of that motion, her own hands in the air.

She hardly ate and did no cooking. Dad picked up the slack, but halfheartedly. He would come home from campus and look in the cupboards. I remember dinners of peanut butter on saltines, cans of tomato soup for starters and cans of clam chowder for mains. Every meal a passive-aggressive cri de coeur.

Grandma Donna began coming over every day to watch me, but, in Bloomington in 1979, watching me didn't mean I could never be out of her sight. I was allowed the roam of the neighborhood, just as I'd been allowed the roam of the farmhouse property, only now it was the street I had to be warned about instead of the creek. Crossing the street without a grown-up was forbidden, but I could usually scare up one of those if needed. I met most of the neighbors by holding their hands and looking both ways. I remember Mr. Bechler asking if I was maybe in training for the talking Olympics. I was gold-medal material, he said.

There weren't many children on the block and none anywhere close to my age. The Andersens had a baby girl named Eloise. A ten-year-old boy named Wayne lived two houses down; a high-school boy lived on the corner across the street. There was no one I could reasonably be expected to play with.

Instead I got acquainted with the neighborhood animals. My favorite was the Bechlers' dog Snippet, a liver-and-white spaniel with a pink nose. The Bechlers kept her tethered in their yard, because, given half a chance, she ran off and she'd already been hit by a car at least once that they knew of. I spent hours with Snippet, her head on my leg or my foot, her ears cocked, listening to every word I said. When the Bechlers realized this, they put a chair out for me, a little chair that they'd gotten back when the grandchildren were young. It had a cushion on the seat shaped like a heart.

I also spent a lot of time alone, or alone with Mary (remember Mary? Imaginary friend no one liked?), which was not something I'd ever done much of before. I didn't care for it.

Grandma Donna would change the beds and do the laundry, but only if our father wasn't there; she couldn't stand to be in the same room with him. If Lowell was angry that Fern had been sent out of our lives, Grandma Donna was angry that she'd ever been let in. I'm sure she'd deny this, say that she'd always loved Fern, but even at five I knew better. I'd heard too often about my first birthday, how Fern had dumped out Grandma Donna's handbag and eaten the last photograph ever taken of Grandpa Dan, a Polaroid that Grandma Donna kept in her purse to look at whenever she was feeling low.

If there'd been a second photo, I probably would have eaten one too, Lowell said, as I followed Fern's lead in most things. And Lowell also said that Dad had found it very telling that Grandma left her bag, filled as it apparently was with poisonous objects, where Fern could reach it, but I could not.

Our father had planned to name Fern and me after our grandmothers, one of us Donna and one of us Fredericka, a coin toss to see which was which, but both grandmothers insisted that I be the one with their name. Dad, who'd meant it as something nice, maybe even compensatory, was annoyed when it turned into an argument. He'd probably expected this of Grandma Donna, but not of his own mother. A hole was about to open, a rupture in the space-time continuum of the Cooke family, until our mother stepped in to plug it, saying that I would be Rosemary and Fern would be Fern, because she was the mother and that was the way she wanted it. I learned of the earlier plan only because Grandma Donna once referenced it in an argument as further evidence of Dad's peculiarity.

Personally, I'm glad it came to nothing. I suppose it's because she is my grandmother that Donna seems like a grandmother's name. And Fredericka? A Rose by any other, if you say so. But I can't believe that being called Fredericka my whole life wouldn't have taken a toll. I can't believe it wouldn't have mind-bent me like a spoon. (Not that I haven't been mind-bent.)

So Grandma Donna would clean the kitchen, maybe unpack some dishes or some of my clothes if she felt energetic, since it was clear by now that no one else planned to open those boxes. She'd make me lunch and cook something medicinal, like a soft-boiled egg, take it to the bedroom, put our mother in a chair so she could change the bedsheets, demand the nightgown for the wash, beg Mom to eat. Sometimes Grandma Donna was all sympathy, delivering in salubrious doses her preferred conversation—details on the health and marital problems of people she'd never met. She was especially fond of dead people; Grandma Donna was a great reader of historical biographies and had a particular soft spot for the Tudors, where marital discord was an extreme sport.

When that didn't work, she'd turn brisk. It was a sin to waste such a beautiful day, she'd say even when it wasn't such a beautiful day, or, your children need you. Or that I should have started nursery school a year ago and already be in kindergarten. (I didn't, because Fern couldn't go. Or Mary, either.) And that someone had to put the brakes on Lowell, he was only eleven, for God's sake, and shouldn't be allowed to rule the house. She would have liked to see one of her children running the emotional blackmail game Lowell got away with; he should have a close encounter with his father's belt.

She drove once to Marco's, intending to force Lowell home, but she came back defeated, face like a prune. The boys had been out on their bikes, no one knew where, and Marco's mother said Dad had thanked her for keeping Lowell and she'd send him home when it was our father who asked. Marco's mother was letting the boys run wild, Grandma Donna told Mom. Plus she was a very rude woman.

Grandma always left before our father returned from work, sometimes telling me not to say she'd been there, because conspiracy is folded into her DNA like egg whites into angel food cakes. But of course, Dad knew. Would he have left me there otherwise? Later he'd bring whatever she'd cooked back down from the bedroom and shovel it into the disposal. He'd get himself a beer and then another and then start on the whiskey. He'd put peanut butter on a cracker for me.

At night, from my bedroom, I'd hear arguing—Mom's voice too soft to be heard (or maybe she wasn't speaking at all), Dad's laced (I know now) with liquor. You all blame me, Dad said. My own goddamn children, my own goddamn wife. What choice did we have? I'm as upset as anyone.

And finally, Lowell, home at last, climbing the stairs in the dark without anyone hearing him and coming into my room, waking me up. "If only," he said—eleven years old to my five, socking me high on the arm so the bruise would be hidden by my T-shirt sleeve—"if only you had just, for once, kept your goddamn mouth shut."

I have never in my life, before or after, been so happy to see someone.

4

I DEVELOPED A PHOBIA about the closed door to our parents' bedroom. Late at night, I could hear it, pulsing in its frame like a heart. Whenever he let me, I huddled with Lowell in his room, as far away from that door as I could get and still be home.

Sometimes Lowell felt sorry for me. Sometimes it seemed that he, too, was frightened. We each carried the weight of Fern's disappearance and our mother's collapse, and occasionally, for short periods, we carried it together. Lowell would read me a book or let me jabber away while he played complicated games of solitaire that required two or three decks of cards and were nearly impossible to win. If just anyone could win a game, then Lowell couldn't be bothered.

Sometimes, if he wasn't completely awake, he'd let me climb into his bed after dark to get away from our father's shouting, though other times he'd remember to be mad, send me silently sobbing back upstairs. Bed-hopping was an established custom in the house—Fern and I had rarely ended the night in the bed where we'd started. Our parents felt that it was natural and mammalian not to want to sleep alone, and though they would have preferred we stay in our own beds, because we kicked and thrashed, they'd never insisted on it.

While Lowell slept, I'd calm myself by fiddling with his hair. I liked to catch a bit between two scissored fingers and run my thumb over the scratchy ends. Lowell had Luke Skywalker's haircut, but the color was pure Han Solo. Of course, I hadn't seen the movie back then. Too young for it and besides Fern couldn't have gone. But we had the trading cards. I knew about the hair.

And Lowell, who'd seen it several times, had acted it out for us. I liked Luke best. *I'm Luke Skywalker. I'm here to rescue you.* But Fern, who was more sophisticated in her tastes, preferred Han. *Laugh it up, fuzzball.*

Unfairness bothers children greatly. When I did finally get to see *Star Wars*, the whole movie was ruined for me by the fact that Luke and Han got a medal at the end and Chewbacca didn't. Lowell had changed that part in his retelling, so it came as quite a shock.

LOWELL'S ROOM SMELLED of damp cedar from the cage where three rats, washouts from our father's lab, would chirp and creak in their spinning wheel all night long. In retrospect, there was something incomprehensibly strange about the way any of the laboratory rats could transform from data point to pet, with names and privileges and vet appointments, in a single afternoon. What a Cinderella story! But I didn't notice that until later. Back then, Herman Muenster, Charlie Cheddar, and little hooded Templeton represented nothing to me but were only themselves.

Lowell smelled too, not bad, but sharp to my senses, because his smell had changed. At the time, I thought the difference was that he was so mad; I thought that it was anger I was smelling, but of course he was also growing up, losing the sweetness of childhood, beginning to sour. He sweated in his sleep.

Most mornings, he left before anyone else was awake. We didn't know this right off, but he was having breakfast with the Byards. The Byards were a childless couple, devout Christians, who now lived across the street from us. Mr. Byard's eyesight was bad and Lowell read the sports page aloud to him while Mrs. Byard fried up bacon and eggs. According to Mrs. Byard, Lowell was sweet as a peekin pie and always welcome.

She'd known a bit about the situation at our house. Most of Bloomington did, though no one really understood it. "I'm praying for you all," she told me, appearing at our door one morning, holding a tin of chocolate chip cookies and backlit like an angel by a soft autumn sun. "You just remember you were the one made in God's image. You hold tight to that and it'll carry you through the storm."

My Lord, anyone would think Fern had died, Grandma Donna said. Which is maybe what you, too, are thinking, that at five, of course, I wouldn't have figured that out without being told, but anyone older would have.

I can only assume that our parents explained to me about Fern's disappearance, possibly many times, and I've repressed it. It simply isn't plausible to think they hardly said a word. But this I remember clearly—waking up each morning and going to sleep each night in a state of inchoate dread. The fact that I didn't know what I was dreading made it no less dreadful. Arguably, more so.

Anyway, Fern was not dead. Still isn't.

Lowell started seeing a counselor and this became a frequent topic in our father's nightly monologues. Lowell's counselor would suggest something—a family powwow, a session with the parents alone, some exercises in visualization or hypnosis—and our father would explode. Psychoanalysis was completely bogus, he would say, good only for literary theory. Maybe it was useful, when plotting books, to imagine that someone's life could be shaped by a single early trauma, maybe even one inaccessible in memory. But where were the blind studies, the control groups? Where was the reproducible data?

According to our father, the nomenclature of psychoanalysis had taken on a scientific patina only when it was translated into English Latinates. In the original German, it was refreshingly modest. (You must picture him shouting this. In the house I grew up in, it was perfectly ordinary for a tantrum to include words like *Latinates*, *nomenclature*, and *patina*.)

Yet the counselor had been our father's idea. Like so many other parents of troubled children, he'd felt the need to do *something*, and like so many other parents of troubled children, a counselor was the only something he could think of to do.

For me, he engaged a babysitter, Melissa, a college student with owlish glasses and blue streaks zigzagging, like lightning, through her hair. The first week, I went to bed the minute she arrived and got up again only when she left. I was, let's agree, a babysitter's dream.

It was a learned behavior. Once, when I was four, as a stratagem for shutting me up, a babysitter named Rachel had spooned several kernels of popcorn onto my tongue and told me they would pop if I only kept my mouth closed long enough. This seemed like an entirely desirable goal and I lasted as long as I could and took the failure hard until Lowell told me it never would have happened. That put me off babysitters entirely.

As I got used to Melissa, I decided I liked her. This was a bit of luck. I'd concocted a plan that involved fixing my family with the only valuable thing I had to offer—my talking—and I couldn't do it alone. I tried to explain to Melissa the games I was supposed to be playing for my father, the tests I was supposed to be taking, but she couldn't or wouldn't get it.

We settled on a compromise. Every time she came, she would teach me a new word from the dictionary. The only rule was that it had to be a word so lonely, so dusty with neglect that she, too, hadn't known it beforehand. I didn't care what the words meant; that saved a lot of time and bother. In return, I had to not talk to her for an hour. She would set the oven timer to make sure, which generally resulted in me asking her every few minutes when the hour would be up. The things I had to say would collect in my chest until they were so crowded together I was ready to burst.

"How was your day, Rosie?" Dad would ask when he came home from work and I'd tell him it was ebullient. Or limpid. Or dodecahedron. "That's good to hear," he'd say.

None of this was meant to be informative. Obviously, it didn't even need to cohere. Catachresis? Bonus points.

I was merely trying to show him that I, at least, was continuing with our work. Whenever he was so disposed, he would find me, sleeves rolled up and hard at it.

ONE AFTERNOON, Grandma Donna came and forced our mother into an outing—coffee and a shopping trip. Summer had gone and autumn was headed toward its sell-by date. Melissa was supposed to be watching me but was watching television instead.

Melissa was now an established part of the household and

watched TV every afternoon, although daytime TV had never been allowed before, children being expected to make their fun up from scratch.

Melissa had gotten hooked on a soap. It wasn't the same soap as my grandparents'—there was no Karen, no Larry. Melissa's soap was all about Ben and Amanda, Lucille and Alan. And if my grandparents' soap had been regrettably sexed up, this one was an orgy. Melissa let me watch it with her because I wouldn't understand a thing; because I didn't understand a thing, I rarely wished to watch. We disagreed as to how quiet I should be while the show was on.

Melissa was beginning to slip the tether. She'd just taught me a word and then made me promise not to ever say it to our parents. The word was *ithyphallic*. Years later, if *ithyphallic* had come up on the SATs, I'd have been all over it, but no such luck. It's not really a very useful word.

And just ask Lowell if I'm the sort of person who keeps her promises. The minute I saw our father, I told him that my day had been ithyphallic, instead of the official day's word, which was *psychomanteum*, but whether that figured in the impending decision to let Melissa go, I cannot say.

Anyway, before I said *ithyphallic* to our father, I said it to Lowell. Lowell was supposed to be at school, but had come home early, sneaking in through the back door, motioning at me to follow him outside, which I did, though not as quietly as he'd wanted. Lowell was uninterested in my new words, waved them past with an impatient flick of his hand.

One of the neighbors was out front, the boy from the white house on the corner, the big boy from the high school. Russell Tupman, leaning against Mom's blue Datsun, lighting a weary cigarette and sucking it in. I'd never thought to see Russell Tupman in my own driveway. I was charmed. I was flattered. I fell instantly in love.

Lowell held up his hand and shook it. The car keys rang in his fist. "You sure about her?" Russell asked, indicating me with his eyes. "I hear she's a talker."

"We need her," Lowell said. So I was told to get in the back and Lowell fastened my seat belt, which he was pretty conscientious about doing even when Russell wasn't the one driving. I learned later that Russell didn't technically have his license yet. He'd taken driver's ed and everything; he knew how to drive. I don't remember a moment's anxiety about his driving, no matter how much fuss it caused after.

Lowell said that we were going on a secret adventure, a spy caper, and I was allowed to bring Mary, because Mary knew how to keep her mouth shut and was an example to us all. I was pretty happy about the whole thing, pretty honored to be going off with the big boys. Looking back, I can see that Lowell was only eleven years old, while Russell was sixteen, and that this must have been an enormous gap, but at the time I thought of them as equally glamorous.

I was also, in those days, desperate to get out of the house. I'd had a dream in which I heard someone knocking on our parents' door from the inside. It started with a jaunty rhythm, like the sound of tap shoes, only each tap was louder than the last until they were so loud I thought my eardrums would burst. I woke up terrified. The sheets beneath me were soaked and I had to get Lowell to change my pajamas, strip the bed.

Russell switched from our mother's radio station to WIUS,

the student one, and some song I didn't know came on, but not knowing the song didn't stop me singing along in the backseat until Russell finally told me I was hell on his nerves.

Hell. I repeated that several times, but under my breath so Russell wouldn't have to deal with it. I liked the way it made my tongue curl.

I couldn't see out the front window, only the back of Russell's head bopping in time against the headrest. I tried to think of how to make him love me. Something inside me knew that big words weren't the way to Russell's heart, but I couldn't think what else I could offer.

More songs on the radio and an ad for an original radio mystery play to be aired on Halloween. Then a caller who wanted to talk about a professor who was making his entire class read *Dracula*, even the Christians who thought it imperiled their souls. (Let's just pause here for a moment to imagine how a person who felt imposed on by vampires back in 1979 feels today. And then, right back to my story.)

More callers. Most people liked *Dracula* though some didn't, but nobody liked professors who thought they could tell you what to read.

The car began to bounce and I heard gravel under the tires. We came to a stop. I recognized the bright crown of the tulip tree by our old farmhouse drive, its golden leaves floating in a white-blue sky. Lowell got out to open the gate, got back in.

I hadn't known this was where we were coming. My good mood turned anxious. Though no one had said so, as no one was saying much of anything, I'd assumed Fern had been left behind in the old farmhouse to live with the graduate students. I'd pictured her life going on much as before, maybe even with less disruption than I'd had—missing Mom, for sure (and weren't we all?), but with Dad still stopping by to oversee the drills, the games with colored poker chips and raisins. When, in a couple of months, she'd turn six, I'd assumed like every other year she'd have a birthday cake with the icing roses she and I so loved. (I don't know for a fact that she didn't.)

So my thinking was that it was sad that she never got to see our mother, and I wouldn't have wanted to be her, but it wasn't *that* sad. The graduate students were nice and they never shouted, because they weren't allowed to and they loved Fern. They loved Fern more than they loved me. Sometimes I had to wrap myself around their legs and refuse to let loose, just to get their attention.

Now we were bumping up the driveway. Fern was always quick to hear a car approach; she'd already be at the window. I wasn't sure I wanted to see her, but I knew for certain that she wouldn't want to see me. "Mary doesn't want to see Fern," I told Lowell.

Lowell twisted around, pinned me with a narrow-eyed look. "Oh my God! You didn't think Fern was still here, did you? Fuck, Rosie."

I'd never heard Lowell say *fuck* before; in retrospect, I'm sure he was trying to impress Russell. *Fuck* was another word that felt good in my mouth. Fuck, fuck, fuck. Quack, quack, quack. "Don't be such a baby," Lowell said. "There's nobody here at all. The house is empty."

"I'm not a baby." This was reflexive; I was too relieved to be insulted. No angry reunion, then. The familiar treetops were overhead like golden clouds; beneath us, the familiar crunching of the gravel under the tires. I remembered how I used to find pieces of quartz in the driveway here, clear and crystalline. Like four-leaf clovers, this happened just often enough to keep me looking. There was no gravel at the new house and, so, no point.

The car stopped. We got out and walked around the side to the kitchen door, but it was locked, all the doors were locked, Lowell told Russell, and the windows, even the upstairs windows, had been, in our last year there, fitted with bars, the route from the apple tree to the bedrooms cut off before I'd ever mastered it.

The only remaining hope was the dog door into the kitchen. I don't remember ever having a dog, but apparently, we did once, a large terrier—Tamara Press was her name—and apparently, Fern and I had loved her to distraction and slept on top of her until she died of cancer just before I turned two. Unlike most dog doors, the latches for this one were on the outside.

Lowell undid them. I was told to go through.

I didn't want to. I was frightened. I felt that the house must be hurt not to be my house anymore, that it must feel abandoned. "It's just an empty house," Lowell told me encouragingly. "And Mary will go with you," as if even I could think Mary would be good in a fight.

Mary was useless. I wanted Fern. When would Fern get to come home?

"Hey," said Russell. Talking to me! "We're counting on you, runt."

So I did it for love.

I SCRAPED THROUGH the dog door into the kitchen, stood up inside a fall of sunlight, dust motes caroming and shining about me like glitter. I had never seen the kitchen empty. The scuffed linoleum was brighter and smoother where the breakfast table ought to have been. Fern and I had once hidden under that table so that no one would see us drawing on the floor with felt-tip markers.

The ghosts of our artwork were still visible if you knew to look for them.

The empty room closed about me like a hum, squeezed me tightly until it was hard to breathe. I felt the whole kitchen thick with rage, only I couldn't tell if it was the house or Fern who was so angry. I opened the door hastily for Lowell and Russell, and as soon as they entered, the house let me go. It was no longer angry. Instead it was terribly sad.

The boys went ahead, talking quietly so I couldn't hear, which made me suspicious and I followed. There were so many things I missed here. I missed the wide staircase. We used to sled down on beanbag chairs. I missed the cellar. In the winter, we'd always had baskets of apples and carrots you could eat without asking, as many as you wanted, though you had to go down into the dark to get them. I wasn't going down into the dark now unless the boys did, and if they did, then I wasn't staying behind.

I missed how big and busy it had always been. I missed having a yard I couldn't see to the end of. I missed the barn, the horse stalls filled with broken chairs and bicycles, magazines, bassinets, our stroller and car seats. I missed the creek and the fire pit, where we roasted potatoes or popped corn in the summer. I missed the jars of tadpoles we kept on the porch for scientific observation, the constellations painted onto the ceilings, the map of the world on the library floor, where we could go with our lunches and eat in Australia or Ecuador or Finland. *My palms cover continents* curved in red letters down the far western edge of the map. My palm didn't even cover Indiana, but I could find the state on the map by shape. Soon I'd hoped to be able to read the words. Before we moved, my mother had been teaching me out of my father's math books. *The product of two numbers is a number.*

"What a freak show," Russell said, which took the shine right off for me. What a dump. My room in our new house was bigger than my room here.

"Is the lawn still electrified?" Russell asked. The front yard was choked with dandelions, buttercups, and clover, but you could see how it was meant to be a lawn.

"What are you talking about?" said Lowell.

"I heard if you stepped on the grass, you got an electric shock. I heard it was all wired up to keep people out."

"No," said Lowell. "It's just regular grass."

EVENTUALLY MELISSA'S SOAP ended and she noticed I wasn't around. She looked all through the neighborhood until the Byards made her call our father, who'd just found out that Lowell was missing from school. He'd had to cancel his class, a point that was repeated to us many times over the next few days—that it was not just him we'd inconvenienced but a whole class of students, as if his not showing up hadn't been the best part of their week. Arriving home, he saw that the car was gone.

So when, on our return, he lifted me out of the backseat, he didn't ask how my day had been. It didn't stop me telling him.

5

THERE'S SOMETHING YOU DON'T KNOW yet about Mary. The imaginary friend of my childhood was not a little girl. She was a little chimpanzee.

So, of course, was my sister Fern.

Some of you will have figured that out already. Others may feel it was irritatingly coy of me to have withheld Fern's essential simian-ness for so long.

In my defense, I had my reasons. I spent the first eighteen years of my life defined by this one fact, that I was raised with a chimpanzee. I had to move halfway across the country in order to leave that fact behind. It's never going to be the first thing I share with someone.

But much, *much* more important, I wanted you to see how it really was. I tell you Fern is a chimp and, already, you aren't thinking of her as my sister. You're thinking instead that we loved her as if she were some kind of pet. After Fern left, Grandma Donna told Lowell and me that when our dog Tamara Press had died, our mother had been devastated—just the way she was now, being the implication. Lowell reported this to our father and we were all so offended Grandma Donna had to give it right up.

Fern was not the family dog. She was Lowell's little sister, his shadow, his faithful sidekick. Our parents had promised to love her like a daughter, and for years I asked myself if they'd kept that promise. I began to pay better attention to the stories they read me, the stories I soon was reading to myself, looking to learn how much parents love their daughters. I was a daughter as well as a sister. It was not only for Fern's sake that I needed to know.

What I found in books was daughters indulged and daughters oppressed, daughters who spoke loudly and daughters made silent. I found daughters imprisoned in towers, beaten and treated as servants, beloved daughters sent off to keep house for hideous monsters. Mostly, when girls were sent away, they were orphans, like Jane Eyre and Anne Shirley, but not always. Gretel was taken with her brother into the forest and abandoned there. Dicey Tillerman was left with her siblings in a parking lot at a shopping mall. Sara Crewe, whose father adored her, was still sent away to live at school without him. All in all, there was a wide range of possibility, and Fern's treatment fit easily inside it.

Remember that old fairy tale I mentioned at the very start—how one sister's words turn to jewels and flowers, the other's to snakes and toads? Here is how that fairy tale ends. The older sister is driven into the forest, where she dies, miserable and alone. Her own mother has turned against her, we are told, a thing so disturbing I'd wished I hadn't heard it and, long before Fern was sent away, had already told Mom never to read us that story again.

But maybe I made that last part up, me being so upset, so alarmed. Maybe later, after Fern left, I saw how I should have felt and revised my memory accordingly. People do that. People do that all the time.

Until Fern's expulsion, I'd scarcely known a moment alone. She was my twin, my fun-house mirror, my whirlwind other half. It's important to note that I was also all those things to her. I would say that, like Lowell, I loved her as a sister, but she was the only sister I ever had, so I can't be sure; it's an experiment with no control. Still, when I first read *Little Women*, it seemed to me I'd loved Fern as much as Jo loved Amy if not as much as Jo loved Beth.

WE WERE NOT the only household during this period attempting to raise a baby chimpanzee as if she were a human child. The aisles of the supermarkets in Norman, Oklahoma, where Dr. William Lemmon was prescribing chimps liberally to his grad students and patients, were full of such families.

We were not even the only household to do so while simultaneously raising an actual human child, though no one but us had twinned the child with the chimpanzee since the Kelloggs had done so in the 1930s. By the 1970s, in most chimped-up households, the human child was considerably older and no part of the experiment.

Fern and I were raised in as much the same way as was deemed rational. I'm sure I was the only chimp sibling in the country who had to decline all birthday party invitations, though this was mostly to prevent me from bringing colds home; little chimps are terribly susceptible to respiratory infections. We went to exactly one party in my first five years, and I don't even remember it, but Lowell told me there'd been an unfortunate incident involving a piñata, a baseball bat, and a lot of flying candy that ended with Fern biting Bertie Cubbins, the birthday girl, on the leg. Biting someone who's not in the family—apparently, a really big deal.

I'm only guessing, of course, that other chimped-up families did things differently. Certainly Fern was hyperaware of any favoritism and responded to it with vigor and vinegar. Unfairness bothers chimps greatly.

My very earliest memory, more tactile than visual, is of lying against Fern. I feel her fur on my cheek. She's had a bubble bath and smells of strawberry soap and wet towels. A few drops of water still cling to the sparse white hair of her chin. I see this, looking up from the shoulder I am leaning against.

I see her hand, her black nails, her fingers curling and uncurling. We must have still been very young, because her palm is soft and creased and pink. She is giving me a large golden raisin.

There is a dish of these raisins on the floor in front of us, and I think they must have been Fern's and not mine, earned somehow in one of our games, but it doesn't matter, because she is sharing them with me—one for her, one for me, one for her, one for me. My feeling in this memory is a great contentment.

Here's a later memory. We're in my father's study, playing a game we call Same/NotSame. Fern's version involves being shown two things—two apples, for instance, or one apple and one tennis ball. She's holding two poker chips, one colored red and one colored blue. If she thinks the two things are the same, she's supposed to give Sherry, today's grad student, the red chip. Blue means different. It's not clear she understands the game yet.

Meanwhile, this game is already too simple for me. I'm working with Amy, who has given me several lists of four items. I'm being asked which thing doesn't fit. Some of the lists are pretty tricky. Piglet, duckling, horse, and bear cub becomes pig, duck, horse, and bear. I love this game, especially since Dad has explained there are no right and wrong answers; it's all just to see how I think. So I get to play a game I can't lose *and* I get to tell everyone everything I'm thinking while I do it.

I'm making my choices and also telling Amy what I know about ducks and horses and the like, what my experience of them has been. Sometimes when you give bread to ducks, the big ones take all of it and the little ones don't get any, I tell her. That's not fair, right? That's not nice. Sharing is what's nice.

I tell her how I was once chased by ducks because I didn't have enough bread to go around. I say that Fern doesn't give her bread to the ducks. She eats it herself, which is sometimes true but sometimes not. Amy doesn't correct me, so I say this again, with more confidence. Fern is not a good sharer, I say, eliding Fern's good record of sharing with *me*.

I tell Amy that I've never ridden a horse, but I will someday. Someday I'll have a horse of my own, probably named Star or maybe Blaze. Fern couldn't ride a horse, could she? I ask. I'm always on the hunt for things I can do that Fern can't. "You may be right," Amy says, writing it all down. Life couldn't be better.

But Fern is getting frustrated, because she's not being allowed to eat the apples. She quits playing Same/NotSame. She comes over, rests the rough shelf of her forehead against my own flat one so that I'm staring straight into her amber eyes. She's so close her breath is in my mouth. I can smell that she's unhappy, her usual sort of wet-towel smell, but with a pungent, slightly acrid undertone. "Stop bothering me, Fern," I say, giving her a little push. I am, after all, working here.

She wanders about the room for a bit, signing for apples and also bananas and candy and other delicious things, but disconsolately, since none of the above is materializing. Then she begins to jump back and forth between the top of our father's desk and the big armchair. She's wearing her favorite yellow skirt with the pictures of blackbirds on it and it flies up to her waist when she jumps, so you can see the diaper underneath. Her lips protrude and funnel, her small face pale and bare. I hear the soft *oo oo oo* sounds she makes when she's anxious.

She's not having fun, but it still looks like fun to me. I climb onto Dad's desk myself and nobody says no, or even be careful, maybe because no one said these things to Fern and so now they can't. It's farther than I thought and I land on the floor on my elbow. As I fall, I hear Fern laughing. This causes some excitement. Typically, a chimp laughs only when there is physical contact. Prior to this, Fern has laughed only when she was being chased or tickled. Mocking laughter is a distinctly human trait.

Our father tells Sherry and Amy to listen carefully when Fern laughs. The sound is constrained by and timed to her breath, so the laughter comes in pants. Perhaps, Dad suggests, Fern can't sustain a single sound through a cycle of repeated exhalation and inhalation. What would this mean for oral speech development? No one seems to care that Fern was being mean, though that seems to me to be the crucial bit.

Later, because no one paid attention when I said my elbow hurt and then it turned out to be broken, Dad apologized by letting me see the damage on my X-ray. The fissures look like the crackle finish on a china plate. I'm somewhat soothed by the seriousness of having broken a bone.

But not completely. The things I can do that Fern can't are a molehill compared to the mountain of things she can do that I can't. I'm considerably bigger, which should count for something, but she's considerably stronger. The only thing I do better is talk, and it's not clear to me that this is a good trade-off, that I wouldn't swap it instantly for being able to scamper up the banister or stretch like a panther along the top edge of the pantry door.

This is why I invented Mary, to even the score. Mary could do everything Fern could and then some. *And* she used her powers for good instead of evil, which is to say only under my direction and on my behalf.

Although my primary motive for her creation was to have a playmate no one preferred to me. The best thing about Mary was that she was kind of a pill.

A FEW DAYS after the trip to the farmhouse, Mary and I can be found in the branches of a maple in Russell Tupman's backyard. We are looking into Russell's kitchen, where his patchwork-vest-wearing elf of a mother has covered a table with newspaper and taken a cleaver to a pumpkin.

Why are we in Russell's maple? Because it's the one tree on the block I can easily climb. The base of its trunk forked into three parts, one almost parallel to the ground, so that I could start by simply walking as if on a trestle, holding on to the branches above for balance. As I got higher, I had to climb, but the branches were numerous, each an easy step to the next. The fact that we could look from those branches into the windows of Russell's house was just a bonus. We were definitely there for the climbing and not to reconnoiter.

Mary went higher than I could, and she said she could see all the way back down the street to the Byards' roof. She said she could see into Russell's bedroom. She said Russell was jumping on his bed.

But she was lying, because the next thing I knew, Russell was coming out the kitchen door and walking straight toward me. The tree still had a smear of red leaves, so I hoped I was hidden. I held very still until Russell was directly beneath me. "What are you doing up there, runt?" he asked. "What do you think you're look-ing at?"

I told him that his mother was cutting up a pumpkin. Only I used the word *dissecting*. Lowell had once found a dead frog by the creek at the farmhouse and he and my father had spent an afternoon dissecting it on the dining room table, slicing open the chambers of its little wet nut of a heart. I hadn't minded that, but now the sight of Russell's mother reaching into the pumpkin was beginning to upset my stomach, send saliva into my mouth. I swallowed hard and stopped looking through the window.

I was standing on one branch, holding with one hand on to a higher one, swaying slightly, casually, as I talked. You would never have known my stomach was roiling. Savoir faire to spare. "Mon-key girl," Russell said, a phrase I would come to know well when I started school. "What a weirdo." But his tone was pleasant enough and I didn't take offense. "Tell your brother I've got his money."

I looked into the kitchen again. Russell's mother had started pulling the intestines from the pumpkin, slapping them by the hand-ful onto the newspaper. My head went empty and my legs shook, and for a moment I thought that I would fall or, even worse, vomit.

So I straddled a branch for more stability, but it was a thin branch, so flexible that it bent unexpectedly under my weight and suddenly I was sliding down it, breaking off little shoots and leaves as I went. I landed back on the ground, feet first, butt second. My hands were covered with scratches.

"What the hell are you doing now?" Russell asked and then flicked a finger toward the crotch of my pants, where the leaves had left a stain. I really can't describe the humiliation of this. I knew my crotch wasn't something to be looked at or talked about. I knew it shouldn't be an autumn red.

. . .

A FEW DAYS LATER, the cops busted Russell. Grandma Donna told me that he'd thrown a Halloween party at the farmhouse. Every window in the place had been broken, she said, and an underage girl had spent a night in the hospital.

Language is such an imprecise vehicle I sometimes wonder why we bother with it. Here is what I heard: that maybe Fern had reached, like a poltergeist, across time and space and destroyed the home in which we'd all lived. A few broken windows might have signified a party to me. Fern and I had thrown a croquet ball through one once and had good fun doing it in spite of what came after. But every window in the place? That didn't sound larkish. That had the precision and persistence of fury.

Here's what Grandma Donna thought she was telling me: that I was not too young to understand the dangers of mixing alcohol and drugs. That she just hoped she'd never live to see the day I had to have my stomach pumped. That such a thing would break our mother's broken heart.

6

THEN ONE MORNING, just like that, Mom came back into focus. I woke to Scott Joplin's "Maple Leaf Rag," decanting note by cheerful note up the stairs. Our mother was up, calling us by piano to breakfast as she used to do, hands arched, foot pedal pumping. She had showered and cooked, would return soon to reading and, finally, talking. Weeks passed then without Dad taking a drink.

This was a relief, but less so than you might think, as you couldn't depend on it now that you'd seen the other.

We spent that Christmas in Waikiki, where Santa wore board shorts and flip-flops and nothing felt like Christmas. We'd never been able to travel with Fern; now we could, and we needed to get away. Last year, Fern had insisted on plugging and unplugging the Christmas lights no matter how many times she was told to cut it out. It was our tradition to let her put the star on the top of the tree.

Fern, sneaking a present into an upstairs closet, hooting with excitement and giving the game away. Fern, on Christmas morning, filling the air with shredded wrapping paper, stuffing it down the backs of our necks like snow.

It was my first time on an airplane, the white clouds a rolling mattress beneath us. I loved the way Hawaii smelled, even in the airport, plumeria on the breeze and dribbled into the hotel shampoos and soaps.

The beach at Waikiki was shallow enough that even I could walk out a good long ways. We spent hours in the water, bobbing up and down, so when I lay at night on the hotel bed that Lowell and I were sharing, my blood still rocked in my ears. I learned to swim on that trip. Our parents stood beyond the breakers and caught me as I kicked from one to the other and I was pretty sure Fern couldn't have done that, though I didn't ask.

I had a revelation that I shared over breakfast—about how the world was divided into two parts: above and below. When you went snorkeling, you were visiting the part below, and when you climbed a tree, you were visiting the part above, and neither was better than the other. I remember being pretty sure that this was an interesting thing for me to say, something someone should be writing down.

When you think of three things to say, pick one and only say that. For months after Fern left, the two things I didn't say were always about her. In Hawaii, I thought—but didn't say—that maybe Fern could climb but I could dive. I wished she were there to see me do that. I wished she were there, hooting over a piece of lava cake, scaling the trunks of the palm trees like Spider-Man.

She would have so loved the breakfast buffet.

I saw her everywhere, but I never said so.

Instead I watched our mother obsessively for signs of breakage. She floated on her back in the ocean or lay on a chair by the pool drinking mai tais, and, on hula night, when the maître d' asked for volunteers, she went right up. I remember how beautiful she was, brown from the sun, flowers dripping from her neck, her hands fluid and fluent—*we throw our nets out into the sea, and all the ama-ama come a-swimming to me.*

She was an educated woman, our father noted gingerly at dinner the night before we came home. An intelligent woman. Wouldn't it be good to have a job so she wasn't stuck in the house all the time, especially now that I'd be going to kindergarten?

I hadn't known I was going to kindergarten until he said this. I hadn't been around other kids all that much. I was stupid enough to be excited.

The sea was shining outside the restaurant window, just turning from silver to black. Mom agreed in that general way that means not to pursue the topic, and he took the hint. We were all alert to her hints back then. We were careful with each other. We tiptoed.

This lasted for many months. And then, one night at supper, Lowell said suddenly, "Fern really loved corn on the cob. Remember what a mess she'd make?" and I got a flash of yellow kernels pasted across Fern's little pegs of teeth like bugs in a screen door. Probably we were having corn on the cob when Lowell said this, which would mean it was summer again—thunderstorms and fireflies and nearly a year since Fern had been sent away. But that's just making a guess.

"Remember how Fern loved us?" Lowell asked.

Dad picked up his fork, held it trembling in his fingers. He put it down again, gave our mother a quick, glancing look. She was staring into her plate, so you couldn't see her eyes. "Don't," he said to Lowell. "Not yet."

Lowell shook him off. "I want to go see her. We all need to go see her. She's wondering why we haven't come."

Our father passed his hand over his face. He used to play a game with Fern and me where he did that. One pass down the face would reveal him scowling. His hand back up would bring a smile. Down, scowl. Up, smile. Down, Melpomene. Up, Thalia. Tragedy and comedy performed as facial expressions.

That night's reveal showed him saggy and sad. "We all want that," he said. His tone matched Lowell's. Calm, but firm. "We all miss her. But we have to think what's best for *her*. The truth is that she had a terrible transition, but she's settled in now and happy. Seeing us would just stir her up. I know you don't mean to be selfish, but you'd be making her feel worse for the sake of you feeling better."

By now Mom was weeping. Lowell rose without another word, took his full plate to the garbage, dumped it in. He put his dish and glass into the dishwasher. He left the kitchen and he left the house. He was gone for two nights and he was not with Marco. We never did find out where he'd slept.

THIS WASN'T the first time I'd heard Dad make that argument. Back on the day when I'd gone to the farmhouse with Russell and Lowell, back on the day when I'd finally understood Fern wasn't living there, I'd asked our father where she was.

He was up in his new study and I'd been sent to remind him that *The Rockford Files* was on, because Lowell couldn't believe that "stay in your room and think about your behavior" might actually mean "miss your favorite TV shows." I considered climbing on the desk and jumping into his lap, but I'd already shown poor judgment, going off without telling Melissa, and I knew Dad wasn't in a playful mood. He'd catch me if I left him no choice in the matter, but he wouldn't be happy about it. So I asked him about Fern instead.

He'd pulled me into his lap, smelling as he always did of

cigarettes and beer, black coffee, Old Spice. "She has a different family now," he said, "on a farm. And there are other chimpanzees, so she has lots of new friends."

I was instantly jealous of all those new friends who got to play with Fern while I did not. I wondered if she liked anyone there better than me.

It felt odd to be sitting on one of Dad's legs without Fern for ballast on the other. His arms around me tightened. He'd told me then, just as he'd told Lowell later (and probably more than once), that we couldn't go see her, because it would upset her, but that she had a good life. "We'll always always miss her," he said. "But we know that she's happy and that's the important thing."

"Fern doesn't like being made to try new foods," I said. This had been worrying me. Fern and I cared a lot about what we ate. "We like what we're used to."

"New can be good," Dad said. "There's a ton of foods Fern has never even heard of and would probably love. Mangosteens. Sweetsops. Jackfruits. Jelly palms."

"But she can still eat her favorites?"

"Pigeon peas. Cake apples. Jamjams."

"But she can still eat her favorites?"

"Jelly rolls. Monkey bars. Summer salts."

"But she can still . . ."

He gave up. He gave in. "Yes," he said. "Yes. Of course. She can still eat her favorites." I remember him saying that.

I believed in this farm for many years. So did Lowell.

WHEN I WAS ABOUT EIGHT, I recovered what seemed to be a memory. It came one piece at a time, like a puzzle I had to fit together. In this memory, I was a tiny child, riding in the car with my parents. We were on a narrow country road, buttercups, grasses, and Queen Anne's lace crowding the car from the sides, brushing against the windows.

My father stopped for a cat that was crossing in front of us. I shouldn't have been able to see this cat, strapped as I was into my car seat in the back, yet I now remembered it clearly as a black cat with a white face and belly. It wandered uncertainly in front of us, back and forth, until my father grew impatient and drove on, running it over. I remembered my shock; I remembered protesting. I remembered my mother defending my father, saying that the cat had just refused to get out of the way, as if there'd really been nothing else they could have done.

When it was complete, I took this memory to the only person I thought might believe it, my grandma Donna. She was sitting in an armchair, reading a magazine, probably *People*. I think that maybe Karen Carpenter had just died; both my grandmas took that hard. I was shaking when I told her, trying not to cry and not succeeding. "Oh, sweetheart," Grandma Donna said. "I think that must have been a dream. You must know your father would never, ever do such a thing."

If anyone was eager to see the worst in Dad, it was my grandma Donna. Her instant dismissal was enormously comforting. It gave me back the things I knew—that my father was a kind man, that he would never do such a terrible thing. To this day, I can feel the bump of the tire over the cat's body. And to this day I am very clear in my mind that it never happened. Think of it as my own personal Schrödinger's cat.

Was my father kind to animals? I thought so as a child, but I knew less about the lives of lab rats then. Let's just say that my father was kind to animals unless it was in the interest of science to be otherwise. He would never have run over a cat if there was nothing to be learned by doing so.

He was a great believer in our animal natures, far less likely to anthropomorphize Fern than to animalize me. Not just me, but you, too—all of us together, I'm afraid. He didn't believe animals could think, not in the way he defined the term, but he wasn't much impressed with human thinking, either. He referred to the human brain as a clown car parked between our ears. Open the doors and the clowns pile out.

The idea of our own rationality, he used to say, was convincing to us only because we so wished to be convinced. To any impartial observer, could such a thing exist, the sham was patent. Emotion and instinct were the basis of all our decisions, our actions, everything we valued, the way we saw the world. Reason and rationality were a thin coat of paint on a ragged surface.

The only way to make any sense of the United States Congress, our father told me once, is to view it as a two-hundred-year-long primate study. He didn't live to see the ongoing revolution in our thinking regarding nonhuman animal cognition.

But he wasn't wrong about Congress.

7

More memories of Fern:

In this first memory, we are three years old. Mother is sitting in the big love-seat in the library so that Fern can squeeze in on one side and me on the other. It's raining, been raining for days, and I am sick of being inside, sick of using my inside voice. Fern loves being read to. She's sleepy and quiet, pressing in as close to our mother as possible, her hands playing with the belt loops on Mom's corduroy pants, smoothing the nap on Mom's thighs. I, on the other hand, am flinging myself about, unable to get comfortable, kicking across Mom's lap at Fern's feet, trying to make her do something that will get her in trouble. Mom tells me to hold still in a voice that could pickle fish.

The book is *Mary Poppins* and the chapter is the one in which an old woman breaks off her own fingers, which then become sugar sticks for the children to suck on. I have a queasy feeling about this, but Fern hears the word *sugar* and her mouth begins to work in a sleepy, dreamy way. I don't understand that Fern doesn't understand about the fingers. I don't understand that Fern doesn't follow the story.

I interrupt constantly, because I wish to understand everything.

What is a perambulator? What is rheumatism? Will I get rheumatism someday? What are elastic-sided boots? Can I have some? Are Michael and Jane mad when Mary Poppins takes their stars? What if there were no stars in the sky? Could that happen? "For God's sake," Mom says finally. "Can you just let me read the damn story?" and because she used the words *God* and *damn*, which she hardly ever does, Mary has to be sacrificed. It's Mary wants to know, I tell her. "Mary is getting on my last nerve," our mother says. "Mary should be nice and quiet like our little Fern here."

Just as I sacrificed Mary, Fern has sacrificed me. She didn't know what rheumatism was, either, but because I was the one who asked, now she does. She gets to know about rheumatism *and* she gets praised for not talking when *she can't even talk*. I think that Fern has gotten praised for nothing and that I never get praised for nothing. It's clear that Mom loves Fern best. I can see half of Fern's face. She is almost asleep, one eyelid fluttering, one ear blooming like a poppy from her black fur, one big toe plugging her mouth so I can hear her sucking on it. She looks at me sleepily from over her own leg, from around the curve of Mom's arm. Oh, she has played this perfectly, that baby who still wears a diaper!

MEMORY TWO: One of the graduate students has gotten a free compilation tape from the local radio station and she throws it into the cassette player. We are dancing together, all the girls—Mom and Grandma Donna, Fern and I, the grad students, Amy, Caroline, and Courtney. We are rocking it old-school to "Splish Splash I Was Taking a Bath," "Palisades Park," and "Love Potion No. 9."

I didn't know if it was day or night. *I started kissin' everything in sight.*

Fern is smacking her feet down, loud as she can, jumping sometimes onto the backs of the chairs and then landing on the floor. She makes Amy swing her, and laughs the whole time she is in the air. I am shaking it, popping it, laying it down and working it out. "Conga line," Mom calls. She snakes us through the downstairs, Fern and I dancing, dancing, dancing behind her.

MEMORY THREE: A day of bright sun and new snow. Lowell is throwing snowballs against the kitchen window. They splatter softly when they hit, leaving trails of shine across the glass. Fern and I are too excited to stand still but twirl about the kitchen, trailing and spinning our scarves. We are so anxious to get outside we are impossible to dress. Fern is stamping and rocking from side to side. She does a backflip, and then another, and then I am looking down on the top of her head as we link hands for a merry-go-round spin.

I am asking where snow comes from, and why it comes only in winter, and if it snows in Australia in the summer, does that mean everything in Australia is opposite to our world? Is it light during the night and dark during the day? Does Santa bring you presents only if you've been very bad? Mom is not answering my questions, but fretting instead, because there is no way to make Fern wear mittens or boots. If you put something on Fern's feet, she screams.

The whole question of clothing has been a touchy one. Excepting those times when Fern would be too cold without (a second exception has been made for the diaper), Mom would rather not dress her; she doesn't want Fern made comical. But I have to wear clothes, so Fern also has to. Besides, Fern wants them. Mom decides to classify Fern's clothing as self-expression, an anthropomorphism Dad dislikes.

On this occasion, Mom settles for pinning her own large gloves to the cuffs of Fern's parka, shoving Fern's hands into them but letting her take them right out again. Mom warns me to stay upright. No loping through the snow on my hands and feet. A smell spreads through the kitchen. I can see that Mom is considering sending Fern out anyway. "She stinks," I say and Mom sighs, unzips Fern's parka, takes her upstairs to change her clothes. Dad is the one who brings her down again, reinserts her into her snow wear. I hear the shower running upstairs. By now I'm so hot I'm sweating.

Lowell has been building a snow ant. The abdomen, which Lowell calls the metasoma, is not as big as he wants—he wants a giant, mutant snow ant as tall as he is—but the snow is so sticky, it's already iced into place. When Fern and I finally burst out into the snow-globe world of the farmhouse yard, we find him trying to dislodge it, keep it rolling. We hop about him as he struggles. Fern swings up into the little mulberry tree above us. There is snow on the branches. Some of it she eats. Some of it she shakes down our necks until Lowell tells her to cut it out.

Fern is not much for cutting things out. Lowell puts up his hood. She drops onto his back, arm around his neck. I hear her laughing—a sound like a handsaw scraping back and forth. Lowell reaches over his head, grabs her arms, and somersaults her to the ground. She laughs more and scrambles up the tree for a repeat.

But Lowell has already moved off to find another white sheet of snow, start another snow ant. "My mistake was to stop and wait for you guys," he tells us. "We got to keep it moving." He ignores Fern's cries of disappointment.

I stay behind, digging a trench around the unfinished metasoma with my mittened hands. Fern climbs down, starts after Lowell. She looks back to see if I'm coming and I sign for her to give me some help. Ordinarily, this would have no impact, but she's still mad at Lowell. She pivots back.

Our father is standing on the porch with his coffee. "'Nothing beside remains,'" Dad says, pointing with his cup to the abandoned snow-ant abdomen. "'Round the decay of that colossal wreck.'"

Fern sits on the ground beside me, rests her chin on my arm, her feet on the metasoma. She stuffs another handful of snow into her mouth, smacks her protuberant, acrobatic lips, and turns to look up at me, eyes shining. Fern's eyes seem larger than human eyes, because the whites are not white but an amber color only slightly lighter than the irises. When I draw Fern's face, the crayon I use for her eyes is burnt sienna. Fern's own drawings are never finished, as she always eats the crayon.

She kicks now at the snowball with her feet. It's not clear this is meant to help, but it does. Beside her, I push with my hands. With less effort than I expected, it rocks a little and breaks free.

I'm able to roll it now so that it gathers girth. Fern is bouncing behind me like a cork on a wave, sometimes on top of the snow crust and sometimes falling through. She leaves a churned wake, the trail of the Tasmanian devil. The gloves pinned to her cuffs flop over the snow like leather fish.

Lowell turns, shading his eyes, because the sun is one bright dazzle on the ice-white world. "How did you do that?" he shouts back. He's grinning at me through the porthole of his jacket hood.

"I tried really hard," I tell him. "Fern helped."

"Girl power!" Lowell shakes his head. "Awesome thing."

"Power of love," says my father. "Power of love."

And then the graduate students arrive. We're going sledding!

No one tells me to calm down, because Fern won't be calming down.

My favorite grad student is named Matt. Matt's from Birmingham, England, and calls me *luv*, me and Fern both. I wrap my arms around his legs, jump up and down on the toes of his boots. Fern hurls herself at Caroline, knocking her into the snow. When Fern stands up, she is powdered head to toe like a doughnut. Both of us are demanding in our own ways to be picked up and swung. We are so excited that, in the strangely illuminating phrase my mother favors, we're completely beside ourselves.

I ALWAYS USED to believe I knew what Fern was thinking. No matter how bizarre her behavior, no matter how she might deck herself out and bob about the house like a Macy's parade balloon, I could be counted on to render it into plain English. Fern wants to go outside. Fern wants to watch *Sesame Street*. Fern thinks you are a doodoo-head. Some of this was convenient projection, but you'll never convince me of the rest. Why wouldn't I have understood her? No one knew Fern better than I; I knew every twitch. I was attuned to her.

"Why does she have to learn our language?" Lowell asked my father once. "Why can't we learn hers?" Dad's answer was that we still didn't know for sure that Fern was even capable of learning a language, but we did know for sure that she didn't have one of her own. Dad said that Lowell was confusing language with communication, when they were two very different things. Language is more than just words, he said. Language is also the order of words and the way one word inflects another.

Only he said this at much greater length, longer than either

Lowell or I, or certainly Fern, wished to sit still for. It all had something to do with *Umwelt*, a word I very much liked the sound of and repeated many times like a drumbeat until I was made to stop. I didn't care so much what *Umwelt* meant back then, but it turns out to refer to the specific way each particular organism experiences the world.

I am the daughter of a psychologist. I know that the thing ostensibly being studied is rarely the thing being studied.

When the Kelloggs first raised a child alongside a chimpanzee, back in the 1930s, the stated purpose was to compare and contrast developing abilities, linguistic and otherwise. This was the stated purpose of our study as well. Color me suspicious.

The Kelloggs believed that their sensationalistic experiment had sunk their reputations, that they were never again taken seriously as scientists. And if I know this now, our ambitious father surely knew it then. So what was the goal of the Fern/Rosemary Rosemary/Fern study before it came to its premature and calamitous end? I'm still not sure.

But it seems to me that much of the interesting data is mine. As I grew, my language development not only contrasted with Fern's but also introduced a *perfectly predictable* x-factor that undermined all such comparisons.

Ever since Day and Davis published their findings in the 1930s, there's been a perception that twinness affects language acquisition. New and better studies took place in the 1970s, but I'm not sure our parents were looking in their direction yet. Nor would such studies have been completely relevant to a situation such as ours, where the twins had such disparate potentials.

Though Fern and I were sometimes separated while the grad students observed us, we spent most of our time together. As I developed the habit of speaking for her, she seemed to develop the expectation that I would. By the time I turned three, I was already serving as Fern's translator in a way that surely retarded her progress.

So I think that, instead of studying how well Fern could communicate, our father might have been studying how well Fern could communicate with me. That there was a vice versa here, a tabloid-ready vice versa was unavoidable but unacknowledged. Here is the question our father claimed to be asking: can Fern learn to speak to humans? Here is the question our father refused to admit he was asking: can Rosemary learn to speak to chimpanzees?

One of the early grad students, Timothy, had argued that in our preverbal period, Fern and I had an idioglossia, a secret language of grunts and gestures. This was never written up, so I learned of it only recently. Dad had found his evidence thin, unscientific, and, frankly, whimsical.

SOMETIMES OOFIE, chimp star of the American Tourister luggage commercials, came on the TV. Fern paid no attention to him. But once, we caught a couple of reruns of *Lancelot Link, Secret Chimp*, with the very handsome Tonga playing Link. These talking apes, in their suits and ties, were more interesting to Fern. She watched intently, puckering and unpuckering her prehensile mouth, making her sign for hat. "Fern wants a hat like Lancelot Link," I told our mother. There was no need to make the request for myself. If Fern got a hat, I would get a hat.

Neither of us got a hat.

A short time later, our father arranged for a young chimp named Boris to visit the farmhouse for an afternoon. The sign Fern made for Boris was the same sign she used for the brown recluse spiders we sometimes found in the barn, which my mother translated as *crawling poo*, and Lowell as *crawling shit* (which seemed more sensible to me. *Poo* was a joke word. *Shit* was serious and Fern was being serious). Boris, Fern said, was dirty crawling shit. And then, deadly crawling shit.

Surrounded as she was by humans, Fern believed she was human. This wasn't unexpected. Most home-raised chimps, when asked to sort photographs into piles of chimps and humans, make only the one mistake of putting their own picture into the human pile. This is exactly what Fern did.

What seems not to have been anticipated was my own confusion. Dad didn't know then what we think we know now, that the neural system of a young brain develops partly by mirroring the brains around it. As much time as Fern and I spent together, that mirror went both ways.

Many years later, I found on the Web a paper our father had written about me. Subsequent studies with larger sample sizes have confirmed what Dad was among the first to suggest: that, contrary to our metaphors, humans are much more imitative than the other apes.

For example: if chimps watch a demonstration on how to get food out of a puzzle box, they, in their turn, skip any unnecessary steps, go straight to the treat. Human children overimitate, reproducing each step regardless of its necessity. There is some reason why, now that it's our behavior, being slavishly imitative is superior to being thoughtful and efficient, but I forget exactly what that reason is. You'll have to read the papers.

The winter after Fern vanished, and half a term late because of the tumult and turmoil at home, I started kindergarten, where my classmates called me the monkey girl or sometimes simply the monkey. There was something off about me, maybe in my gestures, my facial expressions or eye movements, and certainly in the things I said. Years later, my father made a passing reference to the uncanny-valley response—the human aversion to things that look almost but not quite like people. The uncanny-valley response is a hard thing to define, much less to test for. But if true, it explains why the faces of chimps so unsettle some of us. For the kids in my kindergarten class, I was the unsettling object. Those five- and six-year-olds were not fooled by the counterfeit human.

I could and did quarrel with their word choice—were they so stupid, I asked winningly, that they didn't know the difference between monkeys and apes? Didn't they know that humans were apes, too? But the implication that I'd be okay with being called ape girl was all my classmates needed to stick with their original choice. And they refused to believe they were apes themselves. Their parents assured them they weren't. I was told that a whole Sunday school class had been devoted to rebutting me.

Here are some things my mother worked with me on, prior to sending me off to school:

Standing up straight.

Keeping my hands still when I talked.

Not putting my fingers into anyone else's mouth or hair.

Not biting anyone, ever. No matter how much the situation warranted it.

Muting my excitement over tasty food, and not staring fixedly at someone else's cupcake.

Not jumping on the tables and desks when I was playing.

I remembered these things, most of the time. But where you succeed will never matter so much as where you fail.

. . .

HERE ARE SOME THINGS I learned only once I got to kinder-garten:

How to read children's faces, which are less guarded than grown-ups', though not as expressive as chimps'.

That school was about being quiet (and you'd think Mom might have added that to the things she'd warned me about; that rule I'd been given—that rule where you say only one for every three things you want to say—it wasn't nearly sufficient to the cause).

That big words do not impress children. And that grown-ups care a lot about what big words actually mean, so it's best to know that before you use one.

But most of all, I learned that different is different. I could change what I did; I could change what I didn't do. None of that changed who I fundamentally was, my not-quite-human, my tab-loid monkey-girl self.

I hoped that Fern was doing better among her own kind than I among mine. In 2009, a study showed macaque monkeys seem-ingly evidencing the uncanny-valley response themselves, which makes it probable for chimps.

Of course, none of that was in my thinking back then. For years, I imagined Fern's life as a Tarzan reversal. Raised among humans and returned now to her own kind, I liked to think of her bringing sign language to the other apes. I liked to think she was maybe solving crimes or something. I liked to think we'd given her superpowers.

PART THREE

❋

I did not think things through in such a human way, but under the influence of my surroundings conducted myself as if I had worked things out.

—FRANZ KAFKA, "A Report for an Academy"

1

I THINK IT'S inarguable that Mom, Dad, and Lowell were more shattered by Fern's departure than I was. I fared better simply by virtue of being too young to quite take it in.

And yet there were ways in which I was the one who carried the damage. For Mom, Dad, and Lowell, Fern had arrived in the middle of the story. They'd gotten to be themselves first, so they had a self to go back to. For me, Fern was the beginning. I was just over a month old when she arrived in my life (and she just shy of three months). Whoever I was before is no one I ever got to know.

I felt her loss in a powerfully physical way. I missed her smell and the sticky wet of her breath on my neck. I missed her fingers scratching through my hair. We sat next to each other, lay across each other, pushed, pulled, stroked, and struck each other a hundred times a day and I suffered the deprivation of this. It was an ache, a hunger on the surface of my skin.

I began to rock in place without knowing I was doing so and had to be told to stop. I developed the habit of pulling out my eyebrows. I bit on my fingers until I bled and Grandma Donna bought me little white Easter gloves and made me wear them, even to bed, for months.

Fern used to wrap her wiry pipe-cleaner arms around my waist from behind, press her face and body into my back, match me step for step when we walked, as if we were a single person. It made the grad students laugh, so we felt witty and appreciated. Sometimes it was encumbering, a monkey on my back, but mostly I felt enlarged, as if what mattered in the end was not what Fern could do or what I could do, but the sum of it—Fern and me together. And me and Fern together, we could do almost anything. This, then, is the me I know—the human half of the fabulous, the fascinating, the phantasmagorical Cooke sisters.

I've read that no loss compares to the loss of a twin, that survivors describe themselves as feeling less like singles and more like the crippled remainder of something once whole. Even when the loss occurs in utero, some survivors respond with a lifelong sense of their own incompleteness. Identical twins suffer the most, followed by fraternals. Extend that scale awhile and eventually you'll get to Fern and me.

Although it had had no immediate impact on the cut of my jibber-jabber—in fact, it took many years to truly sink in—finally I came to understand that all of my verbosity had been valuable only in the context of my sister. When she left the scene, no one cared anymore about my creative grammars, my compound lexemes, my nimble, gymnastic conjugations. If I'd ever imagined I'd be more important without her constantly distracting everyone, I found quite the opposite. The graduate students disappeared from my life the same moment Fern did. One day, every word I said was data, and carefully recorded for further study and discussion. The next, I was just a little girl, strange in her way, but of no scientific interest to anyone.

2

THERE IS AN ADVANTAGE to sharing a bedroom wall with your parents. You hear things. Hearing things is also the disadvantage. Sometimes Mom and Dad had sex. Sometimes they talked. Sometimes they had sex while they talked.

Years passed, but the things our parents talked about at night didn't change as much as you might think. Dad worried about his professional standing. Not so long ago he'd been a young professor on the rise, gathering in grants and graduate students like eggs at Easter. There were six students in his lab at the end of the Fern years, all scribbling theses about the study in the old farmhouse. Two of them were able to finish their work as planned, but four were not—at best, they had to narrow their focus, jigger something thin and uninteresting from data already collected. The reputation of the whole lab, of the whole department, suffered.

Our father turned paranoid. Although he himself had published solid and exciting work during that five-year period, he was now certain that his colleagues disrespected him. The evidence was everywhere he looked, at every staff meeting, every cocktail party. It drove him periodically to drink.

Lowell continued to be a problem, mostly Lowell, but also me.

Our parents lay beside each other in their bed and fretted. What was to be done about us? When would Lowell revert to the sweet, sensitive boy they knew he was inside? When would I manage to make a friend I didn't make up?

Lowell's counselor, Ms. Dolly Delancy, said that Lowell no longer believed their love for him was unconditional. How could he? He'd been told to care for Fern as a sister. He'd done so, only to see her cast from the family. Lowell was confused and he was angry. Good thing we have a trained professional to tell us that, Dad said.

Mom liked Ms. Delancy. Dad did not. Ms. Delancy had a son, Zachary, who was in the third grade when I was in kindergarten. Zachary used to lie under the jungle gym and whenever a girl swung over him, he'd call out the color of her underwear, even if she was wearing pants and he couldn't possibly know. I know our parents were aware of this, because I was the one who told them. Dad thought it was relevant information. Dad thought it was very telling. Mom did not.

Ms. Delancy said that the qualities making Lowell hard to live with were all very good qualities, some of his best, in fact—his loyalty, his love, his sense of justice. We wanted Lowell to change, but we didn't want him changing the things preventing that change. It made for a ticklish situation.

I didn't have a counselor of my own, so Ms. Delancy shared her thoughts about me as well. I was in the same predicament as Lowell, but while Lowell was responding by pushing the boundaries, I was trying my hardest to be good. Both reactions made sense. Both should be seen as cries for help.

Children do best with clear expectations and predictable consequences, Ms. Delancy said, conveniently ignoring the fact that if you told Lowell, this is where we draw the line, you could count on him stomping instantly over it.

Our parents decided it would be better to leave the line a blur and concentrate on allaying Lowell's insecurities. The house filled with love for Lowell, his favorite foods, books, games. We played Rummikub. We listened to Warren Zevon. We went to fucking Disneyland. It made him furious.

I DON'T SUPPOSE Ms. Delancy's assessment was wrong, but I do think it was incomplete. The part she was missing was our shared and searing grief. Fern was *gone*. Her disappearance represented many things—confusions, insecurities, betrayals, a Gordian knot of interpersonal complications. But it also was a thing itself. Fern had loved us. She'd filled the house with color and noise, warmth and energy. She deserved to be missed and we missed her terribly. No one outside the house ever really seemed to get that.

Because school was not making me feel the things everyone thought I needed to be feeling—valued and indispensable—I was transferred in the first grade to the hippie school on Second Street. The kids there didn't like me any better, but name-calling was not tolerated among the hippies. Steven Claymore taught the kids to scratch their armpits instead, which sometimes kids just did, so it had deniability, and this allowed the adults, including our parents, to console themselves that my situation had improved. I had a wonderful first-grade teacher, Ms. Radford, who genuinely loved me. I was given the part of the hen in *The Little Red Hen*—inarguably, the lead, the star turn. This was all it took to convince Mom that I was flourishing. Her catatonia had been replaced with an implausible buoyancy. Lowell and I were fine. We were such good kids, basically. Smart kids. At least we all had our health! Every gangplank a seesaw.

Is there a character in all of fiction more isolated than the little red hen?

I think Mom and Dad must have instructed the school not to say anything about Fern, because their usual approach to social difference and difficulty was to wade in up to their empathetic eyeballs.

"The reason Tammy can't eat Shania's birthday cupcakes is because she's allergic to wheat. Today we'll learn about wheat—where it grows and how many of the foods we eat contain it. Tomorrow Tammy's mother will bring in cupcakes made from rice flour, for us to taste. Does anyone else have allergies?"

"Today is the first day of the month of Ramadan. When Imad is older, he will observe Ramadan by fasting every day from sunrise to sunset. Fasting means not eating and not drinking anything but water. The dates of Ramadan are tied to the moon, so they change every year. Today we will make a lunar calendar. We will draw pictures of ourselves as astronauts walking on the moon."

"Dae-jung doesn't speak English, because his family comes from Korea. Today we will find Korea on a map. We will learn some Korean words so that Dae-jung isn't the only one learning a new language. Here is how you say 'Welcome, Dae-jung,' in Korean."

Without a specific injunction, it's hard to see how my childhood with Fern didn't ever become a lesson plan.

Dad gave me some tips designed to improve my social standing. People, he said, liked to have their movements mirrored. When someone leaned in to talk to me, I should likewise lean in. Cross my legs if they did, smile when they smiled, etc. I should try this (but be subtle about it. It wouldn't work if anyone saw I was doing it) with the kids at school. Well-meant advice, but it turned out badly, played too readily into the monkey-girl narrative—monkey see, monkey do. Which also meant I'd blown the subtlety part.

Mom had a theory I heard through the bedroom wall. You didn't need a lot of friends to get through school, she told Dad, but you had to have one. For a brief period in the third grade, I pretended that Dae-jung and I were friends. He didn't talk, but I was well able to supply both sides of a conversation. I returned a mitten he'd dropped. We ate lunch together, or at least we ate at the same table, and in the classroom he'd been given the desk next to mine on the theory that when I talked out of turn, it might help his language acquisition. The irony was that his English improved due in no small part to my constant yakking at him, but as soon as he could speak, he made other friends. Our connection was beautiful, but brief.

As soon as he was genuinely fluent, Dae-jung transferred to the public school. His parents had ambitions for him that included the math classes at North. In 1996, my mother phoned me at school in Davis to tell me that Dae-jung was just down the road at UC Berkeley. "You two could get together!" she said. My short-lived belief in our friendship was *that* intoxicating to her. She's never been able to give it up.

The word in Korean for "monkey" is *won-soong-ee*. That's phonetic. I don't know the proper romanization.

3

MEANWHILE, Lowell clawed his way to high school. High school Lowell was easier to live with than middle school Lowell. He stopped demanding that we go see Fern and joined the rest of us in seldom mentioning her. He was chilly but polite; peace settled over the house like a thin mantle of snow. One Mother's Day, he gave Mom a music box that played the theme from *Swan Lake*. She cried for days over it.

Marco was still Lowell's best buddy, though Marco's mom liked Lowell less than she had before they'd shoplifted Twizzlers from the Sahara Mart on Third Street, been picked up and made an example of.

He had an on-again, off-again relationship with a girl. Her name was Katherine Chalmers, but everyone called her Kitch. Kitch was Mormon. Her parents were strict and overwhelmed— they had nine children—so policing her had fallen to her two oldest brothers. Each rose to the challenge in his own special way. One showed up at our door and marched her home whenever she'd missed her curfew. The other bought bottles of Boone's Farm wine for her so she wouldn't have to shoulder-tap strangers. This mix, as our father's studies would tell you, was a poor model for behavior modification. Kitch was a girl with a reputation.

At the Chalmers house, Lowell wasn't allowed anywhere near Kitch's bedroom, but our parents had what Mom called an Open Door Policy, which is to say that Kitch could be in Lowell's room, but only if the door was fully open. Sometimes I was sent to check on this and the door was always as demanded. But sometimes Lowell and Kitch were on the bed together, fully clothed, but vigorously trying to occupy the same space anyway. Mom never asked about that part, so I never said. Somewhere along the way, I'd learned not to tattle.

In fact, at some point, I'd mostly stopped talking altogether. I can't tell you exactly when that happened. Years before, I'd figured out that school went best when I didn't draw attention to myself, but knowing this and accomplishing it were two different things. So it happened gradually, over time, by dint of constant effort. First I eliminated the big words. They were getting me nowhere. Then I quit correcting other people when they used the wrong words. I raised the ratio of things I thought to things I said from three to one, to four to one, to five, to six, to seven.

I still thought as much as ever, and sometimes I imagined the responses I would have gotten if I had spoken up and what I would have then said next, and so on and so on. Without the release of talking, these thoughts crowded my brain. The inside of my head turned clamorous and outlandish, like the Mos Eisley spaceport bar in *Star Wars*.

Teachers began to complain of my inattentiveness. In the old days, even when I talked nonstop, I was still able to pay attention. I had become distractible, Mom said.

Unfocused, said Dad.

Lowell said nothing. Probably he hadn't noticed.

In his senior year, he was the point guard on the South High School basketball team. This was a position of such power and prestige that even my life was made easier by it. I went to all the games. The bouncing echoes of a high school gym, the bells, the smells, the slap of the ball on the wood—these are things I still respond to with a profound sense of well-being. Indiana basketball. Everyone was nice to me when my brother was on the court directing traffic.

Marion, Indiana, had a powerhouse team that year and we had a game with them coming up; I was so excited I buzzed. I'd made a poster of a snake wrapped around a basketball so that it turned into Lowell's number—9—and put it in the living room window. And then, one day, when Lowell was absolutely supposed to be at practice, leading his team through their drills, I heard him come in. I recognized the sound the door made when it was Lowell closing it.

I was upstairs, reading something or other—*Bridge to Terabithia* or *Where the Red Fern Grows*—one of those books where someone dies, because I was already soppy with tears. Mom was out, I don't remember where, but I don't think she could have changed a thing and I'm just as glad she didn't try and have that failure to reproach herself with later.

I went down to see what was what. The door to his bedroom was shut. I opened it. Lowell was lying facedown on his bed, feet on his pillow, head at the foot. He looked up, but not so much that I could see his face. "Get the fuck out of my room," he said. Voice full of nails. I didn't move.

He swung his legs to the floor, stood, and turned toward me. His face was red, wet, and puffy as a cloud. He took me by the shoulders, shoved me out. "Don't you ever fucking come in here again," he said. "Fucking ever." He closed the door.

By dinner he seemed normal. He ate and talked to Dad about the upcoming game. He didn't say he'd missed practice and I didn't say so, either. We watched an episode of *The Cosby Show*. I remember him laughing. It was the last thing we all did together.

That night he took all his money—his bank was a Groucho Marx sock puppet Grandma Donna made for him back when he'd had chicken pox—and put it in his gym bag along with some clothes. He'd always had a gift for making money and he never spent a dime, so I expect he had a goodly sum. He took our father's keys, walked to the lab, and let himself in. He consolidated the rats into a few large cages, which he then took outside. He let the rats go. Then he caught a bus to Chicago and he never came back.

Once again our father's grad students lost data they'd spent years collecting. It was no kindness to the rats, Dad said, not with the weather we were having. It was certainly no kindness to our father, who stayed on at the university but never again had a grad student that any other professor wanted to work with. I'll just say that Mom took Lowell's disappearance hard, worse even than when we lost Fern, and leave it at that. I don't have the words for what it did to her. She's never even managed to pretend to recover.

At first we all thought he'd come back. I had a birthday looming; I was certain he wouldn't miss that. He'd often taken off for a few days, as many as four on one occasion, and then returned without us ever learning where he'd slept. So in spite of the Great Rat Release, it took our parents a while to figure out that this time was different. Two weeks in, they decided the police, who saw him as a habitual runaway and also an adult, since he'd just turned eighteen, were insufficiently concerned. They hired their own investigator, a no-nonsense woman named K. T. Payne, to track him down. At first, Payne called us regularly at home. She hadn't caught up to

Lowell, but she was on the scent. There'd been sightings. There'd been reports. There'd been mischief, or so I gathered by the exact way no one was telling me much. "Hey, kiddo," she'd say to me, if I was the one to answer, "how's it sparking?" and I'd hang around to hear what I could hear, but our parents' side of things would be carefully brief and noninformative.

Then Lowell disappeared entirely. With each new phone call, Mom circled the drain, and eventually Dad asked K.T. to use his office phone instead.

A second investigator was hired.

Weeks became months and still we believed he'd be back. I never moved into his room, though I often slept in his bed, which made me feel closer to him and got me away from that shared wall and Mom's crying. One day I found a note he'd left for me inside *The Fellowship of the Ring*. He knew I reread that trilogy often; he knew that the day would soon come when I'd need the consolation of the Shire, which was as much like Bloomington, Indiana, as any place else in the world. "Fern is not on a fucking farm," the note said.

I kept this to myself as Mom was in no condition to be told. I assumed Fern *had* been on the farm and then sent away again, probably for bad behavior. Besides, Lowell was dealing with it. Lowell would take care of Fern and then he would come back and take care of me.

It never once occurred to me that our father had been lying all along.

WHEN I WAS EIGHT OR NINE, I used to spend the time before I went to sleep at night imagining that Fern and I lived on her farm together. There were no adults and no other humans, only young chimps, chimps with a great need for someone to teach them songs, read them books. The bedtime story I used to tell myself was that I was telling the baby chimps a bedtime story. My fantasy was drawn in part from *Peter Pan*.

A second inspiration was the Swiss Family Robinson, Disney version. When we'd gone to Disneyland, the tree house had been my favorite thing in the whole park. If only I'd had no parents watching my every move, if only I'd been a happy, carefree orphan, I'd have hidden under the player piano until everything closed, and then taken up residence there.

I transplanted the whole thing, root, trunk, and branch, to Fern's farm, where my nighttime ruminations focused on the pulleys and wires, how we'd get running water and grow vegetables— in my fantasy life, I liked vegetables—all without leaving the tree. I'd fall asleep with visions of gadgetry and logistical challenges dancing in my head.

Ironic then that many years later, the Swiss Family Robinson were forcibly moved out of the Disney tree house so that Tarzan and his saintly ape mother, Kala, could move in.

MARION CRUSHED Bloomington South and went on to win the state championship—the first year in a three-year streak known as the Purple Reign. I don't think Lowell could have altered that outcome. Even so, his disappearance didn't help my social standing. The morning after the game, there was toilet paper dripping like tinsel from the branches of our mulberry tree, and three bags of shit, probably dog but who really knows, by the front door. That day we played dodgeball at school and I came home one large walking bruise. No one had tried to stop it. I suspect some of the teachers might have liked to join in.

Months became years.

On my first day of seventh grade, someone taped a page from *National Geographic* to the back of my jacket. It was a glossy view of a fertile female chimp butt, pink and swollen and target-like. For the next two hours, whenever I was in the hall, kids poked at my back as I went past, in a fucking motion, until, finally, in French class, my teacher noticed the picture and removed it.

I figured the rest of my time at middle school would be more of the same. Add gum and ink and water from the toilet bowl. Stir vigorously. I came home that first day, locked myself in the bathroom, took a shower to cover the noise, and cried and cried for Lowell, who I still thought would someday be back. When he came home, Lowell would make them stop. Lowell would make them sorry. I just had to keep going until then, keep sitting in those classes and walking in those hallways.

I never told my parents. My mother wasn't strong enough to hear it; she would never come out of her room again if I told. The only thing I could do for her now was to be okay. I worked at that as if it were my job. No complaints to management about worker conditions.

There was no point in telling my father. He'd never let me quit after only one day. He couldn't help me and he'd make some terrible blunder if he tried. Parents are too innocent for the Boschian landscapes of middle school.

So I kept my mouth shut. I was always keeping my mouth shut by then.

Fortunately for me, that first day turned out to be as bad as it got. There were other students, kids even more offensively weird than I, who took the full weight of middle school in my place. Occasionally, someone would ask, in tones of great concern, if I was in estrus, which was my own fault; no one would have even known the word if I hadn't used it once, apparently memorably, back in the fourth grade. But mostly no one spoke to me at all.

In their bedroom, in the dark, Mom and Dad worried about how quiet I'd become. It was bound to happen, they assured each other. Typical teenage sullenness; they'd been much the same themselves. I'd grow out of it. Hit some reasonable midpoint between the constant talking I'd done before and my current silence.

Occasionally, we heard from Lowell. A postcard would come, sometimes with a message, sometimes without, always unsigned. I remember one with a picture of the Nashville Parthenon and a St. Louis postmark. "I hope you're happy," he'd written on the back, which is a hard thing to parse, and you have to work to take it at face value, but it could mean just exactly what it said. Lowell could have been hoping we were happy.

WE STOPPED LOOKING for him one day in 1987, early June. Lowell had been gone more than a year. I was out on the driveway, throwing a tennis ball against the garage door and catching it, which is how you play catch when there's only one of you. I was thirteen years old, had a whole hot summer stretching ahead of me before I went back to school. The sun was shining and the air was wet and still. I'd been to the library that morning and had seven books waiting in my room, three of which I'd never read before. Across the street, Mrs. Byard waved at me. She was mowing their lawn and the motor of the mower had a sleepy distant hum, like bees. I wasn't happy, exactly, but I was remembering how happiness felt.

Two men parked a black car in front of the house and came up the walk. "We need to talk to your brother," one of the men said to me. He was dark-skinned, but not black. Hair shaved so short he was almost bald, and sweating in the heat. He took a handkerchief out, wiped the top of his head with it. I would have liked to do that, too, run my hand over his hair. I would probably have liked the way that stubble felt in my palm.

"Can you get him for us?" the other man asked.

"My brother's with Fern," I said. I rubbed my hands on the thighs of my pants to get the itch off. "He's gone to live with Fern."

Mom came out of the house and gestured for me to join her on the porch. She took me by the arm, put me behind her, so that she stood between the men and me.

"FBI, ma'am," the almost bald man told her. He showed her a badge. He said my brother was a person of interest in a fire that had caused $4.6 million of damage to the John E. Thurman Veterinary Diagnostic Laboratory at UC Davis. "It'd go best for him if he came to talk to us of his own accord," one of the men said. "You should tell him that."

"Who's Fern?" asked the other.

MOST OF THE RATS that Lowell had released were recaptured, but not all. Despite our father's dire predictions, some survived that winter and the next one, too. They went on to have full lives—sex, travel, and adventure. For many years after, there were hooded-rat sightings in Bloomington. One rat was found in a shoe in a dorm room closet, another in a downtown coffee shop. Under the pew in the campus chapel. In the Dunn cemetery, eating the buttercups on a grave dating back to the Revolutionary War.

4

THEN I WAS FIFTEEN, biking on my own through the beautiful, autumnal IU campus. Someone shouted my name as I pedaled past. "Rosemary! Wait up," this someone called. "Wait up!" So I waited up and it was Kitch Chalmers, now a student at the U and seeming genuinely glad to see me. "Rosemary Cooke!" she said. "My old buddy from back in the day!"

Kitch took me into the student union, bought me a Coke. She chitchatted a bit and I listened. She told me that she regretted the wildness of her youth and hoped I wasn't making the same mistakes. She warned me that some things, once done, couldn't be undone. But she was on a better path now. She was in a sorority and her grades were good. She was getting an education degree, which was something I, too, should think about. You'd probably be a great teacher, she said, and to this day I have no idea why anyone would have thought that, though it is what I eventually did.

She had a nice boyfriend, who was off on his mission in Peru, she told me, and he didn't let a week go by without calling her. Finally, she asked if we ever heard from Lowell. She never had. Not one word since the day he'd left. She thought she deserved better than that. We all deserved better, she said, we were a nice family.

And then she told me something I didn't know about the last time she'd seen Lowell. They'd been walking together to his basketball practice, she said, when they ran into Matt. Matt my favorite grad student, Matt from Birmingham. Matt whom, after Fern left, I'd never seen again.

Matt who'd known I loved him, but hadn't even said good-bye.

It turned out, Kitch said, that Matt had left Bloomington with Fern. He'd seemed surprised when Lowell didn't already know that. Other chimps, separated suddenly from their families, had sometimes just died with no clear cause but grief. So Matt had been sent along, had volunteered, in fact, to help with the transition. He'd taken Fern to a psych lab in Vermillion, South Dakota. This lab housed more than twenty chimps, and was run by a Dr. Uljevik, about whom Matt had nothing good to say.

Although Fern was clearly suffering from the shock and terror of the move, Dr. Uljevik insisted on limiting the time Matt had with her to a few hours a week. He'd put Fern at once into a cage with four larger, older chimps, and when Matt told him that she'd never been with chimps before and couldn't they introduce her slowly, Dr. Uljevik said no. He said she had to learn her place. She had to learn what she was. Dr. Uljevik said, "If she can't learn her place, we can't keep her here." He never once, in all the time Matt had spent there, had called Fern by her name.

"Then," Kitch said, "Lowell just lost it." She'd tried to make him go on to basketball practice. She was afraid he'd be benched for the Marion game. She'd told him he had a responsibility to his teammates, to the whole school, heck, to the whole town.

"'Don't effing talk to me about responsibility,'" he'd said (which I doubted. Lowell never said *effing* in his life). "'That's my sister in that cage.'" They'd had a fight and Kitch had broken up with him.

Kitch had never known Fern, and so, like everyone else in town, she'd never really understood; Lowell's reaction still struck her as extreme and inexplicable. "I told him I didn't want to be the girl-friend of the guy who lost the game to Marion," she'd told me. "I wish I hadn't said that, but we were always saying horrible things to each other. I thought we'd make it up later, like we always did. He sure used to say some horrible stuff. It wasn't just me."

But I barely heard that part, because I was still hearing what she'd said earlier. "Out there in South Dakota," Kitch had said, "Matt said they treated Fern like some kind of animal."

IT'S HARD ENOUGH here to forgive myself for things I did and felt when I was five, hopeless for the way I behaved at fifteen. Lowell heard that Fern was in a cage in South Dakota and he took off that very night. I heard the same thing and my response was to pretend I hadn't heard it. My heart had risen into my throat, where it stayed all through Kitch's horrible story. I couldn't finish my Coke or speak around that nasty, meaty, beating lump.

But as I'd biked home, my head cleared. It took me all of five blocks to decide it wasn't such a bad story, after all. Good old Matt. Twenty other chimps for friends, a new chimp family. The cage clearly just an interim measure before she was moved into Dad's farm. Lowell had no gift for belief and faith. Lowell, I thought, Lowell was capable of leaping to some crazy conclusions.

Besides, if there *had* been a problem with Fern, Lowell had surely taken care of it by now. He'd gone to South Dakota and done whatever needed to be done. And then he'd moved on to Davis, California. The FBI had told us so. My own government. Would they lie?

At dinner, I adopted my usual strategy of saying nothing. The spoken word converts individual knowledge into mutual knowledge, and there is no way back once you've gone over that cliff. Saying nothing was more amendable, and over time I'd come to see that it was usually your best course of action. I'd come to silence hard, but at fifteen I was a true believer.

5

AND THEN I TRIED to never think of Fern again. By the time I left for college, I'd come surprisingly close to achieving this. It had all happened so long ago. I'd been so young. I'd spent many more years without her than with her, and most of the years I'd had with her were years I didn't remember.

I left home, the last of the children to do so. Though Mom had acquiesced to this out-of-state nonsense, her voice on the phone that first year was ragged. I couldn't come back for the summer and still qualify for in-state tuition during my sophomore year, so I didn't. Mom and Dad came to visit in July. "At least it's a dry heat," they kept telling me, though once the thermometer tops a hundred I think that's just crazy talk. We drove around campus; wound, without noting it, past the old arson crime site, the lab now fully operational.

Then they went back to Bloomington, where, in August, they moved house. It was a strange feeling, to know that once again I lived somewhere I'd never seen.

With no conscious decision regarding the matter, I found myself avoiding classes that dealt with primates. No genetics, no physical anthropology, and certainly no psychology. You might be surprised at how hard dodging primates can be. Take Introduction to Classical Chinese and find yourself devoting a week to Sun Wukong, the Monkey King, and the chaos he wreaks in Heaven. Take a European literature class and find on the syllabus Kafka's "A Report for an Academy," with its ape narrator, Red Peter, which your professor will tell you is a metaphor for being Jewish and you'll see how it might work that way, but it's not the most obvious reading. Take astronomy and maybe there's a section devoted to exploration, to those pioneering dogs and chimps of space. You might be shown the photos of the space chimps in their helmets, grinning from ear to ear, and you might feel an urge to tell the rest of your class that chimps grin like that only when they're frightened, that no amount of time among humans will change it. Those happy-looking space chimps in those pictures are frankly terrified and maybe you just barely stop yourself from saying so.

So it's not true that I never thought of Fern. More that I never thought of her unless prompted and then I never lingered there.

I came to UC Davis both to find my past (my brother) and to leave it (the monkey girl) behind. By monkey girl, I mean me, of course, not Fern, who is not now and never has been a monkey. In some unaccessed part of my brain, somewhere in that thinking that's below language, I must have still believed it was possible to fix my family and myself, live our lives as if Fern had never been part of us. I must have believed that this would be a good thing to do.

Checking into the freshman dorms, I made a decision never to talk about my family. I wasn't a talker anymore and I anticipated little difficulty in this. But I was surprised to find that the families we'd all left behind were, often as not, the topic du jour and harder to avoid than I'd hoped.

My first roommate was an *X-Files* obsessive from Los Gatos.

Her name was Larkin Rhodes, a natural blonde who dyed her hair red and made us all call her Scully. In states of high emotion, Scully's cheeks turned from a scrubbed pink to white to pink again, so quickly it was like time-lapse photography. She started talking about her family practically the minute we met.

Scully had gotten in first, chosen a bed, and thrown her clothes onto it in a heap (they stayed that way for months; it was like a nest she slept in), and was putting up posters when I opened the door. One poster was, of course, the famous "I Want to Believe" from *The X-Files*. The other was from *Edward Scissorhands*, which she said was her very favorite Johnny Depp. "What's yours?" she asked and I might have made a better first impression if I'd had one.

Fortunately, Scully was the oldest of three sisters and accustomed to compensating for lesser minds. She told me that her father was a contractor who worked on high-end houses—houses with rolling ladders in the libraries, red carp in the fountains, closets the size of bathrooms, bathrooms the size of bedrooms. He spent his weekends at Renaissance Faires, wearing velvet hats and saying good morrow to the wenches there.

Her mother designed cross-stitching kits and marketed them under the company name of X-Rhodes (pronounced *Crossroads*). She gave craft workshops all over the country, but was particularly popular in the South. Scully had a pillow on her bed with a cross-stitched aerial view of the Great Wall of China, a display of thrilling chiaroscuro—really, it was as if you were there.

Her mother had once made Scully miss a high school dance in order to clean the bathroom grout with bleach on a toothbrush. "That there tells you everything you need to know about Mama. She has Martha Stewart on speed dial," Scully said. And then, "Not like for real. Just kind of psychically." She fixed her sad blue eyes on me. "You know how everything seems so normal when you're growing up," she asked plaintively, "and then comes this moment when you realize your whole family is nuts?" By the time I'd heard all that, I had known her for maybe twenty minutes.

Scully was appallingly gregarious—so outgoing she was practically incoming. Everything seemed to happen in our room. I'd come back from class or dinner, or I'd wake up in the middle of the night, and there'd be a half-dozen freshmen, sitting with their backs against the walls, carrying on about the Whac-A-Mole dynamics of the homes they'd just left. Their parents were so weird! Like Scully, they'd just figured that out. Every single one of them had weird parents.

One of them had a mother who'd once grounded her a whole summer because she'd gotten a B-plus in biology. Her mother had grown up in some part of Delhi where they didn't abide B-pluses.

One of them had a father who made the whole family stand at the refrigerator and down a glass of orange juice before going out for breakfast, because restaurant orange juice was too expensive to order, but you could hardly call it breakfast without.

One night the girl across the hall, Abbie something or other, told us she had an older sister who, at sixteen, said that back when she was three, their dad used to make her touch his penis. Abbie was lying across the foot of my bed when she said this, her head on one hand, black hair falling like a fountain around her bent arm. She was probably wearing a tank top and flannel plaid pajama bottoms. She slept in these, but she also wore them to class. She said that everyone in L.A. went to school in their pajamas.

"And then, after everyone goes into therapy and takes sides, and no one is speaking to anyone anymore," Abbie said, "she suddenly remembers he didn't; she maybe only dreamed he had. And she's like *still* pissed off at everyone who didn't believe her, because what if it had been true? She's a crazy person," Abbie said. "Sometimes I truly hate her. Like the rest of the family is fine, you know? And then this one crazy sister ruins it all."

This was so serious no one knew how to respond. We all sat and watched Scully paint her toenails with gold glitter, and no one said a word. The silence went on too long, turned awkward.

"Whatev," Abbie said, which in 1992 meant you didn't really care no matter how much it had sounded as if you did. She didn't just say this; she used a hand sign as well—index fingers up, hands joined at the thumbs into a W. That we had forced her to *whatev* us made our silence so much worse.

Whatev was the first hand sign I learned at college, but there were several popular then. There was the thumb-and-index-finger L held against the forehead, which meant *Loser*. The *whatev* W could be flipped up and down, W to M to W to M, in which case it meant *Whatever, your mother works at McDonald's.* 'Cause that's the way we rolled back in '92.

Doris Levy spoke up. "My father sings in the grocery store," she offered. She was sitting with her arms around her knees on the floor by Scully's golden toes. "Top-of-his-lungs loud." Old-school rock and roll piped in over the intercom, and her father in the deli, picking up all the cheeses and smelling them, belting away. *Mama told me not to come. Wake me up before you go-go.*

"Maybe he's gay," Scully suggested. "He sounds kind of gay to me."

"One night at dinner, out of nowhere, he asks me if I respect him," Doris said. "What the fuck am I supposed to say to that?" She turned to me. "Your parents are probably pretty weird, too?" she asked. I caught the whiff of collusion. I got that we were filling the silence as a team so that Abbie wouldn't regret having told us what she'd told us. I got that it was my turn now.

But I flubbed the handoff. I was still hearing Abbie's voice—*and then this one crazy sister goes and ruins it all*—and everything else was someone shouting at me from a distant, stormy shore.

"Not really," I said, and stopped so as to not talk about my parents. Who were, after all, as ordinary a pair of people who'd tried to raise a chimp like a human child as you were ever going to find.

"You are lucky to be so fucking normal," Scully told me and everyone else agreed.

What a scam I'd pulled off! What a triumph. Apparently, I'd finally erased all those little cues, those matters of personal space, focal distance, facial expression, vocabulary. Apparently, all you needed to be considered normal was no evidence to the contrary. This plan of moving halfway across the country and never talking to anyone ever again was working like a dream.

Except that now I'd achieved it, normal suddenly didn't sound so desirable. Weird was the new normal and, of course, I hadn't gotten the memo. I still wasn't fitting in. I still had no friends. Maybe I just didn't know how. Certainly I'd had no practice.

Maybe sedulously making sure that no one really knew me was an impediment to friendship. Maybe all those people coming in and out of my room *were* friends and I just hadn't realized it, because I'd been expecting more. Maybe friendship was not as big a deal as I'd thought and I actually had lots of friends.

Inferential data suggests otherwise. I wasn't asked along when Scully and a Brady Bunch of other freshmen went off to Tahoe for a weekend to ski. I learned of it only afterward, the plans carefully not laid in my room, not discussed in my presence. On the trip, Scully had hooked up with an older guy from Cal Poly, who slept with her one night and then wouldn't speak to her the next morning. This had to be so thoroughly talked through that I overheard, and Scully saw me overhearing. "We didn't think you'd be into it," Scully said, "coming from Indiana and all. Like *you* need to go somewhere and see snow." Awkward laugh, eyes darting about like pinballs, cheeks aflame. She was so embarrassed I felt bad for her.

IF YOU'VE EVER been a college undergraduate taking Philosophy 101, you've probably encountered the concept of philosophical solipsism. According to solipsism, reality exists only inside your own mind. What follows then is that you can only be certain of your own status as a conscious being. Everyone else might be some sort of mindless marionette operated by alien overlords or cat parasites, or possibly running about with no motivation at all. You'll never prove otherwise.

Scientists have solved the problem of solipsism with a strategy called *inference to the best explanation*. It's a cheap accommodation and no one is happy about it, with the possible exception of those alien overlords.

So I can't prove that I'm different from you, but that's my best explanation. I infer this difference from the responses of other people. I assume my upbringing is the cause. Inference and assumption, smoke and Jell-O, nothing you could build a house on. Basically, I'm just telling you that I feel different from other people.

But maybe you feel different, too.

The average chimp friendship lasts about seven years. Scully and I shared a bedroom for nine months. We never had a serious quarrel or falling out. And then we packed up, sashayed off into our separate lives, and haven't spoken since. Say good-bye to Scully.

We won't be seeing her again until 2010, when she friends me on Facebook for no discernible reason and with nothing much to say.

FOR MY SECOND YEAR, I answered an apartment-share advertisement I'd found on the Food Co-op bulletin board. Todd Donnelly, a junior majoring in art history, turned out to be a nice, quiet guy, a guy who took people at their word, which is a dangerous but generous way to live in the world. I heard a lot more about his Irish father, from whom he got his freckles, and his Japanese mother, from whom he got his hair, than he heard about my parents, but he heard more than most. By then I'd figured out the way to talk about my family. Nothing simpler really. Start in the middle.

One night Todd managed to procure, through his own mysterious methods, an animated version of *The Man in the Iron Mask*, done by Burbank Films Australia. Alice Hartsook, his girlfriend at the time (Todd was such an idiot to let her go), came over. They took the couch, heads at either end, feet heaped in the middle, toes wriggling. I lay on the rug with some pillows. We ate microwaved popcorn and Todd discoursed on animation in general and the Burbank style in particular.

You know the story. One twin is the king of France. One twin is thrown into the Bastille and forced to wear an iron mask so no one will ever see his face. The twin in prison has all the kingly qualities. The real king is a real asshole. Toward the middle of this cartoon there is a lovely ballet under a firework sky. Oddly, that was the moment at which I found I couldn't breathe. On the television— pirouettes, arabesques, and a shower of colored stars. On the floor—me, sweating, heart running uphill, gulping for air but unable to open my lungs. I sat up and the room went dark, revolving slowly about me.

Alice thrust the discarded popcorn bag at me with instructions to breathe into it. Todd slid to the floor behind me, his legs to either side of my legs. He rubbed my shoulders. This was kind, since Todd wasn't a toucher. And I do like to be touched; it's a monkey-girl thing.

The shoulder-rub relaxed me enough that I began to cry. I was still breathing into the popcorn bag and my sobbing came as all manner of lovely ocean sounds, sometimes waves and sometimes seals. "Are you all right?" Todd asked me, which I clearly wasn't and yet people do ask that. "What happened?" Todd's thumbs pressed into the back of my neck.

"Are you all right?" asked Alice. "Should we call someone? What happened?"

I honestly didn't know. I didn't want to know. Something was rising from the crypt, and what I did know was that I didn't want to see what it was. Nor did I want to see the rest of *The Man in the Iron Mask*. I said I was fine, all better now, and that I had no idea what had set me off. Made some excuse and left to go lie down where I continued to cry, only more quietly so as to not further upset Todd and Alice.

When there is an invisible elephant in the room, one is from time to time bound to trip over a trunk. I took my old escape route and I still knew the way. I fell asleep just as fast as I could.

6

SOME YEARS PASSED.

Enter Harlow.

Now that you know me better, let's take a second look at that first encounter. I'm sitting in the cafeteria with my grilled cheese sandwich and my milk. Harlow blows through the door like a hurricane, if hurricanes were tall, sexy girls in blue T-shirts and angelfish necklaces.

So maybe I'm less alarmed than you'd imagined the first time you heard this story. Maybe I could see that Harlow wasn't as angry as she was pretending to be. The smashing of the dishes, the throwing of the coats—it was all performative. Maybe I could see how she was enjoying herself.

It was a good performance and she was enjoying that part, too, the satisfaction of a job well done, but it wasn't a great performance or I wouldn't have seen through it. Still, as a fellow impostor, I appreciated her vigor. I admired her choices though I wouldn't have made them. Freak or fake, I'd been asking myself ever since I arrived at college, and suddenly here was someone bold enough to be both.

But I was still as much in the dark about my own reactions as you were the first time you heard this. Too busy ducking, chafing at the handcuffs, phoning Dad, filling out the paperwork. Fast-forward now to me returning to Davis after Thanksgiving vacation and finding Harlow in my apartment. No one would have liked that. Maybe I liked it even less. Here we go again, I said to myself. I said this so distinctly in my head that I heard it as well as said it. As if I was quite used to finding someone with no sense of bound-aries in my space, fiddling with my things and breaking most of them. Here we go again.

And this, finally, was the moment the hypnotist snapped her fin-gers. My ease with Harlow's tantrums and impositions had nothing to do with our shared humbuggeries. I was okay with her acting-out because I'd seen it before. Harlow could have pissed in the cor-ner, and it would have been nothing I hadn't seen before. Since she hadn't, by the family metric, her behavior hardly even counted as a scene.

I was struck less by the familiarity of it all than by the time it had taken me to recognize that familiarity. It was one thing to con-ceal my essential monkey-girlness from others. It was quite another to completely forget it myself. (And yet, wasn't that exactly what I'd been hoping for? Turned out I didn't like it. I didn't like it one bit.)

My father hadn't been fooled. "I suppose someone put you up to it," Dad had said on the phone, but I hadn't noticed. I hated it when Dad understood me better than I did myself and often chose not to listen when he talked rather than run that risk.

When the revelation finally came, it complicated my feelings to-ward Harlow more than it illuminated them. On the one hand, I could see she was bad news. In the comments section of my kinder-garten report card I'd been described as impulsive, possessive, and demanding. These are classic chimp traits and I've worked hard over the years to eradicate them. I felt that Harlow was maybe demonstrating the same tendencies without the same commitment to reform. In her company, I might fall back into bad old ways.

Yet I felt comfortable with her in a way I never felt comfortable with anyone. It's hard to overstate how lonely I was. Let me just repeat that I'd once gone, in a matter of days, from a childhood where I was never alone to this prolonged, silent only-ness. When I lost Fern, I'd also lost Lowell—at least I lost him in the way he'd been before—and I'd lost my mother and father in that same way, and I lost all the grad students for real, including my beloved Matt from Birmingham, who, when the moment came, chose Fern over me.

So I could see that Harlow was fundamentally untrustworthy. Simultaneously, she seemed like someone with whom I could be my true self. I had no intention of doing so and, with an equal and counterbalancing intensity, a great longing for it. It would be so interesting to see who my true self was, I thought with that part of my brain that came from my father. And with the part that came from my mother—has our little Rosemary made a friend at last?

AND HERE WE ARE, finally back in the middle where we left me, a bright-eyed undergraduate saddled with her very own arrest record and someone else's powder-blue suitcase. The prophetic stars are hopping about the sky like fleas.

One: The appearance and immediate disappearance of my mother's journals.

Two: A muffled message from Lowell, the knock on the dungeon wall from an adjacent cell.

Three: Harlow.

When a portent repeats itself three times, like something out of *Julius Caesar*, even Caliban, a couple of plays over, is bound to notice.

MOSTLY I WAS focused on my brother's return. I was sick with excitement, sick with the sort of Christmas-morning anticipation you might have if, in your family, sometimes Christmas turns out more like *Nightmare on Elm Street*.

My for-real Christmas break was less than two weeks away. If Lowell visited during finals, I'd have all sorts of free time for him. We could play poker and Rummikub. Maybe go to San Francisco, hike in Muir Woods. There's a place up by Lake Berryessa where, on a clear day, if you drive on a road marked PRIVATE, NO TRESPASSING and climb over a fence posted TRESPASSERS WILL BE PROSECUTED, you can see across the entire state—the Sierra Nevada to the east, the Pacific to the west. Very very trippy. Lowell would love it.

If he visited after, I'd be in Indiana.

So I hoped Ezra was telling the truth when he'd said that Lowell would be back in a couple of days, and I hoped a couple of days meant two. I hoped Lowell would guess I'd be spending Christmas with Mom and Dad. I hoped he knew I *had* to do that, if only because he never did. I hoped he cared.

A few weeks after my first arrival in Davis, I'd found my way to the newspaper archives in the basement of Shields Library and spent most of a weekend holed up there, reading the local coverage of the April 15, 1987, firebombing of the John E. Thurman Veterinary Diagnostic Laboratory. This didn't get much play in Indiana, where they hadn't connected it with Bloomington's most hated high school point guard ever. Even in Davis, details were thin on the ground.

The lab was under construction at the time it was destroyed. The damage was estimated at $4.6 million. The letters ALF had been painted inside the burned hull and some nearby university vehicles were also tagged with Animal Liberation Front graffiti. "Research on animals benefits animals, people, and the environment," the university spokesman had said.

The ALF claimed that the diagnostic lab was meant to service the animal/food industry, but I knew that only from the Letters to the Editor; there was no mention in the stories themselves. According to *The Davis Enterprise*, the police had no suspects but the action had been classified as domestic terrorism and turned over to the FBI.

I widened my search to the string of firebombings throughout Northern California that had followed. The San Jose Veal Company warehouse, the Ferrara Meat Company, and a poultry warehouse were all hit in rapid succession. A fur store in Santa Rosa was burned. No arrests for any of these firebombings had ever been made.

I went upstairs to ask the reference librarian to help me find stuff on the ALF, to see if they seemed like Lowell's sort of people. ALF tactics included animal rescue and release, and also the theft of notebooks and lab records. They took photographs of vivisections for release to the press. They destroyed lab equipment, including something called the primate stereotaxic device—I didn't know then nor want to know now what that is. They harassed researchers, furriers, and cattle ranchers with hate mail, leaving death threats on their answering machines, sometimes vandalizing their homes or tacking up shocking photographs of animal abuse in the playgrounds where their children went to school.

Some of the press coverage seemed sympathetic. Most did not. Reuters had described the ALF raids as the story of the ark, only with Rambo instead of Noah at the helm. But everyone agreed it was only a matter of time before someone was killed. Someone who mattered. Someone human. There had already been a number of close calls.

I came to a report on a 1985 break-in at UC Riverside. Among the many animals stolen was an infant macaque named Britches. Britches's little eyes had been sewn shut the day he was born, in order to test some sonic equipment designed for blind babies. The plan was to keep him alive for about three years in a state of sensory deprivation and then kill him to see what that had done to the visual, auditory, and motor-skills parts of his brain.

I didn't want a world in which I had to choose between blind human babies and tortured monkey ones. To be frank, that's the sort of choice I expect science to protect me from, not give me. I handled the situation by not reading more.

In 1985, Lowell had just left home. He'd been accepted to Brown University and we'd known he would be leaving us soon, but we'd thought we still had a few months left. A few months of him running about with Marco and Kitch, making us all believe he was ours, that, even as he left us, we could keep him.

The FBI had told my parents that the West Coast ALF was a slick operation of independent cells, safe houses, and an efficient underground railroad for the movement of animals. They wouldn't say what had led them to Lowell or even confirm he was a suspect. They did say that the most militant of the animal rights activists were young, white, male, and from the middle class.

The Davis diagnostic lab had long ago been finished and was busily doing whatever the ALF hadn't wanted it to do. I could bike over any time. I could bike over, but I couldn't go in. As with all other animal labs these days, the security there was tight.

I WAS JUST about to call the airlines yet again, demand that they produce my real suitcase and take the pretender away, when Harlow showed up with a different idea. Harlow's different idea was to pick the lock on the suitcase we did have, open it, and see what was inside. We would not take the stuff. That went without saying. But it was inconceivable to her that we'd return the case without even looking. Who knew what a strange suitcase from Indiana (assuming it had come from Indiana) might contain. Gold doubloons. A heroin-stuffed doll. Polaroids of some midwestern city council in flagrante. Apple butter.

Wasn't I curious? Where was my sense of adventure?

I was impressed that Harlow knew about apple butter. That's no excuse for the way I let her proceed. I counted on the combination lock stumping her. Tools were needed. Possibly a demolitions expert. In chimp studies, this kind of challenge is referred to as a food puzzle. Chimps are graded on achievement and speed, with bonus points for originality. Plus they get to eat whatever's inside. Chimps would see it as a great injustice, opening the suitcase and not taking anything.

I made a few vague objections, trusted to the arithmetical probability of guessing the right combination (1 in 10,000), and let myself be sent off to the co-op in the rain to pick us up some coffees.

Apparently, you can open a combination lock in a matter of minutes by looking down into the shaft for indentations while rotating the wheel. Ezra demonstrated this to me on my return. Ezra had parlayed his paranoid delusions into a very real jungle-commando skill set. It was frightening to think about the things he could do.

Harlow had found him on the third-floor balcony, practicing tai chi under the overhang, and running through his kill lines. "Wipe that face off your head, bitch. Your ass is as dead as fucking fried chicken." Ezra had told me once that, as he goes about his life, he's constantly running the movie version in his head, but I think a lot of people do that. Though maybe in a genre different from Ezra's.

So in the movie version, this is a romantic scene. Harlow enters, finding him all disciplined and moody and graceful. She twirls her hair, and we cut to the living room, two heads bent over the lock. In the movie version, there's a bomb in the suitcase. I return with the coffees just in time to stop them.

Only I didn't stop them. Instead I let Ezra explain the lock, watched him make the final triumphal spin, watched him open the suitcase—all without saying a word. He unpacked it suspensefully, item by dull item. Mostly what came out were clothes—a tracksuit, socks, a yellow T-shirt with THE HUMAN RACE written in a red curve across the chest. Harlow held this shirt up. Beneath the caption was the globe, spun to the side of the Americas. People of all colors were running the circumference, all of them in the same direction, which was like no human race I'd ever known. "Too big," Harlow said with an admirable lack of disappointment.

Ezra fished deeper. "Okay!" he said. "Okay!" And then, "Close your eyes," which no one did, because you'd be an idiot to close your eyes just on Ezra's say-so.

Ezra lifted something out of the case. It rose like a ghost from a body, like a vampire from a powder-blue coffin. Unfolding its insectile limbs, it bounced in Ezra's hand, eyes flat, mouth clacking. "What the hell do we have here?" Ezra asked.

He was holding a ventriloquist's dummy—antique, by the look of it. It danced above the opened suitcase lid like a spider. There were knitting needles in one of its little hands and a red mob-cap on its little head. "Madame Defarge," I told him and then added, "Madame Guillotine," because I always forgot what a reader Ezra was; it seemed so out of character, so uncinematic.

Harlow was pink with happiness. We were in temporary possession of a suitcase belonging to a jogger/ventriloquist. An antique dummy of Madame Defarge was obviously exactly what she'd been hoping we'd find. It brought the roses to her cheeks.

Ezra shoved his hand up the back of Madame Defarge's dress. She leapt toward Harlow's neck, paddled about there. Ezra put words into her mouth. She might have been thanking heaven for little girls. She might have been mouthing the lyrics to "La Marseillaise." Or "Frère Jacques." That's how bad Ezra's French accent was; it might as well have been French.

And talk about your uncanny valley response. I've never seen a more unseemly display of puppetry. I've never seen a creepier sight.

I turned priggish. "We shouldn't be playing with it," I said. "It looks old. Probably irreplaceable," but Harlow said that only a moron would put something irreplaceable in a checked suitcase.

And anyway they were being really careful with it. She took the dummy from Ezra, made it shake its little fists at me. From the look on Madame Defarge's face, I could see that everything was going exactly as she'd planned. "Don't spoil my fun," Madame Defarge said.

I had no time for this nonsense; I had a class to get to. I went into the kitchen, phoned the airport, where my call was very important to them, and left a message. And then Harlow came into the kitchen after me. She promised to put Madame Defarge back in the suitcase and I promised to meet her later for a night of bar-hopping, because, for God's sake, Rosemary, no harm had been done and I should take a chill pill.

And also because I wanted Harlow to like me.

7

IF YOU ASKED me about ninety-nine percent of the college lectures I once attended, I couldn't tell you a thing. That particular afternoon in that particular class falls into the one percent that remains.

It was still raining. Not a hard rain but a clammy one, and me, soaking it in like a sponge on a bicycle. A flock of seagulls were grazing on the soccer fields as I pedaled past. I'd seen that many times during storms, the gathering of the gulls, but it always amazed me. Davis, California, is profoundly inland.

By the time I reached the lecture hall, water had run down the legs of my jeans and puddled in the bottoms of my shoes. Chem 100, where all the biggest classes were held, was a large auditorium that sloped down to where the professor stood. You entered from the highest point, the back of the room. Ordinarily, on a rainy day, attendance would be sparse; students seemed to think classes were canceled like ball games for rain. But this was the last class of the session, the last class before the final. I was late so I had to descend the stairs, sit near the front. I raised the arm-desk and prepared to take notes.

The name of the class was Religion and Violence. The professor, Dr. Sosa, was a man in his middle years with a receding hairline and an expanding belly. He was a popular teacher, who sported *Star Trek* ties and mismatched socks, but all ironically. "Back when I was at Starfleet Academy," he'd say while introducing some piece of ancient data or beginning some historical anecdote. Dr. Sosa's lectures were enthusiastic and wide-ranging. I counted him among the easy-listening portion of my professors.

My father had once suggested, as an experiment, that I should nod every time a professor looked in my direction. I would find, he said, the professors looking my way more and more often, helpless as Pavlov's dogs. Dad may have had an agenda. The only way your absence was likely to be noticed in a class of a hundred or more was if your professor had been carefully conditioned to look for you. Dr. Sosa and I had a silent rapport. My father was a crafty man.

The lecture that day began with a discussion of violent women. Without openly acknowledging it, this underscored the fact that the rest of the class had all been about men. But that first part is not what I remember. I think maybe Dr. Sosa talked about the WKKK, the Temperance Movement, an odd assortment of religious mobs and girl-on-girl mayhem. I think we ranged from Ireland to Pakistan to Peru. But Dr. Sosa clearly thought of all these less as independent movements and more as adjuncts to whatever the men were doing. His heart was just not in the violent women.

Soon he'd returned to the topic of religiously motivated violence against women, a standard thread throughout the class. And then, suddenly, with no warning at all, he was talking about chimpanzees. Chimpanzees, he said, shared our propensity for insider/outsider violence. He described what the border-patrolling male chimps do and their murderous raiding parties. He asked us rhetorically if doctrinal differences simply provided cover for our primate and viciously tribal selves, which was so much like something my father would have said I felt an unreasonable impulse to object on those grounds alone. Dr. Sosa glanced at me and I did not nod. He said that among chimpanzees, the lowest-status male was higher than the highest-status female and he was looking right at me the whole time he said this.

There was a fly in the room. I could hear it. My feet were freezing and I could smell my sneakers, essence of rubber and socks. Dr. Sosa gave up and looked away.

He repeated a thing he'd said many times before—that most religions were obsessed with policing female sexual behavior, that for many it was their entire raison d'être. He described the sexual herding done by male chimpanzees. "The only difference," he said, "is that no chimp has ever claimed he was following God's orders."

Dr. Sosa had wandered off from the podium. He returned to it, consulted his notes. He said that rape, like domestic abuse, was a chimp behavior, and he shared a recent observation from Goodall's team in Gombe of one female in estrus forced to have sex with various males 170 times in one three-day period.

I had to put my pen down. My hands were shaking so hard my pen was vibrating on the paper, marking it with a frantic Morse code of blots and dashes. I missed a few of the things Dr. Sosa said next, because of the way my blood was rampaging through my brain and, when the students around me turned to look, I realized that I'd been breathing too loudly, wheezing or hissing or panting or something. I closed my mouth and the students turned back.

I HOPE YOU haven't assumed that just because I had no friends I'd had no sex; the bar for sexual partners is much, much lower. Though it's surprisingly hard to have sex without friends; I'd often wished for someone who'd give me pointers and reassurance. Instead I'd had to make the whole thing up on my own, wondering why I never experienced the glossy sex of the movies. What is a normal sex life? What is normal sex? What if asking the question already means you aren't normal? It seemed as if I couldn't get even the instinc-tual, mammalian parts of my life right.

"You're very quiet," my first said. We'd met one evening at a frat party shortly after I discovered Jell-O shots. We'd locked our-selves in the bathroom and the sex had been plenty noisy from my perspective, what with the constant banging on the door and peo-ple cursing us when they couldn't get in. I'd had my back against the sink, the rim digging into my spine and then, that angle having proved too difficult for beginners, we ended up on the floor on a filthy bath mat, but I hadn't complained. I'd thought I was being a good sport.

Earlier in the evening, he'd called me shy, as if it were a compli-ment, as if he found my silence strangely compelling or mysterious, or, at the very least, cute. I remembered the noises I'd often heard on my parents' side of the bedroom wall and I could have made them myself if I'd understood they were desirable. I'd just thought of them as creepy and parental.

I knew the first time would hurt; I'd been prepped for that by advice columns in various magazines, so I wasn't alarmed by that part. And it did hurt a hell of a lot. But I'd also been prepped for blood, and there wasn't any. And then it hurt the second time and the third time, too, even though that was with a different guy and a smaller penis. No magazine had suggested it would still be hurting by then.

I finally went to see a doctor at student health. She looked inside and told me that the problem was my hymen, which was so small it had frayed but not broken, so the deed was done in her office with special implements of hymen destruction. "That should clear the way," she said cheerfully, along with a lot of cautionary advice about not letting myself be pressured into things that made me uncomfortable and the importance of protection. Pamphlets were pressed into my hands. I had a terrible ache below, as if a cramp had tied itself in a knot and then tightened. But mostly it was humiliating.

My point being: I'm no stranger to bad sex.

But I am one of the lucky ones. I've never in my life been forced into any sex I haven't wanted at the time.

WHEN I COULD hear again, Dr. Sosa had moved on from common chimps to their (and our) close relations, the bonobos. "Bonobo society," he said, "is peaceful and egalitarian. These laudable qualities are achieved through continual and casual sexual congress, much of it same-sex. Sex among the bonobos is just a form of grooming. Mere social glue," said Dr. Sosa. And then, "*Lysistrata* had it backwards. The road to peace is through more sex, not less."

This went down well with the male students. They were surprisingly okay with being told, by inference, that they were simple creatures entirely controlled by their dicks. Ithyphallic, one might be tempted to say.

They were okay with being told, by inference, that reluctance, mostly female, was the root of all evil. This reaction was less surprising.

A young woman a few rows to my right raised her hand and then didn't wait to be called on. She stood. Her blond hair was braided and beaded in complicated ways. The one ear I could see was rimmed with silver cuffs. "How do you know which came first?" she asked Dr. Sosa. "Maybe female bonobos find their males more attractive than women find men. Maybe it's sexy to be peaceful and egalitarian and not so concerned with policing female sexuality. Maybe you guys should give that a try." Someone in the back made a sound much like the chimpanzee food hoot.

"Bonobos are matriarchal," the young woman said. "How do you know it's the sex and not the matriarchy that makes a society peaceful? Female solidarity. Females protecting other females. Bonobos have it. Chimps and humans don't."

"Okay," Dr. Sosa said. "Fair point. You've given me something to think about." He glanced my way.

DR. SOSA ENDED the last lecture of the quarter by telling us that our preference for our own kind begins at birth. We find it in three-month-old babies who prefer faces from the racial category they see most often to all others. We find it among young children who, when divided into groups along the most arbitrary of criteria—shoelace color, for example—vehemently prefer the people inside their group to the people outside. "'Do unto others as you would have others do unto you' is our highest, most developed morality," Dr. Sosa said. "And really the only one necessary; all the others flow from that; you don't need Ten Commandments. But if you do believe, as I do, that morality starts with God, then you have to wonder why He simultaneously hardwired us against it.

"'Do unto others' is an unnatural, inhuman behavior. You can understand why so many churches and churchgoers say it but so few achieve it. It goes against something fundamental in our natures. And this, then, is the human tragedy—that the common humanity we share is fundamentally based on the denial of a common shared humanity."

End of class. Everyone clapped, either because they'd liked the lecture or else because it was over. Dr. Sosa said a few more words about the final. It wouldn't be a simple regurgitation of dates and facts. He wanted to see the quality of our thinking. He looked at me again. I could have given him one last reassuring nod, but I was still upset. Extremely upset. Profoundly, heart-racingly upset.

I'd never even heard of bonobos. Suddenly everyone seemed to know a lot more about chimpanzees than I did. This came as a surprise and a surprisingly unpleasant one. But that was the least of what I'd been given to think about.

PART FOUR

❋

I'll say it again: imitating human beings was not something which pleased me. I imitated them because I was looking for a way out, for no other reason.

—FRANZ KAFKA, "A Report for an Academy"

I

TODAY, IN 2012, with the whole of the Internet laid out before me like a Candy Land board (or maybe Chutes and Ladders is the better metaphor—or maybe Sorry!—anyway, one of those games that never ends because you never win), I've been trying to find out what happened to other famous cross-fostered chimps. Information about the experiments is easy to come by, not so easy to learn the fates of the subjects. When there is information, it's often disputed.

One of the earliest chimps, clever, docile little Gua, appears to have died in 1933 from a respiratory infection shortly after the Kellogg family returned her to the Yerkes research lab, where she'd been born. She'd lived in the Kellogg home for about nine months alongside their toddler son, Donald, effortlessly outshining him at using a fork and drinking from a cup. She was two years old at the time of her death.

VIKI HAYES WAS born in 1947 and died in her home of viral meningitis when she was either six and a half or seven, depending on what website you choose. After her death, her parents divorced; at least one friend said that Viki had been the only thing keeping that marriage together. She was an only child.

MAYBELLE (BORN IN 1965) and Salome (1971) both died of a severe diarrhea that developed within days of their respective families' going on vacation and leaving them behind. No underlying physical condition for the diarrhea was found in either case.

AFTER HIS RETURN to a research facility, Ally (born 1969) also developed a life-threatening diarrhea. He pulled out his own hair and lost the use of one arm, but none of these things killed him. There are rumors, unsubstantiated, that he died in the 1980s in the medical labs, victim of an experimental but fatal dose of insecticide.

AT TWELVE YEARS OF AGE, Lucy Temerlin (born in 1964) was sent from her home to live with the chimps in Gambia. She'd been raised in Oklahoma by the Temerlin family. Lucy liked *Playgirl* magazine, tea that she brewed herself, and straight gin. She was a tool-using chimp who took sexual pleasure from the household vacuum. She was a wild girl.

But she knew nothing of life in the wild. She'd been born at the Noell's Ark Chimp Farm and taken from her mother into a human home two days later. In Gambia, Janis Carter, a psych grad student, took great care over many years trying to gently habituate her. During this time, Lucy suffered a deep depression, lost weight, and pulled out her hair. She was last seen alive, in the company of other chimps and apparently resigned to being so, in 1987.

Some weeks later, her scattered bones were found and collected. The suspicion that she was killed by poachers, into whose arms she eagerly ran, has been widely transmitted. It has also been strongly contradicted.

NIM CHIMPSKY (1973–2000), star of book and screen, died at the far-too-young age of twenty-six. At the time of his death he was living at the Black Beauty Ranch for horses in Texas, but he'd had many homes and many surrogate families. He learned twenty-five or a hundred twenty-five signs—reports differ—but his linguistic capabilities were a disappointment to Dr. Herb Terrace, the psychologist who'd picked him for study. When Nim was four years old, Terrace announced that the experiment was over. Nim was then sent off to live at the Institute for Primate Studies (IPS) in Oklahoma.

Nim's perceived failures had consequences for many of the signing chimps. Money for these experiments dried up as a direct result.

He was eventually sold to the medical labs, where he lived in a small cage until one of his former grad students threatened a lawsuit and launched a public fund that finally got him out.

WASHOE (1965–2007), the most famous of the cross-fostered chimps, also spent time at the IPS in Oklahoma. The first nonhuman ever to learn American Sign Language, she had a vocabulary of 350 ASL words and died of natural causes in 2007, when she was forty-two. Roger Fouts, who'd started working with her as a grad student, eventually devoted his life to her protection and well-being. She died at the sanctuary he created for her on the Central Washington University campus in Ellensburg, surrounded by humans and chimps who knew and loved her.

About Washoe, Roger Fouts has said, she taught him that in the phrase *human being*, the word *being* is much more important than the word *human*.

THE IMPULSE TO WRITE a book appears to run like a fever through those of us who've lived with apes. We all have our reasons. *The Ape and the Child* is about the Kelloggs. *Next of Kin* is about Washoe. Viki is *The Ape in Our House*. *The Chimp Who Would Be Human* is Nim.

Maurice Temerlin's *Lucy: Growing Up Human* ends in 1975, when Lucy was eleven years old. The Temerlins adopted her believing, as did many of the cross-fostering families, as did my parents, that they were making a lifelong commitment. But at the end of his book, Temerlin expresses a longing for a normal life. He and his wife haven't shared a bed for years, because Lucy won't have it. They can't take a vacation or ask friends to dinner. There is no part of their lives that Lucy doesn't affect.

Lucy had an older brother, human, whose name was Steve. Post-1975, I can find no mention of him. I do find a site that says that Donald Kellogg, the child raised for a year and a half with little Gua—a period of time he would, of course, have had no memory of, though it is well documented in papers, books, and home movies—killed himself around the age of forty-three. Another site claims that Donald had had a distinctly simian gait, but it's a white supremacist site—there is no reason to give that any credence at all.

2

A FEW HOURS after Dr. Sosa's lecture, I met up with Harlow at a beer-and-hamburger place in central Davis called The Graduate. The streets were dark, cold, and wet though the rain had stopped. On another occasion, I might have been more appreciative of the black magic around me, each streetlamp wrapped in its own bubble of mist, my bike-light briefly igniting the puddles on the black streets as I passed. But I was still teetering on the ragged cliff-edge of Dr. Sosa's lecture. My plan for the evening was to drink. In Davis, biking while drunk results in the exact same ticket as driving while drunk, but this was so patently ridiculous I refused to acknowledge it.

By the time I locked my bike, I was shivering mightily. I remembered the scene in *It's a Wonderful Life* when Clarence Odbody orders a flaming rum punch. A flaming rum punch would have really hit the spot. I would have bathed in it.

I opened the heavy door to The Graduate and slid into the din. I'd been considering telling Harlow what I'd just learned about chimp sex. Much would depend on how drunk I got. But I was all about female solidarity that evening, and I thought it might make me feel better to talk frankly to another woman about the horribleness of male chimps. So I was not happy to see that Reg was joining us. Reg did not seem like someone with whom you could profitably discuss chimp sex.

I was even less happy to see Madame Defarge. She was sitting on Harlow's lap, weaving her head from side to side and unhinging her jaw like a cobra. Harlow was wearing a pair of worn jeans just barely held together with embroidered patches of mountains, rainbows, and hemp leaves, so her lap was an interesting place. "I'm being careful with her," Harlow told me, apparently irritated by something I hadn't even had the time to say yet. She was making assumptions about my no-fun-at-all-ness. They were good assumptions. Our relationship had started so promisingly, what with both of us breaking things in best monkey-girl fashion and swinging off to jail together. But I could see she was reassessing me now. I was not as gamesome as she'd thought. I was beginning to disappoint.

She graciously put all that aside for the moment. Harlow had just learned that the drama department would be putting on a gender-reversal version of *Macbeth* in the spring. Of course, she didn't say *Macbeth*; she said "the Scottish play" in that annoying way drama majors do. The male roles would all be taken by women, the women's by men. Harlow had been chosen to help with the sets and costumes and I'd rarely seen her so excited. Everyone was assuming, she told me, that they would be cross-dressing the actors, but she hoped to talk the director out of that.

Reg leaned in to say that there was nothing an audience liked better than a man in a dress. Harlow brushed him away as the minor annoyance he was.

"Wouldn't it be more challenging," she said, "more of a mindfuck, if the costuming didn't change?" That would suggest a place in which the dominant paradigm was female; all those things that coded here in our world as female would represent power and politics. Female would be the norm.

Harlow said that she was already doing sketches of the castle in Inverness, trying to imagine a fantastical, female space. This could have segued into a conversation about chimp rape, but not without harshing the mellow. Harlow was incandescent with hopes and plans.

Men were buying drinks for Madame Defarge.

Reg offered me one of them, a dark ale with a strong hoppy smell. The chilled glass mug was warmer than my hands and I'd lost all feeling in my thumbs. Reg raised his own beer in a toast. "To superpowers," he said, lest I get the impression we were letting bygones be bygones. Let the wild ruckus commence.

Soon I was sweating. The Graduate was packed; there was a DJ, and some ill-advised line dancing. The room smelled of beer and bodies. Madame Defarge gamboled on the tables and the backs of the chairs. Green Day's "Basket Case" pounded from the speakers.

Harlow and Reg had some words, shouting them over the music. I heard most of them. The gist was that Reg thought she was flirting with every guy in the bar and Harlow thought it was Madame Defarge doing the flirting. Harlow herself was simply engaged in performance art and the guys in the bar all knew it.

"Oh, yeah," said Reg. "Bunch of real sophisticates. Real art lovers." Reg said that men associated performance art with women who painted their faces in menstrual blood and they didn't like it. Sluts, though, sluts they liked.

Harlow thought there was an important distinction to be made between a slut and a woman operating a slutty puppet. Reg thought there was no difference, or that maybe women thought there was a difference but men didn't care.

"Are you calling me a slut?" Madame Defarge snapped. "Like you should fucking talk!"

The music slowed without quieting. Harlow and Reg tended to their drinks. A white guy in a backward baseball cap—"fucking milk chicken," Reg told me, loud enough for the guy to hear, which means very loud—came and asked for a dance. Harlow handed him Madame Defarge.

"See?" she said to Reg. "She's dancing with him and I'm dancing with you." She held out her hand and Reg took it, hauled her in. They moved away from the counter, wrapped themselves tightly together, her hands on his shoulders, his in her shredded back-pockets. The guy in the backward baseball cap stared at Madame Defarge in bewilderment until I took her from him.

"She's not for dancing with," I said. "She's very valuable."

The DJ hit the strobe lights. The Graduate morphed into some ballroom of the damned. Reg returned and talked to me at length, the strobe making a slide show of his face. I nodded until nodding made me dizzy, then focused on the bend in his sharp nose to re-orient myself. He wasn't shouting, so I didn't hear a word.

I nodded some more and the whole time I was making this agreeable gesture, I was telling him that his position on superpowers was balderdash and had no bearing on the real world. "Poppycock," I said. "Flapdoodle. Bollocks. Piffle. Crapola. Codswallop."

My gaze had dropped to his chest. A bright yellow road-sign was printed on his T-shirt, with the silhouette of a family running across it. The father was in front, pulling his wife by the hand behind him. The wife was pulling their child and the child had a doll, also by the hand. I'm from Indiana, and Davis is not San Diego. I didn't know this was an actual road-sign, an encouragement to not hit illegal immigrants with your car. Both child and doll were airborne; that's how fast the family was running. I could see their legs pumping, the child's braids whipping behind her. I should maybe say here that I'd taken a couple of pills Harlow gave me. It's a lucky thing I'd never faced peer pressure before; I turned out to suck at it.

"Bullshit," I said. "Baloney. Hooey. Horse feathers."

Reg said he couldn't hear me, so we went outside, where I told him about the mirror test. I can't remember how that had come to mind, but I gave him quite the lecture. I told him that some species, like chimps and elephants and dolphins, recognize themselves in the mirror and others, like dogs and pigeons, gorillas and human babies, don't. Darwin himself had begun to think about this one day when he put a mirror on the ground in the Zoological Gardens and watched two young orangutans look at themselves in it. And then, a hundred years later, a psychologist named Gordon Gallup had refined the test, observed some chimps using the mirror to look inside their own mouths, see those parts of the body only the mirror could show them. I told Reg that we'd been using the mirror test to determine self-awareness ever since *fucking Darwin* and I couldn't believe a guy like him, a college guy who thought he knew everything, wasn't familiar with something so fundamental.

And then I added that a psychomanteum was a mirrored room in which people tried to communicate with spirits, for no particular reason except that I knew it.

I wondered suddenly what the impact of identical-twinness on the mirror test might be, but didn't say so, since I didn't know the answer and he might pretend he did.

Probably I was trying to reestablish my shattered sense of authority on these matters after the revelations of Sosa's class.

Definitely I was being a jerk. I remember Reg saying I sure talked a lot and I remember clapping my hand over my mouth as if I'd been found out. Then Reg said we should go back inside, because I was shivering again. And because he now thought he knew everything he needed to know about the mirror test.

3

THE REST OF the night remains in my brain as that disconnected montage the movies have trained us to have. *The Monkey Girl Returns*, an episodic, demented Iditarod through the town.

HERE I AM, trying to get a rice bowl at Jack in the Box. Reg had left in a snit sometime earlier. Harlow is on my bike, with me balanced on the handlebars. We put a long order in through the intercom, changing our minds many times and trying to be sure the woman on the other end has it all straight, and then she won't serve us because we aren't in a car; she says we have to come inside. An argument ensues, which ends with the woman fetching another woman, a woman of more authority, who tells us to go to hell. The words *go to hell* come crackling out of Jack's big snowball of a head. Harlow takes out the intercom armed with nothing but her house key.

HERE I'M IN the G Street Pub, being chatted up by some black guy in a letterman's jacket, which probably meant he was in high school, but we kissed intensely and for quite some time so I really hope not.

. . .

HERE I'M HUDDLED by myself on a damp bench at the train station, my face on my knees. I'm sobbing and sobbing, because I've gone and let myself imagine a thing I've never let myself imagine before. I've let myself imagine the day Fern was taken away.

I'll never know for sure what happened. I wasn't there; Lowell wasn't there. I'm betting Mom wasn't there and maybe even not Dad.

Fern must have been drugged. Fern must have woken up in a strange place just the way I did that first afternoon in my new bedroom. Only when I'd cried, our father had come. Who had come for Fern? Maybe Matt. I allow myself this one small consolation, to imagine Matt beside her when she first woke up.

I'm picturing her as I last saw her, exuberantly five years old. But she's not in the Swiss Family Robinson tree house now; instead she's in a cage with older, larger chimps, none of whom she knows. Crawling shit, she says, and then she has to learn her place, not only that she's a chimp, but female and lower in status than any male. I know that Fern would never have accepted that without a fight.

What did they do to her in that cage? Whatever it was, it happened because no woman had stopped it. The women who should have stood with Fern—my mother, the female grad students, me— none of us had helped. Instead we had exiled her to a place completely devoid of female solidarity.

I'M STILL CRYING, but I seem to have moved to a booth somewhere I can't identify—not a bar, because I can hear everything everyone says. I'm with Harlow and two guys about our same age. The better-looking one is seated by her, has his arm stretched along the seat back behind her shoulder. He has longish hair and shakes his head frequently to keep it out of his eyes. The other guy is obviously meant for me. He's quite short. I don't care about that. I'm quite short myself. I prefer beta males to alphas. Only he keeps telling me to smile. "Nothing's as bad as all that," he says. If I were five years old, I'd have bitten him by now.

I'm also insulted because it's so clear that I'm the consolation prize. No one is even making an effort to pretend otherwise. It's like we're in a musical and Harlow and her guy are the romantic couple and will get all the best songs and the big story lines. Everything about them will matter. My guy and me are the comic relief.

"I don't even know your name," I say to him as an explanation of why I don't owe him a smile. Though, in all fairness, we probably were introduced at some point when I wasn't listening.

Maybe I didn't say that out loud, because no one responds. He's blinking fast, as if he's got something in his eyes. I'm wearing contacts myself and between them and all the crying I've been doing, it's as if I've scraped the Mojave Desert over my eyeballs. Suddenly that's all I can think about—my aching, stinging, burning eyeballs.

Harlow leans across the table, takes my wrist in her hand, shakes it. "Listen to me," she says firmly. "Are you listening? Paying attention? Whatever you're upset about, you're just imagining it. It's not real."

I can see how tired of me the guy next to Harlow is. "For fuck's sake. Get a grip," he says.

I refuse to be lower status than that insufferable twit. I refuse to smile. I'd rather die.

WE'RE STILL IN the same booth, but now Reg is there. He's seated by Harlow, and the guy with the long hair is by me, and the short guy has gotten a chair and is seated at the open end. I can't remember how all this happened, and I'm angrier than ever over the upgrade. I like the short guy better than the guy with the long hair, but who even asked?

The men all seem tense; any moment now, they'll be firing up their lightsabers. Reg keeps playing with the saltshaker, spinning it and saying whoever it stops at is a douche bag, and the guy with long hair says that *he* doesn't need a saltshaker; *he* knows a douche bag when he sees one just by looking. "Chill out, man," the short guy says to Reg. "You can't have them both"—and Reg raises the temperature by making the *Loser* sign with his hand against his forehead. Not just the simple, two-fingered L but his middle finger, too, pointing out and straight at the guy, which retains its classic meaning but also transforms the simple *Loser* into the *Loser any way you look at it* sign. The guy with long hair catches his breath loudly. We are this close to fisticuffs.

I wonder if I had sex with all three of them, would they calm down? Because it really doesn't seem like they would.

Apparently, this I do say out loud. I try to explain that I was being hypothetical. I try to tell them about Sosa's lecture, but I don't get far, because *bonobo* is such a funny word and they all have such funny looks on their faces, it makes me laugh. At first everyone else laughs, too, but then they stop and I don't. Nobody liked my crying and now that I'm laughing, I can see that I'm still irritating the hell out of everyone.

Now I'm in a bathroom stall, puking up pizza by the slice. When I finish, I go out to the sinks to wash my face and there are three men at the urinal. Wrong bathroom.

One of the men is Reg. I point to his face in the bathroom mirror. "Who's that?" I ask him. And then, helpfully, "It's an intelligence test." I take my contacts out and drop them down the drain, because it's what you do with disposables; you get rid of them. Besides, what's there to see? My own face in the mirror is a badly lit mug shot, egg-white and staring. I reject it entirely. No way do I look like that. That must be someone else.

Reg gives me an Altoid, which is maybe the most thoughtful thing any man has ever done for me. Suddenly I find him very attractive. "You're standing a little close," he says. "Has anyone ever told you that you kind of crowd people? Get in their personal space?" And just like that, I'm over him.

I remember something. "You need a fucking lot of space," I say. And then, before he gets the idea that I care what he needs, I change the subject. "It's really easy to persuade people to be hateful," I tell him, partly as a diversionary tactic and partly just because it is, and it can't be said often enough. "You can train any animal into any behavior on cue if it's a natural behavior to begin with. Racism, sexism, speciesism—all natural human behaviors. They can be triggered any time by any unscrupulous yahoo with a pulpit. A child could do it.

"Mobbing is a natural human behavior," I say sadly. I've started crying again. "Bullying."

Empathy is also a natural human behavior, and natural to

chimps as well. When we see someone hurt, our brains respond to some extent as if we'd been hurt ourselves. This response is not located merely in the amygdala, where emotional memories are stored, but also in those regions of the cortex responsible for analyzing the behavior of others. We access our own experiences with pain and extend them to the current sufferer. We're nice that way.

But I didn't know this back then. Nor, apparently, did Dr. Sosa.

"Time for you to go home," Reg says, but I'm not feeling that. I don't think it's that time at all.

HARLOW AND I are walking through the tunnel of the Shell station car wash. The tunnel has a very distinctive smell, soap and tires, and we're stumbling a bit, because we're stepping on rocker brushes and conveyor belts and other things we can't see. We're agreeing that when we were kids we loved sitting in the car as it went through the car wash. It was the best. It was like being in a spaceship or a submarine, the way the giant cloth squids slapped the windows. I'm fingering the giant cloth squids as I say this; they are as damp and rubbery as you'd expect.

How the water pours down and pours down, sheeting the windows, and you stay cozy and dry. What could be better? Fern loved it, too, but I force that thought out of my head. It comes right back in, Fern's clever hands undoing the various clasps on her car seat so she can ricochet from one side of the car to the other, not miss a thing.

Harlow says that sometimes you thought the car was moving but it was the optical illusion of the brushes passing by you, and I say I'd had that exact same experience. *Exact same*. I shove Fern out of my mind again, and I'm high on Harlow's concurrence, freebasing her approval. We are so much alike! "When I get married," I say, "I want the wedding to be in a car in a car wash," and Harlow thinks that's a great idea, she wants that, too.

I'm BACK AT the G Street Pub. Harlow and I have been playing pool and I'm having a hard time keeping the balls on the table, much less sinking them into the pockets. "You're an embarrassment to the game of pool," Harlow says, and then I lose track of her, can't find her anywhere.

I'm looking down on a skinny guy with hair so bleached it's almost white. I fall into his arms and, without thinking, I call him by his real name. I press into his chest as hard as I can, wanting to smell the way my brother smells, laundry soap and bay leaves and Corn Chex. He's bleached his hair and lost weight, not so much of an athlete now, and I would know him anywhere, anytime.

I burst into tears. "You're all grown up," he says into my ear. "I didn't recognize you at all till you climbed onto the table."

I have such a grip on his shirt; I don't plan on ever letting go. But then Officer Arnie Haddick is standing before me. "I'm taking you in," he says, shaking his big, round cop head. "You can sleep it off at county and maybe you'll use the time to think about the decisions you're making. The company you're keeping." Officer Haddick says he owes it to Vince (my father, in case you've forgotten his name) to get me safely off the streets. He says that a drunk woman is a woman asking for trouble.

He leads me outside, helps me gallantly into the back of the cop car, no handcuffs this time. Harlow is there ahead of me. We'll soon be sharing a cell, even though, as Officer Haddick will make clear the next morning, Harlow is the company I shouldn't be keeping. "We have to stop meeting like this," Harlow says.

I want to ask Officer Haddick if he saw a guy with white-blond hair, but obviously I can't. My brother has vanished so completely I'm afraid I imagined him.

4

No DOUBT I would have escaped my second incarceration by falling quickly asleep if only I'd been able. But Harlow's little white pills were still bucking like broncos in the synapses of my brain. Worse, Fern kept riding them into my consciousness. After all those years of keeping her out of my head, suddenly she was everywhere. I couldn't *not* see how I'd been put, drugged, into a cage just the way she'd once been put, drugged, into a cage. I was confident of my release come morning, and I wondered if she'd also been confident. It was far worse than imagining her frightened, to think of her certain that this was all a mistake and we were on our way to rescue her, that she'd soon be home in her own room and her own bed.

Also like Fern, I was not alone in my cell. In addition to Harlow, there was an elderly woman who took a motherly interest in getting us settled. She was wearing a bald terry-cloth bathrobe of a faded pink and had a smear of dirt across her forehead as if it were Ash Wednesday. Her gray hair sprang from her head like a blown dandelion, only dented on one side. She told me I was the spitting image of Charlotte. "Charlotte who?" I asked.

She didn't answer, so I was left to guess. Charlotte Brontë?

Charlotte of *Charlotte's Web*? Charlotte, North Carolina? I found myself remembering how Mom had cried as she'd neared the end of *Charlotte's Web*. She'd stopped reading with a sudden choke and I'd looked up, surprised by her red eyes, wet cheeks. I'd had a horrible premonition then of what this might mean, with Charlotte feeling so poorly, but not really, as I'd never before been read a book in which someone died, so it wasn't in my range of possibility. In this, I was as innocent as Fern. Across our mother's lap, Fern, lazily repeating her sign for spider. *Crawling poo. Crawling shit.*

Fern had particularly loved *Charlotte's Web*, probably because she'd heard her own name so often when Mom read it. Was that where Mom had gotten the name? It had never occurred to me to wonder. And what had she meant by it then, naming our Fern after the only human in the book who can talk with nonhumans?

I realized that my own hands now were making the same *crawling shit* sign. It didn't seem as if I could stop them. I held them up and stared at the way my fingers were moving.

"Let's talk in the morning," the woman suggested, unaware that I *was* talking. "When we're fresh for it." She told us each to pick out a cot, of which there were four and none of them inviting. I lay down, forcing my eyes shut, but they popped right back open. My fingers strummed. My legs twitched. My thoughts jumped from *Charlotte's Web* to the famous experiments in which innocent, unsuspecting spiders were forcibly drugged with various agents. And then to the famous photographs taken of the webs they'd made under the influence.

I was spinning a pretty crazy web myself, a sustained hypnagogic state in which I struggled to make sense of the images and associations coming at me like flotsam in a flood. Here a chimp. There a chimp. Everywhere a chimp chimp.

I thought that if, as Reg kept insisting, superpowers are fixed rather than relative, then Spider-Man is no more gifted than Charlotte. In fact, compared to Charlotte, Peter Parker is a piker. I repeated that a few times in my head. Peter Parker is a piker. Peter Parker is a piker.

"That's enough of that," the elderly woman told me and I was unsure if I'd spoken aloud or she was reading my mind. Both seemed equally possible.

"Harlow. Harlow!" I whispered. There was no answer. I thought that Harlow might be asleep and how that would mean she hadn't taken the same pills she'd given me. Maybe there weren't enough and she'd meant to be nice, letting me have them and bravely going without. Or maybe she'd known better than to take them herself, and it was just easier to hand them to me than to flush them. Maybe I was just closer than the toilet.

Or maybe she was awake. "I still think superpowers are relative," I told her, just in case. "Charlotte isn't a superhero just because she's a spider and can leap from wall to wall on her web. Her superpower is that she can read and write. Context matters. Context is all. *Umwelt.*"

"Will you shut up?" Harlow asked wearily. "Do you even know you've been talking all fucking night? And making no sense at all?"

I responded to this with an odd mixture of monkey-girl alarm and nostalgia. And resistance. I hadn't been talking so very much. If Harlow pushed me, I could show her what talking all fucking night really meant. I pictured how, if Fern had been here, she would have swung effortlessly up the wall, rained holy hell down on Harlow from above. I wished for Fern so hard it stopped my breath.

"No more talking!" the elderly woman snapped. "Eyes closed and no more talking. I mean it, buster."

My mother always said that it's very rude when people who can't sleep wake up people who can. My father had a different perspective. "You can't imagine," he'd told her once over a bleary breakfast, when he'd poured his orange juice into his coffee and then salted it as well. "You can't imagine the white-hot fury someone who can't sleep feels toward the beautiful dreamer beside him."

So I tried to be quiet. I began to see a kaleidoscope of webs. A great choreography of spiders can-canned across my open eyeballs, kicking leg after leg after leg after leg in waltz time. I could pan in on their honeycomb eyes, their ghastly mandibles. Pan out, see them from above, turn the waving legs into fractal patterns.

No one put the lights out. The music from the spider chorus-line transitioned from ballroom to gabber. Someone began to snore. I had the impression that the snoring was what was keeping me up. My thoughts turned rhythmical in a Chinese water-torture way: *Umwelt. Umwelt. Umwelt.*

The rest of the night was an endless dream sequence directed by David Lynch. Periodically, Fern twirled in. Sometimes she was five years old, turning her backflips, rocking from foot to foot, trailing her scarves, or biting my fingers gently, just as a warning. Sometimes she had the squat, heavy body of an older ape and stared at me so listlessly she was almost lifeless and had to be moved through the scene like a doll.

By morning, I'd managed to get my thoughts organized into a neat if tiresome grid. X-axis: things missing. Y-axis: last seen.

One: Where was my bicycle? I couldn't think where I'd last had it. Maybe at Jack in the Box. I remembered the vandalized intercom with a start. Probably best to avoid Jack in the Box for a bit.

Two: Where was Madame Defarge? I hadn't seen her since we'd left The Graduate. I wanted to ask Harlow, but was too tired to figure out how. It was a question that was bound to annoy her in the best of situations, and this was not that.

Three: Where were Mom's journals? Would she really never ask me about them again or would I have to confess at some point to having lost them? Which would be so unfair, as I rarely lost things and, in the immortal words of Han Solo, it wasn't my fault.

Four: Where was my brother? My relief that he'd seemed happy to see me was now shot through with worry. What had he made of my coziness with the local police? What if he'd never been there at all?

The elderly woman's son arrived and took her back to the nursing home with many apologies for the things she'd apparently said and the things she'd apparently broken. The snoring went with her.

When the door to the cell finally opened for me, I was so tired I had to lever myself through with my arms. Officer Haddick and I had a chat in which I was too beat to participate, though that didn't seem to shorten it.

Reg came to fetch Harlow and gave me a ride home as well, where I took a shower, dizzy and swaying in the hot water. Went to bed, but still couldn't close my eyes. It was the most horrible feeling, to be so utterly wrung-out and still mentally trudging on.

I got up, went to the kitchen, took the burners off the stove and cleaned beneath them. I opened the refrigerator and stared into it even though I had no desire for food of any kind. I thought that at least Harlow hadn't given me a gateway drug. More of a slammed-door drug. I would never ever take it again.

Todd got up and burned some toast, so that the smoke alarm went off and had to be beaten into silence with a broom handle.

No one was answering the phone at Casa Harlow and Reg. I called three times and left two messages. I knew that I should walk right on over to The Graduate, see if anyone had turned a dummy in. I was in a panic, thinking that I'd lost her and her so valuable and all. My bike was one thing, but Madame Defarge didn't even belong to me. How could I have been so careless? And then, I guess, the drug finally wore off, because the next thing I knew, I was waking up in my bed and it was night again.

The apartment had a nobody-home sort of silence. In spite of having slept for hours, I remained exhausted. I dozed again, had a dream that slipped from me like hypnopompic water as I surfaced from it to a memory. Once upon a time, Lowell had come in the night and shaken me awake. I think I was six years old, which would have made him twelve.

I'd always suspected that Lowell roamed after dark. His bedroom was off by itself on the first floor, so he could leave by the door or the window with no one hearing him. I don't know where he went. I don't know for a fact that he did go. But I knew he missed the acreage we'd had at the farmhouse. I knew he missed the days of exploring in the woods. He'd found an arrowhead once and some rocks stamped with the bones of a little fish. That would never have happened in our current cramped yard.

On this occasion, he told me to get dressed quietly, and I was full of questions but managed to keep my mouth shut until we were outside. A few days back, I'd put my foot down in the grass and felt a sharp pain shoot up my leg. When I lifted my foot, screaming, there was a stinger in the arch, the bee still attached by a thread, jerking at the end of its tether and buzzing as it died. Mom had pulled the stinger, with me still screaming, and carried me inside, where she soaked my foot and wrapped it in a baking-soda poultice. I'd been queen bee of the household ever since, carried from chair to chair, books fetched, juice poured. Apparently, Lowell had had enough of my invalidism. We went out to the street and turned to walk up Ballantine Hill. My foot felt fine.

It was a summer night, hot and still. Sheet lightning crackled at the horizon, the moon was out and the black sky smeared with stars. Twice we saw the lights of an oncoming car and ducked behind trees or shrubs so as to not be seen.

"Let's get off the street," Lowell said. We cut across a lawn into a strange backyard. Inside the house a small dog began to bark. A light went on in an upstairs window.

Of course, I'd been talking the whole time. Where were we going? Why were we up? Was it a surprise? Was it a secret? How much past my bedtime was it? This was the latest I had ever been up, right? This was very late for a six-year-old to be up, right? Lowell put his hand over my mouth and I smelled toothpaste on his fingers.

"Pretend we're Indians," Lowell said. He was whispering. "Indians never talk when they're moving through the forest. They walk so quietly you can't even hear their footsteps."

He removed his hand. "How do they do that?" I asked. "Is it magic? Can only Indians do it? How much Indian do you have to be to do that? Maybe you have to wear moccasins."

"Shhh," said Lowell.

We went through a few more backyards. It wasn't so hard to see in the dark as I'd supposed. The night wasn't so quiet. I heard the call of an owl, soft and round as the sound you made blowing across a bottle top. The deep bass of a frog. The friction of insect legs. Lowell's footsteps, I noticed, were no quieter than mine.

We came to a hedge with a gap that we scrambled through on our hands and knees. Since it was big enough for Lowell, it must have been plenty big enough for me. Still, I got scratched by the barbed leaves. I didn't say so; I thought Lowell might send me home if I complained. So I pointed out instead how I wasn't complaining even though I had a scratch on one leg, which was stinging. "I don't want to go home yet," I told him preemptively.

"Then stop talking for a minute," said Lowell. "Look and listen."

The frog was loud now, big-sounding, but I remembered from the creek at the old farmhouse that a big voice could often be tracked to a little frog. I stood up on the far side of the hedge. We were in a bowl of a yard, a secret garden like the one in the book. The slopes were planted with trees and a softer grass than we had at home. At the bottom of the slope was a pond too perfect to be natural. Cattails rose at the edge. In the moonlight, the water was a silver coin, patched with the black of lily pads.

"There are turtles in the pond," Lowell told me. "And fish." He had some broken crackers in a pocket. He let me throw them into the water and the surface pocked as if it were raining, only upward, rain falling up from below. I watched the small and expanding rings made by the fish mouths.

On the slope past the pond there was a walkway, guarded on both sides by a pair of statues—two dogs shaped like Dalmatians, only bigger. I went to pet them, their stone backs smooth, cool, and wonderful to touch. Past the dogs, the walkway twisted like a snake, ending at a screened back porch on a large house. At every curve of the path, there was a bush shaped into something else—an elephant, a giraffe, a rabbit. I was filled with longing for this to be my house. I wanted to open the screen door, step inside, and find my family, my whole family waiting there.

Later I learned something about the people whose house it was. They had a factory that made television sets and were very rich. The dog statues had been carved from pictures of their actual dogs and marked their actual dogs' graves. They had a party every Fourth of July with lobsters flown in from Maine, a party that the mayor and the police chief and the provost all attended. They'd no children of their own but a gentle attitude toward wayward kids who wandered through. Sometimes they'd offer you lemonade. They had thick Hoosier accents.

Lowell was stretched out on the sloping grass, his hands behind his head. I went to lie next to him and the grass was not as thick and soft as it had seemed, though it still smelled thick and soft. It smelled like summer. I put my head on my brother's stomach and listened to his innermost workings.

I was happy then, and happy now, lying on my bed remembering this. How one night I'd gone to fairyland with my brother, and the very best part was that he'd had no particular reason to ask me along, nothing he'd needed me to do. He'd brought me with him just because.

I'd stretched out on the grass beside him, head on his stomach, and tried to keep my eyes open, afraid that if I fell asleep, he'd go home without me. Fairyland was all well and good, but I didn't want to be alone there. Even this part made me happy to remember. My brother could have left me behind that night, but he didn't.

In my head, I finished the grid I'd started in the holding cell, the grid of what was missing and for how long. One, my bicycle; two, Madame Defarge; three: the journals; four: my brother.

Five: Fern. Where was Fern? Probably my brother knew. I should want to know, too, but I was too afraid of the answer. If wishes were fishes, I'd soon see my brother again and nothing he had to say about Fern would hurt me to hear.

But I knew that, both in fairyland and the real world, too, wishes were slipperier things.

5

I PHONED HARLOW AGAIN, and again got the machine. One more time I asked without pique, without drama, nothing but calm dignity as far as the eye could see, where Madame Defarge was. The monkey girl had made another unscheduled appearance, and it had landed her in jail again. When would she learn to behave with restraint and decorum?

It was still raining—large, icy pellets—and I had no bike, so I phoned The Graduate next, to see if a ventriloquist's dummy of Madame Defarge had been left at the bar a couple of nights before. I don't think the man who answered the phone understood the question. I don't think he gave it the good old college try. It seemed I was going to have to go and look for myself, whatever the weather.

I spent the next two hours wandering about the town searching for various things I couldn't find. I was soaking wet, cold to the bone, my eyes already starting to sting again because I'd stabbed new contact lenses into them. A living, breathing puddle of self-pity. Obviously, someone had taken Madame Defarge. I would never be able to afford the ransom. I would never get her back.

Davis was an infamous hotbed of bicycle theft. Bicycles were taken on a whim; people would steal one just to get to their next class. The police swept up the abandoned bikes and sold them at auction once a year, the money going to the local women's shelter. I'd see my bike again, but I'd be outbid and I wouldn't even get to complain, as it was all for such a good cause. Did I want women to have shelter or didn't I? I loved that bike.

I faced the very real possibility that the sight of Officer Haddick chatting so familiarly with me might have spooked my brother. He must know I'd never deliberately turn him in. But how many times had Lowell said to me, "You just can't keep your goddamn mouth shut"? When I was five, six, eight, ten, a hundred thousand times? I *had* learned to keep my mouth shut, but Lowell had never noticed.

I returned to my apartment, empty-handed, teary-eyed, and frozen through. "My feet will never be warm again," I told Todd and Kimmy. "Toes will be lost." They were sitting at the kitchen table, playing a vigorous sort of card game. Most of the cards were on the floor.

They paused long enough to click their tongues sympathetically and then moved on to their own complaints—an aggrieved list of everyone who'd come by while I was out.

First Ezra, on some lame excuse but clearly looking for Harlow. As a result, he'd seen the damaged smoke alarm. There'd been a lecture. Todd and I were putting not only our own lives at risk, but the lives of every single person in the building. And who was responsible for the safety of these people? On whom were they depending? Not me and Todd, that was for damned-sure certain. No, it was Ezra himself in whom they'd put their faith. Maybe we didn't care if Ezra let them down, but it wasn't going to happen. We could take that to the bank.

Next, some loser, some white-guy *baka* in a backward baseball cap, looking for Harlow, had given Todd this puppet-thing he'd said Harlow had asked him to return. "Ugly on a stick," said Todd, presumably about the puppet. And, about Harlow, "Is this like her office now? Her business address?

"Because then Herself drops in. Goes and gets a beer without even asking, takes the puppet to your bedroom, and says to tell you it's back in the suitcase as promised."

"And 'no harm done,'" said Kimmy. "'As promised.'"

And then, another knock on the door! Skinny, bleached-blond, maybe thirty years old? Name of Travers. Looking for me, but since I wasn't around, he and Harlow had gone off together. "Putty in her hands," Todd said. "Poor sad sap."

The fact that Harlow had hardly touched her purloined beer seemed to bother Todd more than anything else. She hadn't even asked and now it just had to be poured down the sink as if it were a Bud Light or something instead of the last specialty wheat beer Todd had, a Hefeweizen, from the Sudwerk microbrewery. He wouldn't finish it himself, because who knew where Harlow's mouth had been? "It's been Grand Central Station for *kisama* here all evening," Todd said. He turned back to his card game, slamming the jack of clubs onto the table.

"You bastard," said Kimmy either to Todd or to his ruthless jack, though I did, just for a minute, think she was talking to me.

Kimmy was one of those people I made uncomfortable for reasons they themselves couldn't figure out. She never looked at my face, but maybe she was that way with everyone, maybe she'd been raised to think it was impolite. Todd said his grandmother, his mother's mother, would never look someone in the eye or show someone her feet, although he also said she was the rudest person to clerks and waitresses that he'd ever met. "We're in America," she would remind him loudly if he seemed embarrassed. "Every customer is the king."

Kimmy cleared her throat. "They said to tell you if you got back in the next hour, which you barely did, you should join them at the crepe place. They're having dinner there."

So I had only to walk out the door, make another trek downtown in the cold, hard rain, and there Lowell would be. I had a stirred-up feeling, a little excited, a little sick to my stomach, a sort of ipecac syrup of happiness. There Lowell would be.

With Harlow.

How could we talk about anything if Harlow was there?

But did I really want to talk about *anything*?

I felt all kinds of urgency. I also felt not quite ready. So I went to my bedroom, toweled my hair and changed into dry clothes, and then opened the powder-blue suitcase where Madame Defarge was sprawled over the folded clothes, ass up. I took her out. She smelled of cigarettes and had a damp spot on her dress. She'd obviously had a big night. Still, she was fine, hardly a hair out of place. She could go right back home whenever the airline picked her up, and no harm done, as promised.

Suddenly, weirdly, I felt a pang at the thought of losing her. Life is all arrivals and departures. "I hardly knew you," I said. "And now you're leaving me." Her uncanny valley eyes stared up. She snapped her reptilian jaw. I made her wrap her arms around my neck as if she were also sorry. Her knitting needles poked my ear sharply until I shifted her. "Please don't go," she said. Or maybe I said that. It was definitely one of us.

THE FLIP SIDE to solipsism is called theory of mind. Theory of mind postulates that, even though these cannot be directly observed, we readily impute mental states to others (and also to ourselves, since the bedrock proposal is that we understand our own mental states well enough to generalize from them). And so we constantly infer someone else's intentions, thoughts, knowledge, lack of knowledge, doubts, desires, beliefs, guesses, promises, preferences, purposes, and many, many more things in order to behave as social creatures in the world.

Children younger than four have trouble sequencing a jumbled set of images. They can describe any given picture, but they fail to see a character's intentions or goals. This means they miss the very thing that links and orders the images. They miss the story.

Young children have the innate potential for a theory of mind, just the way Noam Chomsky says they do for language, but they haven't developed it yet. Adults and older children sequence images easily into a coherent narrative. I myself took this test many times as a child and I never remember not being able to do it, though if Piaget says there was a time I couldn't, then there was a time I couldn't.

In 1978, when Fern was still safely tucked into our family, psychologists David Premack and Guy Woodruff published a paper titled "Does the Chimpanzee Have a Theory of Mind?" In it, they relied primarily on a series of experiments done with a fourteen-year-old chimp named Sarah, in order to see if she could infer human goals in observed situations. They concluded that, within limits, she could.

Subsequent research (that would be my father) raised doubts. Perhaps chimps were merely predicting behavior based on past experience rather than by imputing another's desire and intention. Years of further experimentation have been mostly about improving the methodology for prying into the minds of chimps.

In 2008, Josep Call and Michael Tomasello took another look at a whole range of approaches to this question and the results. Their conclusion was the same as Premack and Woodruff's thirty years before. Does the chimpanzee have a theory of mind? They answered with a definite yes. Chimps do see that mental states, such as purpose and knowledge, combine to produce deliberate action. They even understand deceit.

What chimps don't seem capable of understanding is the state of false belief. They don't have a theory of mind that accounts for actions driven by beliefs in conflict with reality.

And really, who lacking that will ever be able to navigate the human world?

AROUND THE AGE of six or seven, human children develop a theory of mind that encompasses embedded mental states. They've long ago mastered the basic first-order stuff—i.e., Mommy thinks I've gone to bed. Next they learn to handle (and exploit) an additional layer—Daddy doesn't know that Mommy thinks I've gone to bed.

Adult social interactions call for a great deal of this awareness of embedded states. Most adults do this effortlessly and unconsciously. According to Premack and Woodruff, the typical human adult can work with four levels of embedded imputation—someone believes that someone else knows that someone else thinks that someone else feels unhappy—before becoming uncomfortable. Premack and Woodruff describe this four-level facility as "not impressive." Gifted adults can go in as deep as seven layers, but that appears to be about the human limit.

HEADING INTO THE Crepe Bistro for dinner with Harlow and my brother was a challenging exercise in theory of mind. Had Lowell told Harlow how long it had been since he'd seen me? How excited was it okay for me to be? Although I trusted in Lowell's discretion, I didn't believe he had the same trust in mine. We both had secrets that the other might not know were secrets. So I had to figure out what Lowell had already told Harlow about our family, and he had to figure out what I'd already told her, and we both had to guess what the other didn't want said, and all this had to be communicated quickly and in full view of Harlow, but without her knowing.

Test question: How many levels of imputation do you find in the following sentence? Rosemary is afraid that Lowell might not guess that Rosemary really doesn't want him to tell Harlow about Fern because Rosemary believes once Harlow hears about Fern she'll tell everyone else and then everyone else will see Rosemary as the monkey girl she really is.

And all I wanted was to be alone with my brother. I hoped Harlow had a sharp enough theory of mind to figure that out. If necessary, I planned to help her get there. I expected Lowell to help, too.

6

BY THE TIME I arrived at the restaurant, I had walked so much that evening that my feet ached all the way up to my knees. I was so cold my ears throbbed. It was a relief to come inside the little room where the candles were lit, the windows fogged with steam and breath. Lowell and Harlow were seated in a corner, sharing a cozy fondue.

Lowell had his back to the door, so I saw Harlow first. Her face was flushed, her dark hair loose and curling around her throat. She was wearing a boatneck sweater that had slipped off one shoulder so you could see her bra strap. (Flesh-colored.) I watched her pick up a bit of bread and throw it at Lowell, smiling that dazzle of teeth. In an instant, I was four years old, left behind on the ground while Lowell and Fern climbed the apple tree, laughing. "You never choose me," I was shouting at Lowell. "It never gets to be my turn."

I didn't see Harlow notice me, but she leaned in, said something, and Lowell turned. Friday night in the bar, I'd recognized him instantly, but tonight he looked older, more tired, and less like himself. He was incontrovertibly a grown-up now and this had all happened without me there to see it. Despite the bleached hair, he looked like our father; he had our father's nighttime stubble of beard. "Here she is!" he said. "Hey, squirt. Get over here!"

He stood for a brief hug, moved his backpack and coat from the third chair to the floor so that I could sit down. All very casual, as if we saw each other often. Message received.

I tried to shake the feeling that I'd interrupted something, that *I* was the intruder.

"The kitchen was closing," Harlow said, "so Travers ordered you dinner." They appeared to have already downed several glasses of the bistro's excellent hard cider. Harlow's spirits were high. "But we were just about to give up and eat it. You got here just in time."

Lowell had gotten me a salad and a lemon crepe. It was very close to what I would have ordered myself. I felt the prickling of tears over that, how, after all these years, my brother could still order dinner for me. He'd done only one thing wrong and that was to put bell pepper in the salad. I'd always picked the bell pepper out of our mother's spaghetti sauce. Fern was the one who liked bell peppers.

"Hey!" Lowell was leaning back, rocking his chair onto its hind legs. I was afraid if I looked at his face, I wouldn't be able to look away again, so I didn't. I looked at his plate, dribbled with melted cheese. I looked at his chest. He was wearing a black, long-sleeved T-shirt with a colored landscape and the words WAIMEA CANYON underneath. I looked at his hands. They were a man's hands, rough-looking, and on the back of the right one, a large raised scar ran from his knuckles up his wrist until it vanished under his cuff. I was blinking hard; these things swam in and out of focus. "Harlow tells me she didn't even know you had a brother. What's that about?"

I took a breath, tried to find my balance. "I save you for special occasions. My best, my *only* sibling. You're too good for every day." I wanted to match Lowell's insouciance, but I don't think I succeeded, because what happened next was that Harlow pointed out that I was shaking so much my teeth were clicking.

"It's freezing outside," I said, more crossly than I meant to. "And I had to walk all over town, in the rain, searching for Madame Defarge." I could feel Lowell looking at me. "Long story," I told him.

But Harlow had started speaking before I finished. "You should have just asked me! I knew where she was!" And to Lowell, "Rosemary and I were out on the town Friday for a wild night of puppetry."

We were both of us speaking only to Lowell now. "Harlow hasn't told me about her family, either," I said. "We really haven't known each other long."

"Not a long friendship," Harlow agreed. "But superdeep. Like they say, you never know a person till you've done time with them."

Lowell smiled affectionately at me. "Done time? Little Miss Perfect here?"

Harlow took hold of his wrists, so he turned instantly back to her. "She has an arrest record"—moving his hands until they were about a foot apart—"this big," Harlow said. They were staring into each other's eyes. I felt my heart beat three times—tick, tick, tick. Then she let go of him, gave me a quick smile.

I thought the smile was a question—is this okay?—though I wasn't sure about which part. Okay to tell him about our arrest or okay to hold his hands and stare into his eyes? I tried for a look back that said no, absolutely not to both, but either she didn't understand or had never been asking in the first place. Or was no longer looking in my direction.

She went on to tell him about our first trip to the pokey. The big house. The slammer.

But she managed to do this without mentioning Reg, so I went back and folded him in. The good Reg, not the bad one. "Her boyfriend," I said, "came right over and bailed her out."

She dealt with it deftly. Reg quickly became not just bad, but scary bad, and me, well, I became someone so generous that I'd let a person I hardly knew hide out in my apartment. "She's awesome, your sister," Harlow said to Lowell. "I said to myself, self, there's a person you want to know better. There's the person you want to have your back in the world."

The story of the lost suitcase followed and then the discovery of Madame Defarge and then the night on the town. Harlow told most of this, but added frequent invitations for me to join in. "Tell him about the car wash," she said, so I did that part while Harlow pantomimed us groping through the soapy tentacles in the dark, planning our weddings.

She even included Tarzan and my theories of relativity, only now it appeared she'd always agreed with me. When she said Tarzan's name, Lowell put his scarred hand on my sleeve and left it there. I'd been about to take off my coat, but then didn't. That weight on my arm seemed like the only attention I had from him; I wasn't about to lose it.

To be fair—every story Harlow told, every detail in every story, redounded to my credit. I was the one with the cool but wacky ideas. I was the one who could be counted on. I stood up for myself and I stood up for my friends. I was a ball. I was a blast.

I was so not what was going on here.

I do believe that Harlow meant to be kind. I do believe that she believed that I wanted her to sell my brother on a bunch of good qualities I didn't truly have. She could neither know nor help how she looked, with the candlelight painting her face and hair all different colors and that reflected shine in her eyes. She made my brother laugh.

Pheromones are Earth's primordial idiom. We may not read them as readily as ants do, but they make their point. I'd come assuming we'd be ditching Harlow as soon as we could. Then the hard cider flowed and the stories wound about themselves until, like Escher prints, they'd swallowed their own tails. And I had another think coming.

The evening ended with all three of us back in my apartment, Madame Defarge liberated once again, sexily kicking up her heels. She touched Lowell's cheek. She told him he was très cool and also, paradoxically, très hot. He was one quick ticket to ooh-la-la land.

Lowell reached out, brushing past Madame Lefarge's skirt and all the way to Harlow. He held her hand for a minute, stroking over her palm with his thumb. He pulled her closer. "Don't toy with me, madame," Lowell said, his voice so soft I barely heard him.

And Madame Defarge's accent went straight to Memphis. "Not yet, sugar," she answered just as softly. "But I surely am planning to."

"Speaking of puppets," Todd said to me, with a contemptuous nod toward Lowell. He still hadn't figured out Lowell was my brother. When the penny dropped, he felt so bad he gave me his bed and went to spend the night at Kimmy's. He even said I could play his brand-new Nintendo 64, because an offer like that would have made *him* feel a whole lot better.

I excused myself and went to the bathroom to peel my contacts off my insulted eyes. My jaw ached from the way I'd been forcing it to smile. Sometime between my salad and crepe, I'd stopped wanting to be Harlow's friend and started wishing I'd never met her. I felt bad about this—my jealousy, my anger—what with her saying all those nice things about me. Though I was pretty sure she didn't like me nearly as well as she was claiming.

Anyway, she didn't know how long Lowell and I had been apart.

But he did. I was even angrier with him. He'd abandoned me to our parents and their sad, silent house when I was only eleven years old. And now, reunited for the first time in a decade, he'd hardly looked at me. And had no more willpower than a bonobo.

Todd's room smelled like pizza, probably because there were two old slices in a box on his desk, tips curling up like the tongues of old shoes. Also on the desk—a lava lamp, very retro, that swelled and splatted and threw off a slight reddish light. No end of comic books in case I couldn't sleep, but no worries on that score. Twice Reg called and woke me up and twice I had to tell him I had no idea where Harlow was. I thought that Harlow must have heard the phone and known it was Reg, known that she was making me lie to him, which gave me the permission I'd been missing to be as mad at her as I liked.

I knew that Reg knew I was lying, and that he knew that I knew that he knew. Maybe science says that the best of us can manage only seven levels of embedded theory of mind, but I say I could go on like that indefinitely.

AND THEN, just like the old days, Lowell came and got me in the night. He was wearing his coat and backpack. He shook me awake without a word, gesturing for me to come, and waited in the living room while I got ready, dressing in my same clammy clothes, since anything dry was back in my own bedroom with Harlow. I followed him out the door. In the darkened hall, he put his arms around me and I smelled the wet wool of his lapels. "How about a piece of pie?" he said.

I CONSIDERED PUSHING him away, answering with something nasty, but I was too afraid he was leaving already. I settled on brief. Sullen but deniable. "Sure."

He obviously knew his way around Davis, knew, in the wee hours of the morning, where the pie was. The streets were deserted and the rain had finally stopped. We moved from streetlight to streetlight toward a spectral mist that drifted continuously in front of us but couldn't be entered. Our footsteps echoed off the silent sidewalks. "How are Mom and Dad?" Lowell asked.

"They moved. To this little place on North Walnut. It's so weird how they've fixed it up—like a model home or something. None of our old stuff is there." Already, against my will and only provisionally, I was softening. It felt good to share my worries and irritations about our parents with someone equally responsible for making them miserable. More so, if we're being honest. This was what I'd hoped for whenever I'd imagined seeing Lowell again, this exact moment when I could stop being an only child.

"How's Dad's drinking?"

"Not too bad. Though I'm not there, what do I know? Mom's working for Planned Parenthood now. I think she likes it. Playing tennis. Playing bridge."

"Of course," said Lowell.

"There's no piano in the new house." I gave Lowell a minute to deal with this disturbing news. I didn't say, She stopped playing the piano when you left. A car passed in a spray of water. A crow, hunching over the warm streetlight as if it were an egg, scolded us from above. Maybe in Japanese. *"Ba! Ka! Ba! Ka!"* We were definitely being called rude names; the only question was the language. I told Lowell this instead.

"Crows are very smart. If they say we're idiots, we're idiots," he answered.

"Or it could just be you." I used the neutral sort of tone you adopt when you want to claim later that you were only joking. Maybe I'd softened, but I hadn't forgiven.

"Ba! Ka! Ba! Ka!"

I could never, in a million years, have distinguished this particular crow from any other, but Lowell told me that crows are good at recognizing and remembering people. They have unusually large brains for their bodies, a proportion similar to chimpanzees.

I felt my pulse stutter at the word *chimpanzees*, but Lowell said nothing further. We walked past a house on B Street, where the trees had all been stuffed with balloons. There was a banner over the front door, still illuminated by a porch light. HAPPY BIRTHDAY, MARGARET! Fern and I used to get balloons on our birthdays, though Fern had to be watched every moment so she didn't bite one, swallow the rubber, and suffocate.

We passed Central Park. Even in the dark, I could see how all the grass had been drowned in the winter mud; the ground was slick and black. Once I'd made mud-shoes for Fern and me from paper plates and shoestrings. Fern wouldn't wear hers, but I'd tied mine onto my feet, thinking I would walk over the mud in them like snow-shoes over snow. You learn as much from failure as from success, Dad always says.

Though no one admires you for it.

"I tried to read Dad's last paper," Lowell said finally. "'The Learning Curve in Stochastic Learning Theory.' I could hardly follow from one paragraph to the next. It was like I'd never seen those words before. Maybe if I'd gone to college."

"Wouldn't have helped." I told him briefly about Thanksgiving and how Dad had annoyed Grandma Donna with his Markov chains. I mentioned Peter's SATs and Uncle Bob's conspiracy theories and I almost told him Mom had given me her journals, but what if he'd wanted to see them? I didn't want to admit, even to him, that they were lost.

We walked into Bakers Square, with their gingham curtains, laminated place mats, and Muzak. It wasn't a bad setting for us, very old-school, as if we'd stepped back a decade or more to our childhoods, though perhaps a bit too brightly lit. The Muzak was even older—Beach Boys and Supremes. "Be True to Your School." "Ain't No Mountain High Enough." Our parents' music.

We were the only customers. A waiter who looked like a young Albert Einstein came immediately and took our order for two pieces of banana cream pie. He delivered them with some cheerful remarks about the weather, pointing out the window to where the rain had started again—"The drought is over! The drought is over!"—and then went away.

My brother's face across the table was more and more like our dad's. They both had the lean and hungry look that Shakespeare found so dangerous. Cavernous cheeks, darkly stubbled chins. Back at the Crepe Bistro, Lowell had already needed a shave. Now he was a wolf-man, the dark beard making an odd but striking contrast with his bleached hair. I thought that he looked exhausted, but not in the way people look exhausted when they've been up all night having great sex. Just in the way people look when they're exhausted.

And he no longer seemed, as he always had done, so very much older than I was. He noticed me staring at him. "Just look at you. College girl, so far from home. Do you love it? Is life good?"

"Can't complain," I said.

"Come on." Lowell forked a bite into his mouth, smiled at me around it. "Don't be so modest. I bet you can complain for days."

7

LOWELL AND I stayed at Bakers Square through the rest of the night. The rain started and stopped and started again. I had eggs, Lowell pancakes, we both had coffee. The morning crowd came in. Our waiter went home and three others arrived. Lowell told me he'd become a vegetarian, and managed to be vegan except when he was on the road, which was most of the time.

Up at the vet school, Davis had a famous fistulated cow, a cow with a deliberate hole punched into its stomach through which digestive processes could be observed. She was a popular destination for school trips, a reliable exhibit on Picnic Day. You could reach right into that cow, feel her intestines. Hundreds of people had done so. And that cow, Lowell said, lived the life of Riley compared to your typical dairy cow.

It was his firm belief that Davis actually had multiple fistulated cows. They were all named Maggie, each and every one of them, to fool people into thinking there was only one cow and not start asking questions about excessive fistulations, Lowell said.

Lowell said that he'd always assumed he'd go to college and he really regretted missing out on that. He did manage to read a lot.

He recommended Donald Griffin's book *Animal Minds* to me. Maybe I could get Dad to read it, too.

Despite not understanding Dad's last paper, Lowell had a number of criticisms about the work Dad did. It seemed to Lowell that psychological studies of nonhuman animals were mostly cumbersome, convoluted, and downright peculiar. They taught us little about the animals but lots about the researchers who designed and ran them. Take Harry Harlow, whom we'd met as children and who, Lowell said, had given us all lemon drops.

I remembered Dr. Harlow. He'd come to dinner at the farmhouse and sat between Fern and me. Later that night, he'd read us a chapter of *Winnie-the-Pooh*, doing Roo's voice so high and breathy it made us laugh every time Roo spoke. I didn't remember the lemon drops, though I'd bet that was the part Fern would remember. I had a fleeting thought that if Dad had really admired Harry Harlow, I might have been named after him. I might be Harlow right now, same as Harlow was. How freaky would that be?

But no one would name a baby after Harry Harlow. He'd taken rhesus monkey infants away from their mothers and given them inanimate mothers instead, mothers made alternatively of terrycloth or wire, to see which, in the absence of other choices, the babies preferred. He claimed, deliberately provocative, to be studying love.

The baby monkeys clung pathetically to the fake, uncaring mothers, until they all turned psychotic or died. "I don't know what he thought he'd learned about them," Lowell said. "But in their short, sad little lives, they sure learned a hell of a lot about him.

"We need a sort of reverse mirror test. Some way to identify those species smart enough to see themselves when they look at someone else. Bonus points for how far out the chain you can go. Double bonus for those who get all the way to insects."

Our new waitress, a young Latina with short, thick bangs, hovered about us for a while, darting in to rearrange the syrups, take the coffee cups, push the bill into a more prominent position on the table. Eventually she gave up, wandered away in search of more suggestible customers.

Lowell had stopped speaking while she was there. When she left, he picked right up without missing a stitch. "Look how much I'm talking!" he'd said, at some point during the evening. "I'm more like you than you are tonight. I don't usually get to talk all that much. I lead a quiet life." He'd smiled at me. His face had changed, but his smile was the same.

"Here's the problem with Dad's approach." Lowell tapped his finger on the Bakers Square place mat, as if the problem were somewhere around the Scrambler Supreme. "Right in the fundamental assumptions. Dad was always saying that we were all animals, but when he dealt with Fern, he didn't start from that place of congruence. His methods put the whole burden of proof onto her. It was always her failure for not being able to talk to us, never ours for not being able to understand her. It would have been more scientifically rigorous to start with an assumption of similarity. It would have been a lot more Darwinian.

"And a lot less rude," Lowell said.

He asked me, "Do you remember that game Fern used to play with the red and blue poker chips? Same/NotSame?"

Of course I did.

"She was always giving you the red chip. No one else. Just you. Remember that?"

I remembered it when he said it. It popped into my head as a brand-new memory, sharper than the old ones, which had all worn thin as Roman coins. I was lying on the scratched hardwood floor by Dad's armchair and Fern had come to lie beside me. It was that time I'd broken my elbow. Dad and the grad students were still discussing Fern's surprising laughter. Fern was still holding the poker chips—the red for same, the blue for not. She rolled onto her back and I could see every little hair in the fuzz on her chin. She smelled like sweat. She scratched the fingers of one hand over my head. A hair came out. She ate it.

Then, with every appearance of careful consideration, she'd given me the red chip. I could see it all again in my head—Fern looking out at me from those bright, shadowed eyes and laying the red chip onto my chest.

I know what our father had thought it meant. Nothing useful. Once, she'd given me a raisin for every raisin she'd eaten, and now she had two poker chips and was giving me one. Two interesting behaviors—that was as far as Dad could go.

Here is what I'd thought it meant. I'd thought Fern was apologizing. When you feel bad, I feel bad, is what I got from that red chip. We're the same, you and I.

My sister, Fern. In the whole wide world, my only red poker chip.

Under the table, my hands, all on their own, found each other and gripped together as I forced myself to ask the question I should have asked the minute we'd found ourselves alone. "How is Fern?"

It came out in a whisper, and even before my mouth stopped moving, I was already wishing I'd kept it shut. I was so afraid of what the answer might be that I kept talking. "Start at the beginning," I told him, thinking to put off any bad news as long as possible. "Start with the night you left."

. . .

BUT YOU'D PROBABLY rather get straight to Fern. I'll condense.

I'd been right to guess that Lowell had gone to Dr. Uljevik's lab when he left us. He knew he had only a couple of days before we'd start looking and it took him about that long to get there. South Dakota was bitterly cold, a landscape of packed snowless dirt, black leafless trees, and a dry, peppery wind.

He'd arrived after dark and took a room at a motel, because he didn't know where the labs were and it was too late to go searching. Besides, he was asleep on his feet after two nights on the bus. The woman at the desk had hair from the 1950s and a dead stare. He was afraid she'd ask his age, but she was barely interested enough to take his money.

The next day, he found Uljevik's office at the university and introduced himself to the department secretary as a prospective student. She was very midwestern, Lowell said. So friendly. Face like a shovel, flat and open. Big, open heart. The kind of woman he was born to disappoint. "Like Mrs. Byard," he told me. "You know what I mean?"

Mrs. Byard had died about five years ago, so he wouldn't be disappointing her again. I didn't say this.

He'd told the department secretary that he was particularly interested in chimp studies. Was there any way he could see the work being done here? She gave him Uljevik's office hours, which he already knew. They'd been posted on the office door.

But then she left her desk to do some errand or other, which allowed him unsupervised access to Uljevik's faculty mailbox. Among other items, he'd found an electric bill, quite high, with a country road address. He got a map and a hot dog at a gas station. The place was six miles out of town. He walked it.

There were almost no cars on the road. It was sunny out, though painfully cold. It felt good to be moving. He swung his arms for the heat of it and wondered how the game with Marion had turned out. That game wouldn't have ended well, even with him playing. At best, they might have avoided downright ugly. Without him? What's uglier than ugly? He thought he maybe shouldn't go back to high school, should take his GED instead, go straight to college, where nobody would know he'd ever played basketball. He wasn't big enough for the college teams anyway.

He arrived finally at a compound with a chain-link fence. Ordinarily, chain-link fences posed no problem to teenage Lowell; he laughed at chain-link fences. But this one was threaded with the telltale electric wire. That told him he was in the right spot, but also that he had no way inside.

The yard was thick with leafless trees, the ground bare dirt and boulders, fringed with yellowed weeds. There was a tire swing hanging from a branch and a net for climbing, like the ones the army uses in its obstacle courses. No one seemed to be about. Across the road, Lowell found a half tree trunk that hid him from the wind and from view. He curled into it and went promptly to sleep.

He woke when he heard a car door slam. The gate to the compound driveway was open. Inside, a man was unloading great bags of Purina dog chow from the back of a green station wagon. He piled them onto a dolly that he pushed across the dirt to what seemed to be a garage. As soon as he disappeared inside, Lowell crossed the road and slipped through the door into the main building. "I just walked right in," Lowell said. "Simple as that."

He found himself in a dark hallway with a set of stairs leading up and also down. He could hear the chimps. They were in the basement.

There was a strong odor in the stairwell, a mix of ammonia and shit. A light switch, but Lowell left it off. The sun came in through a row of small windows set just above ground level. It was bright enough for him to see four cages, all in a row, and at least a dozen dark, squat figures inside them.

"What came next," Lowell said, "was awful. I know you don't like to talk about Fern. Are you sure you want me to go on?"

He meant this as a warning to me. He wasn't really offering to stop.

I RECOGNIZED FERN right away, he said, but not because I actually recognized her in the dim light, just because she was the youngest and smallest.

She was in a cage with four large adults. I don't think I'd ever realized how different one chimp looks from another. Her hair was redder than most, and her ears were set higher, more like teddy bear ears. All very easy to figure out, all very logical even though she'd changed quite a bit. Solid and squat where she used to be so graceful. But she was eerie in the way she recognized me. It was as if she felt me coming. I remember thinking Dad should do a study on chimp precognition.

I was walking across the basement toward the cages and she hadn't even turned in my direction when I saw her go rigid. Her hair started to rise and she began to very quietly make those *oo oo* sounds she makes when she's agitated. Then she spun around and leapt for the bars of the cage. She was shaking them and swinging back and forth, by then she was looking right at me. By then she was screaming at me.

I ran toward her and when I got close enough she reached through, grabbed my arm, and pulled me so hard she slammed me into the bars. I hit my head and things went a bit sideways for me. Fern had my hand inside the cage, inside her mouth, but she hadn't bitten me yet. I think she couldn't decide if she was more happy to see me or more angry. It was the first time in my life I'd ever been frightened of her.

I tried to pull my hand back, but she wouldn't let me. I could smell the excitement on her, a smell sort of like burned hair. She hadn't had a bubble bath in a long time or a good tooth-brushing. She kind of stank, to be honest.

I started talking to her, telling her I was sorry, telling her I loved her. But she was still screaming, so I know she didn't hear. And she was squeezing my fingers so hard there were flashes going off like popguns in my eyeballs, and it was all I could do to keep my voice calm and quiet.

By now, she'd gotten the other chimps pretty worked up. Another one, a big male and fully erect, came and tried to take my hand from her, but she wouldn't let go. So he grabbed my other arm, and then they were both pulling on me, and between them they bounced me repeatedly against the bars. I hit my nose, my forehead, the side of my face. Fern was still holding my hand, but not in her mouth anymore. She turned and bit the male chimp on his shoulder. She really clamped down. More screaming, coming from all the cages, echoing off the concrete walls. It was like a mosh pit in there. A really dangerous mosh pit.

The big guy dropped my arm and backed away with his mouth wide open, showing his canines, I swear they looked like shark teeth. He was standing straight, his hair, like hers, all up. He was trying to threaten her, but she wasn't paying him any attention. She was signing with her one free hand to me. My name, her fingers in the L with that slap against her chest, and then good, good Fern. Fern is a good girl. Please take me home now. I'll be good. I promise I'll be good.

The big chimp came crashing in from behind and Fern couldn't defend herself and hold on to me at the same time. So she didn't defend herself. He opened these long, bloody wounds on her back with his feet. And all this time, she was still screaming, all the chimps were screaming, and I could smell blood and fury and terror, all that acrid copper and musky sweat and ripe feces, and my head was spinning from the blows I'd taken. And still she didn't let go.

By now, people had arrived, two of them, both men, running down the stairs, shouting at me, but I couldn't hear what they were saying. They didn't seem old enough to be professors, maybe grad students. Maybe janitors. They were big, and one of them was carrying a cattle prod, and I remember thinking, how is that going to work? How can they shock Fern and not get me? And how can I stop them from shocking Fern?

Turned out, they didn't need to shock anyone. The male chimp saw the prod and backed right off, whimpering, to the rear of the cage. Everyone got quiet. They showed it to Fern, and she finally let go.

I took some shit in the face. It came from a different cage, landed with a stench, slid down my neck into my shirt collar. I was told to get the fuck out before the police were called. Fern was trying to press herself through the bars, still signing my name and also hers. Good Fern, good Fern. The men began arguing over whether to dart her or not. When they saw the blood, the argument was over.

One of them left to call the vet. He took me with him, dragging me by my undamaged arm. He was a lot bigger than I was. "I'm calling the police next," he said, giving me a shake. "You think you're funny? You think you're a real funny boy, tormenting caged animals like that? Get the fuck out of here and don't you ever come back."

The other man stayed with Fern. He stood over her with the cattle prod. I think he was protecting her from the other chimps, but I know she saw it as a threat. Her signing got sloppy. Despairing.

I still can hardly stand to think about it, Lowell said. How even after everything, she protected me from that alpha male. The price she paid for that. The way her face looked when I left her there.

I never saw her again, Lowell said.

PART FIVE

❋

*Nowadays, of course, I can portray those
ape-like feelings only with human words and,
as a result, I misrepresent them.*

—FRANZ KAFKA, "A Report for an Academy"

I

THERE WAS SOMETHING NotSame about Fern and me, something so outrageous that Lowell hadn't even suspected it until he went to South Dakota. Something I hadn't known until he told it to me ten years later over breakfast at Bakers Square. The NotSame was this: Like a chair or a car or a television, Fern could be bought and sold. The whole time she was living in the farmhouse with us as part of our family, the whole time she was keeping herself busy being our sister and daughter, she was, in fact, the property of Indiana University.

When my father pulled the plug on the family project, he'd hoped to keep working with Fern under some as yet undetermined circumstances at the lab. But maintaining her had always been an expensive proposition and IU said they had no place to house her safely. They went looking for the exit. She was sold to South Dakota on the condition that they take her at once.

Our father had no say in that. He'd had no authority to send Matt along, but he'd done so, and Matt had no official position in South Dakota, but he'd stayed as long as he was able and seen Fern as often as allowed. They'd done the best they could, Lowell said, and of all people, Lowell was the unlikeliest to cut anyone any slack about this. But it was hard for me back then—and still is, honestly—to understand how any parents could have ended up with so little power concerning their own daughter.

"My visit caused nothing but more pain. Turned out Dad was right about not going to see her." Lowell's eyes were red with fatigue and he was rubbing them hard and making them redder. "Except for the part where he said it would make me feel better."

"Do you know where she is now?" I asked and Lowell said that he did, that she was still in South Dakota, still at Uljevik's lab. Added to the emotional reasons not to visit again was this fact—the FBI was clearly waiting for him there. There was no way he could go back. So he had someone keeping an eye on her. He got reports.

Uljevik himself had retired five years ago, good news for everyone in those cages. "He wasn't really a scientist," Lowell said. "More of a supervillain. The kind of scientist who belongs in a prison for the criminally insane."

Sadly, Lowell said, there were lots of those kinds of scientists still running about, wild and free.

"He trained the chimps to kiss his hand when he walked through the cages," Lowell said. "He made Fern do that over and over again. This guy who used to work there told me Uljevik thought that was funny.

"Uljevik hated Fern, and nobody could ever explain to me why. Once I talked this rich guy into putting up the money to buy her, pay a sanctuary in Florida (already full up, like all the other sanctuaries) enough money to make it worth their while to ignore their waiting list and take her. Uljevik refused to sell. He offered the guy a different chimp and the guy figured one rescue was better than none, so the next thing I knew, he'd agreed. Turned out to be sort of a blessing, I guess. It's always dicey introducing a new chimp into an established troop."

I had a momentary flash of my first day in kindergarten—of me, peculiar, undersocialized, and half a term late.

"The chimp that went instead of her was attacked and beaten nearly to death," Lowell said.

LOWELL SAID:

I had a big scare in '89, when Uljevik announced he was closing a budgetary gap by sending some of the chimps to the medical labs. Uma, Peter, Joey, Tata, and Dao were all sold off. Uma is the only one of those still alive.

I was sure Fern would be on the list, but she wasn't, maybe because she was breeding well. Growing up with us fucked with her sexually though; she's not interested. They started inseminating her. I call that rape without the bruises.

She's had three children so far. Her first, a little boy they named Basil, was taken away almost immediately by an older female chimp. I hear that happens even in the best of families. Fern was pretty sad about it, though.

And then he was taken away again. Uljevik sold Basil along with Sage, Fern's second child, to the city zoo in St. Louis, a thing the best of families usually manage to avoid. Arguably, not ours.

"You should go see them there," Lowell told me. "It's not great, but it's not the medical labs."

A man at another table accused his breakfast partner of pulling rainbows and unicorns out of her ass. I don't know if it was exactly this moment when I overheard that, but I've always remembered it. Such a painful image, so exactly what Lowell wasn't doing. So exactly what Lowell never did. So when Lowell told me that everything had gotten better for Fern when Uljevik retired, I knew it was the truth. "The grad students love Fern," Lowell told me. "Didn't they always?"

Lowell said that Fern had had one more child, a little girl named Hazel. Hazel had just turned two and Fern was teaching her to sign. It seemed likely Fern would get to keep her, as an experiment had been designed around them. The lab workers were forbidden now to use any sign in front of Hazel that she hadn't already been seen using herself on at least fourteen occasions by at least four separate witnesses.

Fern had more than two hundred documented signs herself, and the researchers were keeping a list to see how many of those she passed on. Would she only pass on the functional or would she include the conversational?

"Hazel's got the whole lab wrapped around her little finger," Lowell told me. "She's already making up signs of her own. *Tree dress* for leaves. *Big soup* for the bathtub. Smart as can be. Chess-playing Jesuitical.

"Just like her mom," Lowell said.

"DID FERN GIVE you that?" I asked, pointing to the scar on Lowell's hand, and he said no, that was the calling card of a frightened red-tailed hawk. But I never heard that story, because Lowell hadn't finished with Fern's.

Back in South Dakota, after his break-in, Lowell had needed medical attention. In addition to the facial drubbing he'd taken on the bars of the cage, two of his fingers had been broken and his wrist sprained. A local doctor came to tend him at a private home, the treatment taking place out of the office and off the books. He'd slept that night at that same home, with someone he didn't know watching over him, waking him at intervals to check for signs of concussion. All this had come about because someone had maybe seen Lowell at the lab or else earlier that morning at the university or maybe it was someone back in Bloomington, someone impressed by the Great Rat Release. Lowell was very vague on this point. But whoever this person was, s/he didn't like the way lab animals were treated, and thought Lowell might agree that something needed to be done.

"By now, I'd figured out I couldn't rescue Fern alone," Lowell said. "I'd been stupid and childish, as if Fern and I could just go off together, like Han and Chewbacca. Make the leap to hyperspace.

"Obviously, I hadn't been thinking at all. I'd just wanted to see her, see how she was doing, show her she hadn't been forgotten. Say that I loved her.

"Now I saw that I needed a plan. I needed a place to take her and people to help. I saw that according to the law I'd be guilty of theft, and I saw that I didn't give two shits about the law. I was told about this action coming up in Riverside, California, a car headed there with an empty seat. I said I'd go. My thinking was that anything I did would be bank to use on Fern later."

Lowell had his face turned away from me, looking through the big windows to the street, where the morning commute had begun. The tule fog had risen again. The rain was stopped and the sun was up but thin and strained, so the cars all had their lights on. It was as if the whole town had been stuffed into a sock.

Inside Bakers Square, it was getting busier, silverware striking the china plates, the buzz of conversations. The sound of the cash register. The bell over the door. I was crying and not sure when that had started.

Lowell reached over and took my hands in his own, rough ones. His fingers were warmer than mine. "The police showed up at the lab the next day looking for me—I heard about it. I know they were told all about my visit, so Mom and Dad knew I'd been there and that I was basically okay. But I was still too mad to go home. This ride to Riverside seemed like my best bet for getting out of town without getting caught.

"I thought I was thinking things through. Doing what was best for Fern. But I was so angry. At all of you. I kept seeing her face.

"I didn't mean to never come home," Lowell said. "I just meant to take care of Fern first, get her settled somewhere good, somewhere she'd be happy." He gave my hands a small shake. "Some farm."

Around then, there was one of those strange moments when all the noise inside the restaurant suddenly stopped. Nobody spoke. Nobody clicked the sides of their coffee cup with their spoon. Nobody outside barked or honked or coughed. Fermata. Freeze-frame.

Resume action.

Lowell's voice dropped. "I was so stupid," he said tonelessly. "I could have gone to college there. Maybe found a way to work at the lab. Seen Fern every day. Instead I go get made by the FBI and suddenly I can't ever go back. Or to college. Or home."

And then all the air went out of him. "I've tried so hard to rescue her," he told me. "Years and years of trying and what does Fern have to show for it? What a miserable excuse for a brother I turned out to be."

. . .

HOURS AFTER OUR waitress had despaired of it, we paid the bill. Lowell shouldered his backpack and we walked through the fog down Second Street together. Drops of water collected on the dark wool of Lowell's coat.

I remembered a day when I'd been sick with a cold and Lowell had said since I couldn't go outside, he'd bring the snow in. He'd fetched me snowflakes on the backs of his black leather gloves, promised me intricate six-sided crystals, miniature snow-queen castles. But by the time I'd gotten them to the microscope, they were just blank beads of water.

It was before Fern left, but she wasn't in this memory and I wondered about that. It was hard to keep Fern—a twirling, whirling, somersaulting carpe diem—out of anything. Maybe she'd been off working with the grad students. Maybe she had been there and I'd erased her. Maybe it was too painful just now to remember all that hairy exuberance.

"Walk me to the train station," Lowell said.

So he was leaving. He hadn't even stayed long enough for me to completely get past the sex-with-Harlow outrage. "I thought we'd maybe go hiking," I told him, not even trying not to whine. "I thought we'd go to San Francisco for a day. I didn't think you'd leave this fast."

So many things I'd stored up to tell him. I'd hoped, through patiently assembled implication, to make him see that he couldn't abandon me again. Full-press guilt trip. I'd just been waiting for him to stop doing all the talking.

Maybe he'd guessed. Not much got by Lowell, at least not much about me. "Sorry, Rosie. I can't hang around anywhere, but especially not here."

A dozen students were crowded about the door to Mishka's, waiting for the café to open. We cut a path through them—Lowell and his backpack, me beside him with my head down. Mishka's was a popular place during finals week, but you had to be early to get a seat in the back. The front tables were designated no-study zones; this was known as The Rule.

Outside the café, the fog smelled of coffee and muffins. I looked up and right into the face of Doris Levy from my freshman dorm. Fortunately, she gave no sign of recognition. I couldn't have managed a chat.

Lowell didn't speak again until the students were more than a block behind us. "I've got to assume the FBI knows you're here," he said then. "Especially with that splendid arrest record of yours. Your apartment manager saw me. Your roommate. Harlow. It's too risky. And anyway, there's someplace else I have to be."

Lowell was planning another action, he said, something long-term and so deep-cover he'd have to completely disappear. This meant he couldn't be taking those reports on Fern.

So they'd be coming to me. Never mind how, Lowell said, I'd know when I got one. It was all arranged except for this last thing, which was to tell me that watching over Fern was my job now.

It was the reason he'd come.

We arrived at the train station. Lowell bought his ticket while I sat on the very bench where, a few nights back, I'd sobbed my heart out imagining the day Fern was taken away. What with one thing and another, I'd done so much crying since Dr. Sosa's class, you wouldn't have thought I had any tears left, but down they dripped. At least we were at the train station. Airports and train stations are where you get to cry. I'd once gone to an airport for just that purpose.

We went out to the platform and walked down the tracks until we could be by ourselves again. I wished that I were the one leaving. Ticket to anywhere. What would Davis be like without that constant hope that Lowell was coming? Why even stay here?

I'd been seeing Ezra's habit of starring in his own life as a vanity; I'd been amused by it. Now I saw the utility. If I were playing a part, I could establish a distance, pretend to only pretend to be feeling the things I was feeling. The scene was cinematic, despite the sound track of my snuffling. To my right and my left, the tracks vanished into the fog. The train whistle approached. I could have been seeing my brother off to war. To the big city to make his fortune. To search the goldfields for our missing father.

Lowell put his arms around me. My face left a damp and snotty smear on the wool of his coat. I took in a clogged breath, trying to smell him so I'd remember it. He smelled of wet dog, but that was just his coat. Coffee. Harlow's vanilla cologne. I tried but couldn't get to the smell underneath all that—the Lowell smell. I touched his scratchy cheek, fingered his hair the way I used to when I was little, the way Fern used to do to me. Once, in class, I'd reached out to touch a coil of braids on the head of the woman in the seat in front of me. I hadn't been thinking at all, overwhelmed by the need to feel that intricacy of hair. She'd turned around. "My head doesn't belong to you," she'd said icily, leaving me stuttering an apology, horrified at the way my chimp nature still popped out when I wasn't paying attention.

We heard the warning alarms on the crossing nearest us, the engine approaching from the north. I was sorting madly through all the things I'd planned to say, looking for the single most important.

I made a hasty, ill-advised choice. "I know you've always blamed me for Fern."

"I shouldn't have done that. You were five years old."

"But I honestly don't remember what I did. I don't remember anything at all about Fern leaving."

"Serious?" Lowell asked. He was quiet for a moment; I could see him deciding how much to tell me. This was a bad sign, that there were things he maybe shouldn't say. My heart grew thorns, each beat a stab.

The train arrived. The ticket collector set out a step for the debarking passengers. Some people got off. Others got on. Time was running out. Already we were walking toward the nearest door. "You made Mom and Dad choose," Lowell said finally. "You or her. You were always such a jealous little kid."

He swung his backpack on board, hoisted himself up and in, turned to look back down at me. "You were only five years old," he repeated. "Don't go blaming yourself."

He stared at me then, the way you stare at someone you won't see for a long time. *Her face when I left her.* "Tell Mom and Dad I love them? Make them believe it, that'll be the hard part."

He was still in the doorway, his face partly his own and partly, the tired part, our father's. "You, too, squirt. You can't imagine how much I miss you all. Good old Bloomington. 'When I dream about the moonlight on the Wabash . . .'"

Then I long for my Indiana home.

A middle-aged Asian woman in jeans and high heels came running. She took the step in an agile leap, thwacking Lowell on the arm with her swinging purse. "God, I'm so sorry," she said. "I thought I'd missed my train." She disappeared into the coach. The whistle sounded.

"I'm really glad you have a friend," Lowell told me. "Harlow seems to care a lot about you." And then the conductor came and made him take his seat. It was the last thing I remember him saying, my big brother, my personal Hale-Bopp comet, streaming by and gone again—that Harlow cared.

For all the brevity of the visit, he'd managed to get some licks in. I'd planned to make him feel bad about my lonely life, but Harlow and her stupid friendship had nixed that and I was the one left ashamed. I'd always known he blamed me for Fern, but I hadn't heard it aloud in ten years.

The things Lowell had said combined with his leaving combined with my lack of sleep and the aftermath of the itchy, ugly narcotic I'd taken. Any one of those might have done me in. The entirety was overpowering. I was sad and horrified, ashamed and bereft, lonely and exhausted, caffeinated and guilt-ridden and grief-stricken and many other things as well. The system crashed. I watched the fog swallow the train and all I felt was tired.

"You love Fern," someone said to me. It turned out to be my old imaginary friend, Mary. I hadn't seen Mary in almost as long as I hadn't seen Fern and she hadn't aged a day. She didn't stick around. She brought me the one message—"You love Fern"—and then was gone again. I wanted to believe her. But the whole point of Mary had been to reassure me where Fern was concerned. Maybe she'd just been doing her job.

We call them feelings because we feel them. They don't start in our minds, they arise in our bodies, is what my mother always said, with the great materialist William James as backup. It was a standard component of her parenting—that you can't help the things you feel, only the things you do. (But telling everyone what you felt, that was *doing* something. Especially when what you were feeling was mean. Though as a child, I'd always seen this as more of a gray area.)

Now I searched through my weariness, into every breath, every muscle, every heartbeat, and found a reassuring, bone-deep certainty. I loved Fern. I had always loved Fern. I always would.

I stood by the tracks, all by myself, in a sudden shower of images. My life, only with Fern instead of without her. Fern in kindergarten, making a paper turkey from the silhouette of her hand. Fern in the high school gym watching Lowell play basketball and hooting when he scored. Fern in the freshman dorm, complaining to the other girls about our crazy crazy parents. Fern making the hand signs we found so entertaining back then. *Loser. Whatev.*

I had missed her desperately in every one of those places, every one of those moments, and not even known it.

But as far back as I could remember, I'd also been jealous of her. I'd been jealous again, not fifteen minutes past, learning that Lowell's visit had been for her and not me. But maybe this was the way sisters usually felt about each other.

Though clearly not so jealous that one sister forced another into exile. Had I really done that? This was where the fairy tale ran out of road.

I decided not to think about it further until I was better rested. Here is what I thought about instead: what kind of a family lets a five-year-old child decide such things?

2

ON THE BUS TO VERMILLION, Lowell told me, he'd sat for several hours next to a mail-order bride only a year older than he was and just arrived from the Philippines. Her name was Luya. She'd shown him the photo of the man she was marrying. Lowell could think of nothing good to say about a man who wouldn't even meet her at the airport, so he'd said nothing.

Another man on the bus asked her if she was in the business; neither she nor Lowell knew what that meant. And another man leaned in from the seat behind, eyes darting, pupils enormous, to tell them that the lead levels in breast milk were part of a deliberate plot. Women didn't want to be tied down to house and family anymore. If their milk was toxic, that'd be just the excuse they'd been waiting for. "They all want to wear the pants," the man said.

"I'm seeing so much of America today," Luya kept telling Lowell in nervously accented English. It became a personal catchphrase for him—whenever things were not to his liking, he'd say that— I'm seeing so much of America today.

I went back to my apartment. It was a chilly walk. Ghosts of Fern and Lowell swirled around me, all ages, all moods, appearing and disappearing in the fog. I moved slowly to give myself time to recover from Lowell's visit and from Lowell's departure. And also, truth be told, to delay seeing Harlow.

I didn't want to be worrying over Harlow. She shouldn't have been the very last thing Lowell said to me. She should have been the very last thing on my mind. But once I got home, there she would be, lying in my bed and needing to be dealt with.

I didn't like to think of Lowell as one of those guys who has sex with a girl and then immediately ditches her. Leaving without a word was just Lowell's thing and nothing personal. Harlow could join the club.

In Lowell's defense, he'd struck me as crazy. Real, run-out-of-medication crazy. I know I haven't conveyed that. I've made Lowell sound more lucid than I found him. I did so out of love. But I'm trying to be nothing but honest here. And no one is helped by this evasion, least of all Lowell.

So, out of love, let me try again. The whole time we were with Harlow, he'd seemed perfectly ordinary, a completely believable pharmaceutical rep, which is what he'd told Harlow and maybe really was, who knows? The things that disturbed me all happened later, when we were alone at Bakers Square.

It wasn't the flashes of anger—he'd been angry for as long as I could remember, a foot-stamping, middle-finger-thrusting, boy-shaped storm. I was used to that. His fury was my nostalgia.

No, this was something that looked less mad and more madness. It was subtle and deniable; I could pretend not to see it, which is what I wanted very much to do. But even after ten years empty of data, I knew Lowell. I knew his body language as well as I once knew Fern's. There was something wrong in the way his eyes moved. Something wrong in the way he held his shoulders, worked his mouth. Maybe *crazy* isn't quite the right word, after all—too internal. Maybe *traumatized* is better. Or *unstable*. Lowell appeared unstable in the most literal sense, like someone who's been pushed off his balance.

So I would just explain that to Harlow. He's not a cad, I'd tell her. He's just unstable. She, of all people, should understand.

Then I put Harlow out of my mind so that Fern would have more room there. Enough with the tears and regrets. Lowell had said that Fern was my job now. Hadn't she always been so? Past time to do my job.

Periodic reports were all well and good; our Fern could not be left in a cage in a lab. But Lowell had been trying for ten years to free her. He'd come up against any number of problems—how to take her quietly (and now Hazel) and whom to ask for help and how to keep their whereabouts secret so they wouldn't be instantly identified and returned. The few chimp refuges operating in the U.S. were maxed out and none of them would take a stolen pair of animals if they knew they were doing so.

Where to take her would have been an enormous problem even if she hadn't needed to be hidden. The financial difficulties were huge; the danger in introducing two new chimps, one of them a child, into an established troop severe. How could I possibly succeed where Lowell, so much smarter, better connected, and more ruthless, had failed? And would Fern really wish to be uprooted again, taken again from the people and chimps that she'd come to know? Lowell had told me she had good friends at the lab now.

I suspected that all these problems could be solved with cash. Lots of cash. Making-a-movie or starting-a-foundation kinds of cash. You'll-never-see-a-tenth-of-that kinds of cash.

So many problems, however infinitely varied they first appear, turn out to be matters of money. I can't tell you how much this offends me. The value of money is a scam perpetrated by those who have it over those who don't; it's the Emperor's New Clothes gone global. If chimps used money and we didn't, we wouldn't admire it. We'd find it irrational and primitive. Delusional. And why gold? Chimps barter with meat. The value of meat is self-evident.

By now I'd reached my own street. There were three cars parked in front of the apartment house and one had its interior lights on. I could see the driver, a hulking shadow in the lighted cab. My spider sense was tingling. FBI. How close they'd come to catching Lowell. How terrible I would feel if I'd talked him into staying.

Then I looked more closely at the car. An ancient Volvo, white once upon a time. The scrapings of a bumper sticker that someone had committed to and then thought better of, with only the letter V remaining, or else half a W. I knocked on the passenger window and slid inside when the door unlocked. It was warmer in there and smelled gross but with a minty overlay, like morning breath on Altoids. The light was on because the driver was reading—a large book, *Intro to Biology*. He was stalking his girlfriend and studying for his finals at the same time. He was multitasking. "Good morning, Reg," I said.

"Why are you up so early?"

"I've been off with my brother. Eating pie." What could be more innocent, more rosily American than that? "What're you doing here?"

"Losing my self-respect."

I patted his arm. "You did well to keep that for as long as you did," I told him.

OBVIOUSLY, THIS WAS awkward. I'd told Reg on the phone the night before that Harlow wasn't here. His presence on the street, his little stakeout, openly called me a liar. It would have been nice to have the time to feel the insult, marvel at the crazy of his jealousy, but it was all spoiled by the fact that Harlow might, at any moment, walk out the front door.

"Go home," I said. "She's probably already back there now, wondering where the hell you are."

He looked at me hard, then looked away. "I think we're breaking up. I think I'm breaking up with her."

I made some noncommittal sound. A brief sort of hum. He'd been breaking up with her the first time I'd laid eyes on him and most times since. "Hathos," I offered finally and then thoughtfully provided the definition. "The pleasure you get from hating something."

"That's it exactly. I want a normal girlfriend. Someone restful. You know anyone like that?"

"I'd volunteer if you were rich," I told him. "Like hugely rich. I could be restful for massive sums of money."

"Flattered. But no."

"Then stop wasting my time and go home." I got out of the car and went into the apartment. I didn't watch to see what he'd do next, because I thought it would look suspicious if I did. I took the stairs.

There was no sign of Ezra, it being too early in the morning to shoulder the burdens of apartment management. Todd was still out. My bedroom door still closed. Madame Defarge was on the couch with her legs folded friskily over her head. I carried her with me into Todd's bedroom and fell asleep holding her. I had a dream where Reg and I argued as to which was more humane, the guillotine or the electric chair. I don't remember who took what side. I just remember that Reg's position, whichever it was, was not tenable.

3

I OMITTED MORE from my breakfast with Lowell than his instability. I also omitted a great many of the things he'd said. These things were too ghastly to repeat, and really you already know them. I omitted them because they were not things I wanted to hear and you don't want to hear them, either.

But Lowell would say that we all have to.

He'd told me about an experiment here in Davis that lasted thirty years. Generations of beagles were exposed to strontium-90 and radium-226, their voice boxes removed so that no one would hear them suffering. He said that the researchers involved in this jocularly referred to themselves as the Beagle Club.

He talked about car companies that, as part of their crash studies, subjected fully conscious and terrified baboons to repeated, horrific, excruciating blows to the head. About drug companies that vivisected dogs, lab techs that shouted at them to cut the shit if they whined or struggled. About cosmetic companies that smeared chemicals into the eyes of screaming rabbits and euthanized them afterward if the damage was permanent or else did it to them again if they recovered. About slaughterhouses where the cows were so terrified it discolored the meat. About the stuffed battery cages of the chicken industry, where, just as my uncle Bob had been saying for years, they were breeding birds that couldn't stand up, much less walk. About how chimps in the entertainment industry were always babies, because by adolescence they'd be too strong to control. These babies, who should have still been riding on their mother's backs, were shut into isolated cages and beaten with baseball bats so that later, on the sets of movies, merely displaying the bat would assure their compliance. Then the credits could claim that no animals had been harmed in the filming of this movie, because the harm had all happened before the shooting began.

"The world runs," Lowell said, "on the fuel of this endless, fathomless misery. People know it, but they don't mind what they don't see. Make them look and they mind, but you're the one they hate, because you're the one that made them look."

They, my brother said, whenever he talked about humans. Never *us*. Never *we*.

A few days later, I recounted all these same things in my bluebook final exam for Religion and Violence. It was a sort of exorcism to write them down, an attempt to get them out of my head and into someone else's. This ended in Dr. Sosa's office, under a poster-sized full-color print of the Hubble photograph "Pillars of Creation." A quote hung on the opposite wall: "Everyone thinks of changing the world, but no one thinks of changing himself." Dr. Sosa's office was clearly meant to inspire.

I also remember it as festive. Strings of Christmas bubble-lights festooned the bookshelves, and he had candy canes for us to suck on while we talked. "I don't want to flunk you," Dr. Sosa said, and we were on the same page there; I didn't want that, either.

He sat sprawled back in his desk chair, his feet crossed over a makeshift pile of magazines. One hand, resting on the roll of his belly, rose and fell with his breath. The other held the candy cane with which he occasionally gestured. "Your earlier work was good, and your final . . . your final had a lot of passion in it. You raised a bunch of really important issues." Dr. Sosa sat up suddenly, put his feet on the floor. "But you must see that you didn't answer the actual test questions? Not even close?" He leaned forward to force me into friendly eye contact. He knew what he was doing.

So did I. Did I not train at my father's knee? I mirrored his posture, held his gaze. "I was writing about violence," I said. "Compassion. The Other. It all seemed pertinent to me. Thomas More says that humans learn to be cruel to humans by first being cruel to animals." I'd made this point in my blue-book essay, so Dr. Sosa had already withstood Thomas More. But as I'd leaned forward, Christmas lights had sprung from his temples like incandescent, bubbling horns. My side of the argument suffered as a result.

In point of fact, Thomas More doesn't advocate doing away with cruelty to animals so much as hiring someone to manage your cruelty for you. His main concern is that the Utopians keep their own hands clean, which has turned out to be pretty much the way we've done it, though I don't think it's been as beneficial to our delicate sensibilities as he'd hoped. I don't think it's made us better people. Neither does Lowell. Neither does Fern.

Not that I've asked her. Not that I know for sure what she thinks about anything anymore.

Dr. Sosa read the first test question aloud. "'Secularism arose primarily as a way to limit violence. Discuss.'"

"Tangentially pertinent. Do animals have souls? Classic religious conundrum. Massive implications."

Dr. Sosa refused to be diverted. Second question: "'All violence that purports to have a religious basis is a distortion of true religion.

Discuss with specific reference to either Judaism, Christianity, or Islam.'"

"What if I said science could be a sort of religion for some people?"

"I'd disagree." Dr. Sosa sat back happily. "When science becomes a religion, it stops being science." The bubble-lights gave his dark eyes a holiday twinkle; like all good professors, that man did love an argument.

He offered me an incomplete, because I'd been so attentive in class all quarter, because I'd come to his office and put up a fight. I accepted.

My grades came just after Christmas. "Do you have any idea what we're paying for you to go to that college?" my father asked. "How hard we work for that money? And you just piss it away."

I was learning a ton, I told him loftily. History and economics and astronomy and philosophy. I was reading great books and thinking new thoughts. Surely that was the point of a college education. I said that the problem with people (as if there were only one) is how they think everything can be measured in dollars and cents.

Between my grades and my attitude, my name went right onto Santa's naughty list.

"I'm speechless," my mother told me, which wasn't remotely true.

4

BUT I'M GETTING ahead of myself.

Back in Davis, Mr. Benson moved out of 309, the apartment directly below us. I knew Mr. Benson slightly, a man of indeterminate age, which usually means mid-forties, who'd once described himself to me as the only fat man in the city of Davis. He clerked at the Avid Reader bookstore and he often sang "Dancing Queen" in the shower, loud enough that we could hear it upstairs. I liked him.

For the last month he'd been up in Grass Valley, taking care of his mother. She'd died one day after Thanksgiving and clearly there'd been an inheritance, because Mr. Benson quit his job, paid off his lease, and hired a moving company to pack up his stuff. He himself never came back. I heard all this from Ezra, who also said, sadly, that Mr. Benson had turned out to be more of a slob than he'd ever let on.

While 309 was being cleaned, painted, repaired, and recarpeted for some new occupant, Ezra let Harlow move in. I'm guessing the apartment owner didn't know this. Ezra was sorry to have her on the third floor with the miscreants, but ecstatic to have her in the building. He was in and out of 309 all the time; there was so much work to be done there.

Harlow escaped the disruptions, the lack of furniture, and possibly Ezra's attentions by spending a good chunk of the day in our place. Todd glowered, but it was so temporary. Soon we'd all go home for Christmas and when we returned, someone would have moved in for real. Presumably, I told Todd, this someone would want the apartment without Harlow in it, but Todd wasn't so sure about that.

My guess was that she'd eventually go back to Reg. I hadn't seen Reg since that morning in his car, and Harlow had hardly mentioned him. I didn't even know who'd broken up with whom.

Harlow sat on our couch, drinking our beers and talking feverishly about Lowell. He'd warned her he wouldn't be back, but she hadn't believed him. Like everything else he'd said, she passed this under the microscope of obsessional limerence. I was his sister. Of course, he'd be back, if only to see me.

What had he meant when he'd said she made him nervous? When he'd said he felt like he'd known her forever? Weren't those two things contradictory? What did I make of them?

She wanted to know everything about him—what he'd been like as a little boy, how many girlfriends he'd had, how many of them serious. Who was his favorite band? Did he believe in God? What did he love?

I told her he loved *Star Wars*. Played poker for money. Kept rats in his room, most of them named after cheeses. She was enchanted.

I told her he'd had only one girlfriend all through high school, a wild-eyed Mormon named Kitch. That he'd played point guard on his high school basketball team but ditched the most important game. Shoplifted Twizzlers with his best friend, Marco. It was like dealing dope; nothing I said was enough. I grew impatient. I had papers to write.

But what had he said to me about her?

"He said he was glad we were friends," I told her. "He said you really seemed to care about me."

"I do!" Harlow's face was a glowing orb. "What else?"

There was nothing else, but that seemed too cruel to be the right answer. Equally cruel to let her go on hoping. "Travers is gone," I said, right into that glowing face. Maybe I was talking to myself as much as her. I'd spent half my life waiting for Lowell, and now we all just had to learn to live without that waiting. "Here's the thing. He's a wanted man. Like picture-in-the-post-office wanted. Wanted by the *FBI* as a domestic terrorist for the Animal Liberation Front. You can't even tell anyone he was here or I'll be arrested. Again. For real.

"Before this weekend, I hadn't seen him in ten years. I don't have the first fucking clue what his favorite band is. Travers isn't even his name. You really, really, really need to forget about him."

There I go again, not keeping my mouth shut.

Because what could be more *Casablanca*? Suddenly Harlow saw that what she'd always wanted was a man of principle. A man of action. A domestic terrorist.

Every girl's dream, if she can't have a vampire.

THE ANIMAL LIBERATION FRONT has no governing body, no headquarters, no membership roll. The structure is a loose one of autonomous cells. This is the headache for the FBI—one name leads at most to two or three others and then the line goes dead. Lowell had come to their attention by talking too much—a rookie mistake he'd never repeated (and ironic, considering all the times he'd said I couldn't keep my mouth shut).

Anyone can join the ALF. In fact, anyone involved in the liberation of animals, anyone who physically interferes with their exploitation and abuse, is automatically a member so long as the action takes place according to ALF guidelines. The ALF will not countenance physical harm to any animal, human or otherwise.

Destruction of property, on the other hand—destruction of property is encouraged. The infliction of economic damage on those profiting from misery is a stated goal. As is the need to publicize abuse—bring those horrors occurring in their secret chambers out into the open. This is why a number of states are considering laws that make the unauthorized photographing of what goes on in factory farms and slaughterhouses a felony. Making people look at what is really happening is about to become a serious crime.

Just as membership is automatically conferred with direct action, no membership is possible without it. You don't join the ALF by sympathizing. You don't join by writing about how sorry and sad the suffering of animals makes you. You have to *do* something.

In 2004, Jacques Derrida said that a change was under way. Torture damages the inflicter as well as the inflicted. It's no coincidence that one of the Abu Ghraib torturers came to the military directly from a job as a chicken processor. It might be slow, Derrida said, but eventually the spectacle of our abuse of animals will be intolerable to our sense of who we are.

The ALF is not so interested in slow.

How can they be? All that misery, all that misery is now.

HARLOW DETERIORATED. Her face was swollen, her eyes red, her mouth pinched, her skin pallid. She stopped coming to our apartment, hadn't touched the food in our refrigerator in two days, which probably meant she wasn't eating. Ezra, tool belt slung low about his waist, called a summit meeting on the fourth floor—just him and me—to say that he'd recently come upon her lying facedown on the newly installed carpet of 309. She was maybe crying, he said. Ezra was one of those men so deeply unnerved by a woman's tears he didn't even need to see them.

He blamed Reg. For all his blithe confidence that he had his fingers on the pulse of the building and its occupants, Ezra had missed a beat. "You need to talk to her," he told me. "Make her see that every ending is a new beginning. She needs to hear that from a friend." He thought Reg might be a closeted homosexual or possibly a survivor of child abuse. Was he Catholic? If not, there was no explaining such cruelty and Harlow was lucky to have escaped when she did.

Ezra said he'd told Harlow that, in Chinese, *close a door* and *open a door* were represented by exactly the same character. He himself had taken great comfort from that same observation whenever times got tough. I don't know where he got this, though most of his quotes came from *Pulp Fiction*. I'm reasonably confident it's not true.

I told him that, in Chinese, the character for woman was a man on his knees, and that it wasn't clear to me that the solution to Harlow's heartbreak would be found in the ancient wisdom of the East. I didn't go talk to her. I've often wondered what would have happened if I had.

But I was still angry with her. Harlow, I felt, had no right to such grief, no real claim on Lowell. She'd known him for what? Fifteen minutes? I'd loved him for twenty-two years and missed him most of that time. Harlow should be taking care of *me*, is how I saw it.

I wonder sometimes if I'm the only one spending my life making the same mistake over and over again or if that's simply human. Do we all tend toward a single besetting sin?

If so, jealousy is mine and it's tempting to read this sad consistency as a matter of character. But my father, were he still alive, would surely protest. Who did I think I was? Hamlet? Current psychological research suggests that character plays a surprisingly small role in human behavior. Instead we are highly responsive to trivial changes in circumstance. We're like horses in that, only less gifted.

I myself am not convinced. Over the years I've come to feel that the way people respond to us has less to do with what we've done and more to do with who they are. Of course, it suits me to think that. All those people in junior high who were so mean to me? What unhappy people they must have been!

So the studies don't back me up. There'll always be more studies. We'll change our minds and I'll have been right all along until we change our minds again, send me back to being wrong.

Till then let's give this one to my father and let me off the hook. Maybe my jealousy mattered less than the fact that I had finals. I felt honor-bound to complete at least some of my classes. Plus I had a term paper due and while I wouldn't say I'd left it to the last minute, only a paltry number of minutes remained. I was quite interested in my topic, which was surprising, because the professor had forced us to clear that with our TAs some weeks ago, back when there was no way to predict what I'd be interested in by the time I wrote it. My topic was how the theoretical accommodation of evil in Thomas More's *Utopia* expressed itself in the real world of his own life and politics. It was one of those subjects to which everything that slithers across your brain seems relevant. I find this to be true of most topics.

And then there were all those phone calls I had to keep making about my suitcase. The woman who worked in luggage at the Sacramento Airport had started calling me sweet pea, that's how intimate we'd become.

So I back-burnered Harlow, the last person in the world you should back-burner. And then, twenty-four hours before I was supposed to be on a plane to Indianapolis, while I was in the very midst of packing a duffel bag borrowed from Todd, humming "Joy to the World," thinking about what I should and shouldn't say to my parents about Lowell and whether the new house might be bugged, too, the way we'd always assumed the old one was, which drove my father crazy—like we were lab rats or something, under constant surveillance, your tax dollars at work, he'd say—and was probably the real reason they'd moved. As well as trying to figure out how to ask them for a new bike for Christmas, since I'd lost the last one in a drug-induced fugue. While all this was happening, a policeman came to the door.

It wasn't Officer Arnie this time. This officer didn't introduce himself. He had a triangular face, like a praying mantis, wide mouth, sharp chin, and a vibe of pure, implacable evil. He asked me to come with him nicely enough, but I sensed we weren't going to be friends. He didn't tell me his name, which was okay by me. I didn't want to know it.

5

I WASN'T HANDCUFFED this time. I wasn't put into a cell. I wasn't sent to the office to do the paperwork. Instead I was left by myself in an interrogation room, almost empty—two chairs, both in an uncomfortable orange plastic—one table, linoleum-topped. The door was locked to keep me in. The room was very cold and so was I.

No one came. There was a pitcher of water on the table, but no glass. Nothing to read, not even a pamphlet on traffic or gun safety or what a tragic mistake doing drugs would be. I sat and waited. I stood and walked. I have the habit, never broken, of looking up, of noting how far I could climb in any given location, of how high Fern or Mary might get. There were no windows in this room and the walls were bare. None of us could have managed much.

No one was coming for me with a cattle prod, at least I assumed not, but they were trying to teach me who I was, all the same. I was surprised to feel myself solidly unteachable on this matter. I'd never known who I was. Didn't mean someone else did.

There was a pill bug on the floor and eventually I watched it, since watching it gave me something to do. Fern used to eat pill bugs, which Mom tried to prevent but Dad said they weren't really bugs but more like terrestrial crustaceans, that they breathed through gills and had copper in their blood instead of iron, and no one who'd ever eaten shrimp should turn up her nose at a pill bug. I don't remember eating one myself, but I must have, because I know that they crunch in your mouth like Cheerios.

The pill bug walked to the wall and then along the wall until it came to a corner. This either flummoxed or discouraged it. The morning passed. I learned how meager my inner resources were.

The officer who'd picked me up finally appeared again. He had a tape recorder, which he set on the table between us, a great stack of papers, folders, and notebooks. On the top of the stack I could see an old newspaper clipping; I could read the headline. "Bloomington's Sister Act." Apparently, Fern and I had once been profiled in *The New York Times*. I'd never known that.

The officer sat, sifting through his papers. More long minutes. In the old, old days, I would have been filling that silence and I could tell he was waiting for me to do so. It was a game we were playing, and I decided to win; I would not be the one to speak first. How amazed my long-ago babysitter Melissa and my Cooke grandparents would be if only they could see it. I tried to imagine them all in the room with me, offering encouragement. "Keep quiet!" they told me. "Stop your infernal talking! Give me a minute to hear myself think."

Put this one in my column. The officer gave up and turned on the tape recorder. He said the date and the time aloud. He told me to state my name. I did. He asked me if I knew why I was here. I didn't.

"Your brother is Lowell Cooke," he said. This didn't sound like a question, but apparently it was. "Confirm," he told me tonelessly.

"Yes."

"When did you last see him?"

I leaned forward to establish the eye contact Dr. Sosa had recently used to such good effect on me. "I need to use the bathroom," I said. "And I want a lawyer." Maybe I was just a college student, but I'd seen a television show or two. I wasn't afraid yet, at least not for myself. I figured they'd caught Lowell and that was terrible, terrible, but I couldn't let its terribleness get in the way of the one thing I had to do now, which was to make sure I said nothing that could be used against him.

"Why would you do that?" The officer got angrily to his feet. "You're not under arrest. This is just a friendly chat."

He switched the recorder off. A woman with thin, peevish lips and shellacked, Republican hair came and took me to the bathroom. She waited outside the stall, listening to me pee and flush. When she returned me, the room was empty again. None of the papers nor anything else had been left on the table. Even the pitcher was gone.

The minutes ticked away. I went back to my pill bug. It wasn't moving and I began to worry that it was more dead than discouraged. I began to smell insecticides. My back was against the wall. I slid down it until I was seated, touched the bug with one finger, relieved to see it curl. An image came to me of a black cat with a white face and belly, curled up with her tail over her nose.

I heard Lowell saying I couldn't keep my mouth shut. I heard him saying I'd made Mom and Dad choose.

This cat looked a lot like the cat my father had killed with his car, only this cat was only sleeping. Wrong cat, I heard a voice say, deep in my head, each consonant sharply bitten off. Wrong cat.

I don't know that I've ever heard the voice in my head so audibly. She didn't sound like me. Who was that then, steering the clown car between my ears? What did she do when she wasn't talking to me? What mischiefs, what detours? I'm listening, I told her, but not out loud, in case I was being watched. She didn't answer.

Very little outside noise reached through the walls of the interrogation room. The lights were the same unpleasant, sputtering fluorescents I'd noticed on my first visit. I used the time to plan out what I would say to the next person who came through the door. I would ask for my coat and for something to eat. I hadn't had breakfast that morning. I would ask to phone my parents. Poor Mom and Dad. All three of their children incarcerated at once; that really was bad luck.

I would ask again for a lawyer; maybe that's what we were all waiting for now, the arrival of my lawyer even though no one had suggested I was getting one. I saw the pill bug beginning to cautiously uncurl.

The woman who'd taken me to the bathroom came back in. She had a paper plate with a tuna fish sandwich and some potato chips on it. The sandwich was flattened, as if someone had pressed it between the leaves of a book as a keepsake. The potato chips were green at the edges, but that may just have been the lights.

She asked if I needed the bathroom again and I didn't, but it seemed best to go while I had the chance. It was something to do. I came back and ate some of the sandwich. My hands smelled like tuna fish, a thing I did not like to smell on my hands. They smelled like cat food.

I asked the voice in my head a different question—was there a right cat? An image came to me of the moon-eyed stray we'd often seen around the farmhouse when I was little. My mother left food out for her in the winter and had tried several times to trap and spay her, but the cat was too cunning and my mother had too much to do.

Ever since she'd read us *Millions of Cats* with its seductive illustrations, I'd wanted a cat in the worst way. We never got one, because of all the rats that came in and out of the house. "Cats are killers," my father said. "One of the few animals that kill just for the fun of it. They play with their food."

I was becoming agitated. A cat's fur springs up when it's frightened, to make it seem larger than it is. So does a chimp's hair, and for the same reason. The human version of piloerection is goose bumps, which I now had.

I saw the drawing in *Millions of Cats* of the final kitten, the one the old couple keeps. I saw Fern, sitting with my mother in the big chair, putting her hand on the page, spreading and curling her fingers as if she could pick the picture up. "Fern wants a kitten," I told my mother.

The moon-eyed cat had kittens, three of them. I found them one afternoon, stretched out on a sunny, mossy shelf by the creek, nursing. They pressed their little paws into her belly, massaging the milk into their mouths. Two of them were black and just the same. The mother raised her head to look at us, but didn't move. She seldom let me get this close to her. Motherhood had calmed her down.

The kittens weren't newborns. They were old enough to be running about, kittens in their full bloom of kitten cuteness. The longing to have one overwhelmed me. I knew I should leave them alone, but I pulled the NotSame one, the little gray, from the teat, turned him over to see his sex. He protested loudly. I could look down his pink throat, past his teeth and tongue. I could smell the milk on him. Everything about him was tiny and perfect. His mother wanted him back, but I wanted him, too. I thought that if I'd just found him with no mother, if he'd been an orphan alone in the world, we would have to keep him.

Back in the interrogation room, my shivering was severe. "It's really cold in here," I said aloud, just in case someone was watching. I didn't want them thinking their tactics were getting to me. I didn't want to give them the satisfaction. "Could I please have my jacket?"

In fact, I wasn't shaking because I'd been left for hours in a cold and empty room. Nor because the officer who'd brought me here gave off the same vibe you might have gotten from Keyser Söze; nor because he knew about Fern and me; nor because he'd arrested Lowell. I wasn't shaking because of anything happening now or anything that might happen next. I was completely buried in the unremembered, much disputed, fantasyland of the past.

Sigmund Freud has suggested that we have no early childhood memories at all. What we have instead are false memories aroused later and more pertinent to this later perspective than to the original events. Sometimes in matters of great emotion, one representation, retaining all the original intensity, comes to replace another, which is then discarded and forgotten. The new representation is called a screen memory. A screen memory is a compromise between remembering something painful and defending yourself against that very remembering.

Our father always said that Sigmund Freud was a brilliant man but no scientist, and that incalculable damage had been done by confusing the two. So when I say here that I think the memory I had of the thing that never happened was a screen memory, I do so with considerable sadness. It seems unnecessarily cruel to our father, adding the insult of Freudian analysis to the injury of believing he killed cats with his car for no reason.

You will remember how, in the days of Fern's disappearance, back when I was five, I was sent off to stay with my Indianapolis grandparents. I've told you what happened there. I've told you what happened after.

Here now, I believe, is what happened before. It comes with one cautionary note—that this memory is only as vivid to me as the one it replaces.

6

FERN AND I were down by the creek. She was standing on a tree branch above me, bouncing it up and down. She was wearing a pleated tartan skirt, the kind that needs a large pin to hold it together in the front. Fern's had no pin, so the skirt flapped like wings around her legs. She was wearing nothing else. Her potty training had improved and she'd been out of diapers for months.

On the down bounce, I could sometimes, by jumping, reach her feet. That was the game we were playing—she would dip the branch and I would jump. If I touched her feet, I won. If I didn't, the win was hers. We weren't keeping score, but we were both pretty happy, so we must have been about even.

But then she tired of the game and climbed out of my reach. She wouldn't come down, only laughed and dropped leaves and twigs on me, so I told her I didn't care. I went off purposefully to the creek, as if I had important business there, though it was too late in the year for tadpoles, too early in the day for fireflies. On the ledge, I found the cat and her kittens.

I took the gray one and I didn't give him back even though his mother was crying for him. I took him to Fern. It was a way of boasting. I knew how much Fern would want that kitten, but I was the one who had him.

She swung down as fast as she could. She signed for me to give him to her, and I told her he was mine but I would let her hold him. The moon-eyed mother had always been skittish around me, but she'd never gone anywhere near Fern. She would never, even in the hormonal soup of motherhood, have allowed Fern to take her kitten. The only way Fern would ever have gotten her hands on that little gray was if I gave him to her.

The kitten continued to mewl. The mother arrived, and I could hear at a little distance the two blacks down by the creek, bawling on the ledge where she'd dropped them. Her hair was up and so was Fern's. What happened next happened fast. The mother cat was hissing and spitting. The gray kitten in Fern's hand was crying loudly. The mother struck at Fern with her claws. And Fern swung the tiny perfect creature against a tree trunk. He dangled silently from her hand, his mouth loose. She opened him with her fingers like a purse.

I watched her do so in my memory, and I heard Lowell saying again how the world runs on the fuel of an endless, fathomless animal misery. The little blacks were still crying in the distance.

I took off, hysterical, for the house to get our mother, make her come and fix this, fix the kitten, but I ran smack into Lowell, literally right into him, which knocked me to the ground and skinned up my knees. I tried to tell him what had happened, but I was incoherent with it and he put his hands on my shoulders to calm me. He said to take him to Fern.

She was not where I'd left her, but squatting on the bank by the creek. Her hands were wet. The cats, living and dead, were nowhere to be seen.

Fern leapt up, grabbed Lowell by the ankles, somersaulted clownishly through his legs, her freckled butt exposed and then decorously covered as her skirt fell back into place. There were burrs in the hair on her arms. I pointed those out to Lowell. "She's hidden the kitten in the brambles," I said, "or she's thrown him into the creek. We have to find him. We have to take him to the doctor."

"Where is the kitten?" Lowell asked Fern both aloud and with his hands and she ignored that, sitting on his toes, arms wrapped around his leg. She liked to shoe-ride that way. I could do the same with our father, but was too big for Lowell's feet.

Fern rode a few steps and then bounced off with her usual feckless joy. She grabbed a branch, swinging away and back again, dropping to the ground. "Chase me," she signed. "Chase me." It was a good show but not a great one. She knew that she'd done something wrong and was only pretending otherwise. How could Lowell not see that?

He sat on the ground and Fern came, rested her chin on his shoulder, blew in his ear. "Maybe she hurt some cat by accident," Lowell offered. "She doesn't know how strong she is."

This was intended as a sop to me; he didn't believe it. What Lowell believed, what Lowell has always, to this very day, believed, was that I'd made up the whole thing just to get Fern in trouble. There was no body, no blood. Everything was fine here.

I searched through the ragweed, purslane, dandelion, and horse nettle. I searched through the rocks in the creek and Lowell didn't even help me look. Fern watched from behind Lowell's shoulder, her huge, amber eyes glittering and, or so I thought, gloating.

I thought Fern looked guilty. Lowell thought I did. He was right about that. I was the one who'd taken the kitten from his mother. I was the one who'd given him to Fern. It was my fault what had happened. Only it wasn't all my fault.

I can't blame Lowell. At five years old, I'd already established a reliable reputation for making things up. My aim was to delight and entertain. I didn't outright lie so much as add drama, when needed, to an otherwise drab story. The distinction was frequently lost. The Little Girl Who Cried Wolf, our father used to call me.

The more I searched, the angrier Lowell got. "Don't you tell anyone else," he said. "Do you hear me, Rosie? I mean it. You'll get Fern in trouble and I'll hate you. I'll hate you forever. I'll tell everyone you're a big fat liar. Promise you won't say anything."

I truly meant to keep that promise. The specter of Lowell hating me forever was a powerful one.

But keeping quiet was beyond my capabilities. It was one of the many things Fern could do that I could not.

A few days later, I wanted to go into the house and Fern wouldn't let me. It was another game to her, an easy game. Though much littler than I, she was also faster and stronger. The one time I got by, she grabbed my hand as I went past, yanked me back so hard I felt a pop in my shoulder. She was laughing.

I burst into tears, calling for our mother. It was the effortlessness of it all, Fern's easy win, that had me crying in rage and frustration. I told my mother Fern had hurt me, which had happened often enough that, since it wasn't a serious injury, it wasn't a serious allegation. Children roughhoused until someone got hurt; it was the way families worked. Mothers, having warned everyone that this was what would happen, were generally more irritated than concerned.

But then I added that I was scared of Fern.

"Why in the world would you be scared of little Fern?" Mom asked.

And that's when I told.

And that's when I got sent to my grandparents.

And that's when Fern got sent away.

7

BACK IN THE interrogation room, this memory moved like a weather system through my body. I didn't remember it all that afternoon, not the way I've told it here. But I remembered enough and then, strangely, by the time it passed, I'd stopped shaking and crying. I didn't feel hungry or cold or in need of a lawyer or a bathroom or a sandwich. Instead I had an odd sense of clarity. I wasn't in the past anymore; I was acutely in the moment. I was composed and focused. Lowell needed me. Everything else would have to wait.

I felt like talking.

I picked up the pill bug, which made it curl tightly again, remarkably spherical, a piece of art like something Andy Goldsworthy would make. I put it on the interrogation table next to the plate with my leftover tuna fish, because I figured when I was finally released, Lowell wouldn't want the bug left behind. Double bonus for insects. This room was nobody's home.

My plan was to stick with my go-to story—my grandparents and their soap operas, the trampoline and the man in the little blue house and the woman trussed up like a turkey—only tell it with bigger words. Mimesis, diegesis, hypodiegesis—I would not only tell the tale but also comment on it. I would dissect it. And I'd do all this in such a way as to make it seem at every moment that I was just about to answer the questions asked, just about to get to the real, to the relevant. My plan was a malicious compliance.

I'd seen that done often enough. Teenage Lowell had been a Jedi master.

But the interrogating officer never reappeared. Snap! Like the devil, he was gone.

Instead a broad-hipped, listless woman came to tell me I was free to go, and that's not an errand you assign to the implacably evil. I followed her down the hall and out into the night. I saw the lights of a plane overhead, aimed at the Sacramento Airport. I knelt down and put the little ball of bug in the grass. I'd been inside that interrogation room for about eight hours.

Kimmy, Todd, and Todd's mother were all waiting for me. They were the ones who told me Lowell had not been caught.

Someone else had.

ON THE PREVIOUS EVENING, while I'd celebrated the end of the quarter with an early bedtime, Ezra Metzger had tried to break into the primate center at UC Davis. He'd been arrested on site, various implements needed for picking locks, cutting wires, rerouting electrical signals all hanging on his belt if not in his actual hands. He'd managed to open eight cage doors before he was stopped. In the newspaper later, anonymous UC officials described the monkeys as traumatized by the intrusion. They were screaming bloody murder, one unnamed source had said, and had to be sedated. The saddest part of the news story was this: most of the monkeys had refused to leave their cages.

A female accomplice was still at large. She had taken his car or Ezra might have escaped, too.

No, surely not. That last was unkind.

In 1996, UC Davis had just created the Center for Comparative Medicine as a bridge between the medical and the veterinary schools, a way of bringing together all the research on infectious diseases that used animal models. The primate center was a critical component in this. Disease control had been studied there since its founding—specifically, the plague, SIV, kuru, and various zoonoses, like the Marburg virus, that move from monkey to human. The two separate accidents that had exposed Soviet lab workers to the Marburg virus were still relatively recent. Richard Preston's nonfiction bestseller *The Hot Zone* was very much on our minds.

None of this made it into the newspaper articles, not even a hint. It came up quietly in pretrial, that this was not just a prank, that Ezra could have been letting more things loose than he knew.

Seven years later, in 2003, the university's bid for a high-security bio-defense lab in which monkeys would have been infected with anthrax, smallpox, and Ebola, was lost when a rhesus macaque disappeared as her cage was being hosed down. She was never recovered. She'd made a clean escape.

The Davis primate center is today credited with significant advances in our understanding and treatment of SIV, Alzheimer's, autism, and Parkinson's. Nobody's arguing these issues are easy.

FOUR THINGS KEPT me out of jail.

Number One was that Todd and Kimmy could vouch for my

whereabouts on the previous night. I'd gone to bed early, they told the police, but they'd celebrated the end of the quarter by getting all Christmassy with a classics movie night. They'd rented *Psycho*, *Night of the Living Dead*, *The Wicker Man*, *Carrie*, and *Miracle on 34th Street*. They'd watched them in that order, mostly on the living room couch, with only occasional forays into the kitchen to make popcorn. There was no way I could have left the apartment without them knowing. Not unless I was Spider-Man, Kimmy told me she'd told the police.

"I said Tarzan," said Todd. "But Spider-Man is good."

Not unless I was Fern, is what I thought but did not say, even though I figured everyone must know about Fern by now. This was an inference based on a false belief. I'd underestimated the ability of the police to keep their mouths shut.

In fact, I don't think anyone was all that impressed by *Number One*. Once they'd connected me to Lowell, the police were too sure they had their girl. We were probably all part of the same terrorist cell was how the police saw it, and of course we'd cover for each other. They'd had their eyes on our apartment building for quite some time. A nasty group of people lived on the third floor there.

Number Two was Todd's mother. Some slacker had let Todd place a call prior to interviewing him. Todd's mother was a famous civil rights lawyer in San Francisco; I probably should have mentioned that earlier. Picture William Kunstler, only not so lovable. Picture William Kunstler as a tiny female Nisei. She'd arrived by helicopter, generously expanded her threats to include me as well as Todd and Kimmy. When I finally stepped outside, she was there in a fancy rented car waiting to take us all to dinner.

Number Three was Harlow. Not Harlow herself, no one knew where she was, but Todd and Kimmy had said they had no doubt the woman the police were looking for was Harlow Fielding. The police went and talked to Reg and Reg told them he knew nothing, had seen nothing, had heard nothing, but it sounded like Harlow, pussy-whipping some guy until he actually did time for her.

It didn't sound like something I would do, he'd added, which was certainly nice of him and I imagine he believed it. He didn't know Fern had been doing time for me for years.

Ezra also told the police it was Harlow. I wondered what movie he was starring in now. *Cool Hand Luke? The Shawshank Redemption? Ernest Goes to Jail?* I wondered how easily and quickly he'd given Harlow up, but it never occurred to me that he'd done so to save me until Todd suggested that later. Not that Ezra liked me better than Harlow, because he definitely didn't. But he was an honorable guy. He wouldn't have let me be arrested for something he knew I didn't do, not if he could stop it.

Number Four is that the police never read my Religion and Violence blue-book final.

TODD'S MOTHER TOOK us out to dinner, not in Davis, nothing fancy enough for her there, but into Old Town Sacramento, with its cobbled streets and wood-planked sidewalks. We ate that night at The Firehouse, where Todd's mother urged me to get the lobster to celebrate my narrow escape, but I would have had to pick a live one from the tank so I didn't. It would have looked like a very large pill bug on my plate.

She told me I could still go home for Christmas the next day even though I'd promised the police I wouldn't leave town, so I did.

I thanked her many times. "No need," she told me. "Any friend of Todd's."

"You caught that that was bullshit, right?" Todd asked me later, and for just an instant I thought the bullshit part was that we were friends. But no, he just meant that his mother liked to throw her tiny weight around and didn't really care in whose service. I could see how that might not always be a good quality in a mother, but this didn't seem to be one of those times. I thought there were moments to complain about your parents and moments to be grateful, and it was a shame to mix those moments up. I made a mental note to remember this in my own life, but it got lost the way mental notes do.

Weeks later, I asked Todd if we were friends. "Rosie! We've been friends for years," he said. He sounded hurt.

The big black car took us back to the apartment and then slid away under the stars with Todd's mother inside. The third floor was already whooping it up. The music was at a shattering volume; eventually the police would have to be called. Class notes had been shredded and thrown onto the yard like confetti, followed by a single desk chair, which lay across the walkway, its wheels still spinning. We took the front door in a hail of condoms filled with water. This was what it was like to live in a poorly managed apartment building. We would have to get used to that.

We sat around our own table, an island of sad reflection in an ocean of merry din. We drank Todd's Sudwerk beers, and shook our heads over Ezra, who'd once wanted to join the CIA but hadn't managed, in this his first (as far as we knew) commando operation, to free a single monkey. No one mentioned Fern, so I eventually figured out that they still didn't know. But they did know about Lowell and they were pretty stoked to think they'd entertained such a dangerous guy in our very own apartment. They were impressed with me, too, having this whole hidden life. I had depths within depths, is what they thought, and they would never have guessed.

Todd apologized for having thought Lowell was just a puppet in Harlow's hands, when clearly the reverse had been true. "Your brother must have recruited her," he said. "She's part of his cell now—" which hadn't occurred to me and I instantly disliked the suggestion. Anyway, I felt it was unlikely. Harlow's heartbreak had been too convincing. I'd seen Harlow put on a show. I'd seen her not. I knew the difference.

And then we all watched *Miracle on 34th Street* again, Todd and Kimmy having confessed that actually they'd slept through much of it and several of the other movies, too, and I could have come and gone many times without them knowing.

Miracle on 34th Street is a very pro-lawyer movie. Not so kind to psychologists.

EVEN IF LOWELL hadn't put Harlow up to it, he was still the reason she'd done it. We're a dangerous family to know all right, only not in the way Todd thinks. Clearly, Harlow was trying to find Lowell by the only route she had, his breadcrumb trail. I wondered if she'd succeed. I wouldn't have bet against her.

She wasn't really his kind of girl; she only liked to pretend that she was. If she wanted Lowell, she'd have to get real now. No more drama major, everyone-look-at-me bullshit. But I thought she could probably do that. I thought they might even be happy together.

Late that night, when I opened the door to my bedroom, I smelled the ghost of Harlow's vanilla cologne. I went straight to the powder-blue suitcase. Sure enough, Madame Defarge was gone.

PART SIX

❋

. . . I soon realized the two possibilities open to me: the zoological garden or the music hall. I did not hesitate. I said to myself: use all your energy to get into the Music Hall. That is the way out. The Zoological Garden is only a new barred cage. If you go there, you're lost.

—FRANZ KAFKA, "A Report for an Academy"

I

IN THE YEARS after Fern, we'd made a habit of traveling on Christmas. We went twice to Yosemite, once to Puerto Vallarta. Once to Vancouver. Once all the way to London, where I ate my first kippers, and once to Rome, where my parents bought a small cameo of a young girl for me from a vendor outside the Colosseum because he'd said the girl looked like me, that we were both *bellissima*. And Dr. Remak, who taught German literature at IU but had hidden talents, set it into a ring for me when we got home and I felt *bellissima* whenever I wore it.

We'd never been religious, so Christmas had never meant that to us. After Lowell, we mostly gave it up altogether.

When I finally arrived in Bloomington at the bitter end of 1996, the only sign of the season was a small potted rosemary bush pruned into the shape of a Christmas tree. It sat on a table by the front door, perfuming the entryway. No wreath outside. No ornaments on the rosemary. I had decided not to tell my parents that I'd seen Lowell until we'd gotten through Christmas. The lack of visible merriment told me the day itself was still too fragile, my mother too unstable.

There was no snow that year. On the afternoon of the twenty-fifth, we drove to Indianapolis and had our holiday supper with my

Cooke grandparents. It was, as always, a wet meal. The mashed potatoes were soggy, the green beans limp. The plates were heaped with things indecipherable under a lake of brown gravy. My father drank like a fish.

As I recall, he was hoisting his glass that year in honor of the Colts' kickers being chosen for the Associated Press's All-Pro team. Election to the All-Pros was a distinction that generally eluded Indianapolis. He tried to involve his father in the celebration, but Grandpa Joe had fallen asleep at the table, mid-sentence, like a man hit by a spell. In retrospect, this was the descending doom of Alzheimer's, but we didn't know that then and were affectionately amused.

My period was coming on and I had the dull weight of that in my abdomen. It gave me an excuse to go lie down on the bed in the room where I'd slept the summer we lost Fern. Of course, I didn't say I was bleeding, but something so oblique and midwestern that Grandpa Joe didn't understand it at all and Grandma Fredericka had to whisper it to him.

The harlequin print was still on the wall, just as it'd always been, but the bed had a new frame, wrought iron, twisted into posts and headboards and leaved like ivy. Grandma Fredericka was morphing from her faux-Asian period into full-blown Pottery Barn.

This was the room in which I'd once spent all those weeks thinking that I was the sister who spoke in toads and snakes, the one who'd been driven out to die alone and miserable. This was the room in which I'd figured that Lowell had told everyone I was a big fat liar and since Lowell never lied about anything, everyone had believed him. This was the room in which I'd been the mal de vivre to Fern's joie.

That story about Fern and the kitten was such a terrible one. If I'd made it up, that was truly unforgivable.

Had I?

I turned off the bedside lamp and lay down facing the window. Across the street, the neighbors' Christmas lights dripped from the eaves like icicles, casting a pale glow into the room. I thought of Abbie, the girl in my freshman dorm, who'd told us one night how her sister had claimed their father molested her and then changed her mind, said she'd only dreamed it. "And then this one crazy sister goes and ruins it all," Abbie had said. "I hate her."

And Lowell: "If you tell anyone, I'll hate you forever."

It had seemed fair enough to me that evening in the freshman dorm. Fair enough to hate someone for telling such an ugly lie.

And back when I was five, fair enough for Lowell to hate me. I'd promised not to tell and I'd broken that promise. It's not as if I hadn't been warned.

Our winter coats were piled on the bedcovers. I pulled my mother's parka over my feet. She used to splash herself with an eau de toilette called Florida Water, when I was little. The perfume she used now was as unfamiliar to me as the smell of the home-model house where my parents now lived. But this room smelled exactly the same—stale cookies and no staler than when I was five.

We used to believe that memories are best retrieved in the same place where they were first laid down. Like everything else we think we know, that's not so clear anymore.

But this is still 1996. Step into my head as I pretend to be five again, as I try to feel exactly what I'd felt when, at the end of another day in exile, I'd lie down on this bed in this room.

What came to me first was my guilt over not keeping my

promise. Second, the despair of having lost Lowell's love forever. Third, the despair of having been sent away.

More guilt. I'd taken the kitten from his mother, who'd cried about it, and I'd handed him to Fern. And still more, because I'd left this part out when I'd told on Fern, pretended that she'd acted alone. Whatever Fern and I did, we generally did it together and we generally took the heat as a team, too. It was a point of honor.

But then I'd drilled down to outrage. Maybe I did share in the blame, but I hadn't killed the cat. That was all Fern. It was unfair not to believe me, unfair to punish me most. Children are just as finely tuned as chimps to unfairness, especially when we're on the receiving end.

So maybe I hadn't told the whole truth. But I wouldn't have felt that powerful sense of aggrievement if I'd lied.

On the bed with my mother's coat wrapped around my feet, hearing the murmur of dishes being done, sports being discussed, the traditional holiday gang-up of Grandma Fredericka and Mom over Dad's drinking, a rerun of a young, skinny Frank Sinatra caroling from the television, I made myself go over the whole ghastly memory again. I looked for cracks in the finish; I watched myself watching myself. And then something surprising happened. I realized that I did know who I was.

In the face of that screen memory, still vivid enough in my mind to subvert the whole concept of memory with the efficient, targeted flight of a math proof; in the face of all those studies suggesting that character is unimportant in determining action, and also the possibility that I am, from your perspective, just a mindless automaton operated by alien puppet-masters, still I knew I had not made up that kitten. I knew it because the person I was, the person I had always been, *that* person would not do *that* thing.

I fell asleep then, and in the old days my parents would have picked me quietly up, driven the whole way to Bloomington, and carried me into my room, all without waking me. In a Christmas miracle, the next morning, when I opened my eyes, I would have been home and so would Lowell and Fern.

I'D THOUGHT TO tell my parents about Lowell that very night. I was in the mood for it after all that painful soul-searching, and long car rides are as good as confessionals—or so I'm guessing, never having been to confession—for uncomfortable conversations. But my father was drunk. He tipped his seat back and fell asleep.

The next day seemed unpropitious for reasons I don't remember but which probably had to do with my mother's mood, and then my grades arrived and, useful as a diversion would have been, that didn't seem right. So my visit had only a few days left by the time I finally told. We were sitting at the breakfast table and the sun was pouring in through the French doors that overlooked the backyard deck. The trees out back made a screen so thick that sunlight rarely hit the room. When it did, we took advantage. The only animals to be seen were a well-behaved party of sparrows at the bird-feeder.

You already know about Lowell's visit, so instead of repeating all that, I'll tell you what I left out: Harlow, Ezra, the UC primate center, two trips to jail, drug use, drunkenness, and vandalism. These things would be of no interest to my parents, was my thinking on the matter. I started in the middle and I stopped in the middle, too. I stuck mostly to Bakers Square and our long night of conversation and pie.

About that, my report was thorough. I didn't conceal my concern over Lowell's mental condition or the criticisms he had of

Dad's work or the dreadful things we do to our fellow animals. The conversation was hard on Dad. When I got to Fern, there was no ignoring the fact that she wasn't now and never had been on a farm, that she'd left our house for a life of misery and imprisonment. I don't remember exactly how I phrased this, but my father accused me of harping on it. "You were five years old," he said. "What the hell *should* I have said to you?" as if the biggest crime here was the story he'd told.

My parents were instantly undone by the news that Lowell would have liked to go to college. The fact that he would have liked to come home was too much for them to even contemplate and had to wait for another conversation later that same day. Tears all around the table. My mother, tearing the paper towel she'd used as a napkin to shreds, wiping her eyes and nose on the larger bits.

There were surprises for me, too, which surprised me; I'd thought I was the one with the new information. Most startling was my parents' insistence that I was the reason we'd never talked about Fern, that I was the one who couldn't handle it. I hyperventilated at any mention of her name, they said, scratched at my skin until it bled, pulled my hair out by the roots. They were absolutely united in this: over the years they'd made many attempts to talk to me about Fern and I'd thwarted every one.

That dinner when Lowell had said that Fern loved corn on the cob and also us, that dinner when he'd left the house because my mother wasn't ready to talk about Fern yet—my parents didn't remember that dinner the way I did. I was the one, they said, who'd burst into tears and told them all to shut up. I'd said they were making my heart hurt and then I simply screamed incoherently and hysterically and effectively until everyone stopped talking and Lowell left the house.

This assertion flies in the face of many things I remember. I pass it on because there it is, *res ipsa loquitur*, and not because I'm persuaded.

Despite my alleged hysteria, my parents seemed surprised by the depth of the guilt I felt over Fern's exile. Disturbing as it is, no one abandons a child for killing a nonhuman animal. The kitten was not what got Fern sent away. She would have gotten in trouble, just as Lowell had said, and efforts would have been made to keep small, fragile creatures out of her hands, and that would have been the end of it.

But there had been other incidents that my parents swore I knew about and had even witnessed, though I have no memory of them. Aunt Vivi had claimed that Fern leaned into my cousin Peter's stroller and took his whole ear into her mouth. Aunt Vivi had said she would never visit us again as long as that beast was in the house, which had distressed my mother though my father saw it as a win-win.

One of the grad students had been badly bitten in the hand. He was holding an orange at the time, so it was possible Fern had meant to bite the orange. But the bite had been serious enough to require two surgeries and resulted in a lawsuit against the university. And Fern had never liked that guy.

One day, she had flung Amy, a grad student she adored, against a wall, a distance of several feet. This seemed to come out of nowhere, and Amy insisted it was an accident, but other students said Fern had not looked playful or careless, though they were unable to account for the aggressive behavior. Sherie, who saw it, left the program as a result, though Amy stayed.

Fern was still a little girl and a sweet-tempered one. But she was getting bigger. She was getting out of control. "It wouldn't have been responsible to wait for something more serious to happen," my father said. "It wouldn't have been good for Fern or anyone else. If she'd really hurt someone, the university would have put her down. We were trying to take care of everyone, here. Honey, we had no choice."

"It wasn't you," my mother said. "It wasn't ever about you."

Again, not entirely persuasive. As we continued to talk over the final days of my visit, I found that, just as I'd acquitted myself of one lie, I accused myself of another. I'd told my mother Fern had killed a kitten and that wasn't a lie and didn't get her sent off and there was no guilt to be had over having said so.

But I hadn't stopped with that. I'd never thought that Fern would deliberately hurt me. I'd never noticed that she might, any more than I had these thoughts of Lowell or my parents. But her remorselessness, the way she'd stared impassively at the dead kitten and then opened his stomach with her fingers, had shocked me to the core. So this is what I should have said to Mom; this is what I meant to say—

That there was something inside Fern I didn't know.

That I didn't know her in the way I'd always thought I did.

That Fern had secrets and not the good kind.

Instead I'd said I was afraid of her. That was the lie that got her sent away. That was the moment I made my parents choose between us.

2

IN EVERYONE'S LIFE there are people who stay and people who go and people who are taken away against their will.

Todd's mother worked out a deal for Ezra. The legal system had refused to see that opening a door was the same as closing one. Ezra pled guilty, got eight months in a minimum-security prison in Vallejo. Todd's mother said that he would serve five if he behaved himself. It cost him his job, which he had cared a lot about. It cost him any shot at the CIA (or maybe not, what do I know? Maybe it was just the résumé padding they'd been waiting for). No apartment manager I've ever had since has put his whole heart into it the way Ezra did. "The secret to a good life," he told me once, "is to bring your A game to everything you do. Even if all you're doing is taking out the garbage, you do that with excellence."

I went down on visitors' day—this was after Christmas—so he'd already been there about a month, and they brought him out, in his orange jumpsuit, to where we were allowed to sit on opposite sides of what, in another context, I would have called a picnic table. We were warned not to touch and then left alone. Ezra's mustache was gone, his upper lip as raw as if the hair had been ripped off it like a Band-Aid. His face looked naked, his teeth big and leporine. It was clear his spirits were low. I asked him how he was doing.

"It ain't the giggle that it used to be," he said, which was reassuring to me. Still Ezra. Still *Pulp Fiction*.

He asked if I'd heard anything from Harlow.

"Her parents came up from Fresno, looking for her," I said. "No luck, though. Nobody's seen her."

In the days after I'd told Lowell that Harlow never talked about her family, she'd given me the following information: three younger brothers, two older sisters. Half brothers and half sisters, if you wanted to get technical.

She'd said that her mother was one of those women who loved being pregnant but wasn't much for long-term relationships. A hippie-chick, earth-goddess thing. Each of Harlow's siblings had had a different father, but all of them lived with their mother in a falling-down house on the outskirts of town. Two kids back, they'd run out of room, so some of the fathers had transformed the basement into a warren of bedrooms, where the kids lived a largely unsupervised, Peter Pan sort of life. Harlow hadn't seen her own father in years, but he managed a small theater company up in Grass Valley, so he'd give her a job after graduation, no problem. He was, she said, her ace in the hole.

The similarity of Harlow's basement to my long-ago treehouse fantasies had struck me, except that you had to descend to enter Harlow's Never-Never Land. (Which would be a significant difference—recent studies suggest that people behave with more charity if they've just gone upstairs and less if they've just gone down—if studies like that weren't just an enormous pile of crap. There's science and there's science, is all I'm saying. When humans are the subjects, it's mostly not science.)

The basement and the tree house shared another trait: neither was real.

Harlow turned out to be an only child. Her father read gas meters for PG&E. This is a surprisingly dangerous job, because of the dogs, if not a glamorous one. Her mother worked at the local library. When I run the world, librarians will be exempt from tragedy. Even their smaller sorrows will last only for as long as you can take out a book.

Both her parents were tall but stooped, curled over their torsos in exactly the same way, as if they'd just been punched. Her mother had Harlow's hair, only short and practical. She wore a silk scarf around her neck and under that, on a long silver chain, an Egyptian cartouche. I could just make out the hieroglyphic of a bird. I thought how she'd dressed carefully to come and talk to the local police, to see me, see Reg. I imagined her at her closet, deciding what you'd wear to go learn something about your child that just might break your heart. She reminded me of my own mother, though they weren't alike in any other way except for the heartbreak.

Harlow's parents were afraid Harlow had been kidnapped and who knew what else, because it wasn't like her not to phone when she knew they'd be worried. They were, each of them, fragile as blown glass, afraid she might be dead. They tried to get me to think about that without them having to say it aloud. They suggested that Ezra might be accusing her, might have staged the whole primate action, in order to cover up something much more sinister. She would never, never miss Christmas, they said. Her stocking was still hanging on the mantel, where they said it would stay until, one way or another, she came home.

They'd insisted on taking me out for this conversation, so we were at Mishka's, drinking coffee in the quiet of the early days of winter quarter, hardly another customer in the place, the grinding of the beans the only significant noise.

I was drinking my coffee, anyway. Theirs sat untouched and getting colder by the minute.

I told them I had no doubt that Harlow was alive, that she had, in fact, returned to our apartment the day after the monkey business to get something she'd left there. Even though I hadn't seen her for myself, I had evidence, I told them, she'd left me clear evidence, and that was as far as I got. Her mother made a sound—something halfway between a gasp and a shriek—inadvertent, but loud and high-pitched. Then she burst into tears, grabbed my hands, upsetting our cups.

She herself took the worst of that. I suspected her lovely blouse was done for. "But it's just not like her," her father said over and over again as we were mopping up the mess. "Breaking in somewhere. Taking things"—meaning monkeys, I assume; I'd said nothing about Madame Defarge—"taking things that don't belong to her."

I wondered if we were talking about the same person. Nothing seemed more like Harlow to me.

But no one is easier to delude than a parent; they see only what they wish to see. I told Ezra some of this. He was too depressed to be interested. To my surprise, the need to touch him—something I'd certainly never felt before and probably felt now only because it was forbidden—began to overwhelm me. I wanted to stroke his arm, finger his hair, ruffle up some spirit. I sat on my hands to prevent it.

"Where did you think the monkeys would go?" I asked him.

"Wherever the hell they wanted," he said.

3

As soon as I'd said good-bye to Lowell at the Davis train station, there'd been no point in sticking around, prolonging my college education any longer. I had a sister to take care of. It was time to get serious.

I waited for that first report on Fern to arrive, but it never did. Whatever Lowell thought he'd put into place had slipped out of it. Meanwhile, I checked out every book I could find on the monkey girls—Jane Goodall (chimps), Dian Fossey (gorillas), and Biruté Galdikas (orangutans).

I thought of going to work at Gombe Stream after graduation, spending long days observing the Kasakela chimpanzees. I thought I might have something special to contribute there, might find a way, after all this time, to make something good come from Dad's experiment. This, I thought, was the life I was born to live, so like those tree-house dreams that used to rock me to sleep. I thought that I might find the place where I fit in at last. Tarzan in the jungle. The idea vaulted me into elation.

Plummet. I remembered the 170 rapes over three days from Dr. Sosa's lecture. Some scientist had observed all that, had actually watched a chimp raped 170 times and kept count. Good scientist. Not me.

Besides, because I had so assiduously avoided primates in all my classes, this career path would have amounted to starting college over.

And how did it help Fern?

I remembered then that Lowell's old girlfriend, Kitch, had once told me she thought I'd be a great teacher. I'd figured she was just being polite—and also crazy, probably driven crazy like so many before her by sorority living—but after several hours with the university handbook in one hand and my transcript in the other, it seemed that my fastest route through, the major that would accept most of the classes I'd already taken, was education. Of course, then there would be the credential to get. But I couldn't see another degree I'd finish much before Mayan doomsday.

ONE DAY THAT spring I ran into Reg at the library and he suggested that we go together to see the drama department's gender-bending *Macbeth*. He had two tickets, he said, courtesy of some friend of Harlow's.

We met around twilight at the Dramatic Art Building. (A month later, appropriately enough, the name would be changed to the Celeste Turner Wright Hall, one of only three buildings on campus named after a woman. We thank you, Celeste, we women of Davis.) It was a beautiful night, and behind the theater, the redbuds and the currants were blooming in the arboretum. Down the hill, I heard mallards quarreling languidly.

The play was the usual bloody affair, and none of Harlow's ideas had been used. I thought this was a shame. It wasn't a bad show, but it would have been much more interesting the way she'd envisioned it. Reg, though, persisted in his original assessment, that there was nothing funnier than a man in a dress.

I found this appalling, demeaning to women and cross-dressers everywhere. I said that he must be the only idiot in the world who thought *Macbeth* should be played for laughs.

He waved his hands cheerfully at me. "When a guy takes a girl to see a feminist show," he said, "he knows what he's getting himself into. He knows the evening will end in a fight." He asked if I was getting my period, which he also thought was pretty damned funny.

We were headed to his car then. I turned abruptly around. I preferred to walk, I told him. By myself. What a jerk. I was halfway home before I realized what he'd said. "When a guy takes a girl . . ." I hadn't known it was a date.

The next day he called me up and asked me out again. We lasted about five months as a couple. Even now, as I inch toward my forties, this remains a personal best for me. I liked Reg a lot, but we never moved in together. We fought all the time. I wasn't as restful as he'd hoped.

"I don't think this is going to work," he said to me one evening. We were parked in front of my apartment house waiting for the police to leave. They were ticketing the third floor for noise violations.

"Why not?" I asked in the spirit of scientific inquiry.

"I think you're terrific," he said. "And a very pretty girl. Don't make me spell it out." So I'm not sure exactly why we broke up.

Maybe he was the problem. Maybe I was. Maybe it was the ghost of Harlow, shaking her gory locks at us. *Hence, horrible shadow! Unreal mockery, hence!*

The conversation wasn't as hurtful as it sounds in the recounting. When I think of Reg, I think of him fondly. At the time, I was pretty sure I was the one who'd started the breaking up, even though he was the first to say it. Later, though, I heard he was dating a man, so maybe I was too quick to take the credit.

The fact remains that I can't seem to make sex work over the long haul. Not for lack of trying. Don't make me spell it out.

I wonder if Lowell would say that the way I was raised has fucked me up sexually. Or if none of you can make sex work over the long haul, either.

Maybe you think you can, but you really can't. Maybe anosognosia, the inability to see your own disability, is the human condition and I'm the only one who doesn't suffer from it.

Mom says I just haven't met the right guy yet, the guy who sees the stars in my eyes.

True enough. I've yet to meet that guy.

THE MAN WHO saw the stars in my mother's eyes died in 1998. Dad had taken off for a solitary week of camping, fishing, kayaking, and introspection along the Wabash River. Two days in, while portaging the kayak over some rocks, he had a heart attack that he mistook for the flu. He made it home and into bed, where he had a second heart attack a day later, and a third in the hospital that night.

By the time I arrived, he was outdoors again, climbing some dream mountain in the borderlands. It took concentrated, sustained effort, from both Mom and me, to tell him I was there and I'm still not sure he knew me. "I'm really tired," he said. "Could you take my pack? Just for a little while?" He sounded embarrassed.

"Sure, Dad," I said. "Sure. Look, I have it now. I'll carry it for as long as you need." This was the last thing I said to him that I know he heard.

I imagine that sounds like a deathbed scene in a movie—clean, classic, profound, and weighty. In fact, he lived another day, and there was nothing tidy about it. There was blood, shit, mucus, moaning, and hours of audible, painful gasping for breath. Doctors and nurses dashed about, and Mom and I were allowed into the room and then tossed from it with regularity.

I remember an aquarium in the waiting room. I remember fish whose beating hearts were visible inside their bodies, whose scales were the color of glass. I remember a snail that dragged itself along the sides, the mouth in its foot expanding and contracting endlessly as it moved. The doctor came out and my mother stood to meet him. "I'm afraid we've lost him this time," he said, as if there would be a next time.

NEXT TIME, I'll put things right between my father and me.

Next time, I'll give Mom the fair share of blame for Fern that her collapse forestalled this time around. I won't drop the whole of it onto Dad next time.

Next time, I'll take the share that's mine, no more, no less. Next time I'll shut my mouth about Fern and open it about Lowell. I'll tell Mom and Dad that Lowell skipped his basketball practice, so they'll talk to him and he won't leave.

I'd always planned to forgive Dad someday. It cost him so much, but it didn't cost him me, and I wish I'd said so. It's painful and pointless that I didn't.

So I've always been grateful for that one final request. It was a great gift to let me take a burden, however imaginary, from him.

. . .

DAD WAS FIFTY-EIGHT years old at the time of his death. The doctor told us that, due to the combination of diabetes and drink, he had the body of a much older man. "Did he live a stressful life?" he asked us, and Mom asked back, who didn't?

We left his body behind for further scientific analysis and got into the car. "I want Lowell," my mother said and then she melted over the steering wheel, gasping so hard for breath it seemed that she might die along with Dad.

We changed places and I drove. I made several turns before realizing that I was not on my way to the house of stone and air but back to the saltbox by the university, where I'd grown up. I was almost home before I noticed.

Dad had a long, respectful obituary in *The New York Times*, which would have pleased him. Fern was mentioned, of course, but as a research subject, not a "survived by." I felt the jolt of Fern's name coming when I hadn't braced for it, like hitting an air pocket in a plane. The monkey girl was still afraid of exposure, and this seemed like an international reveal.

But by this time, I was at Stanford, where I didn't know much of anyone. No one said a word to me about it.

A few days after the obit ran, we got a postcard of the Regions Building in Tampa, Florida, with its steepled roof and forty-two floors of pewter-tinted windows. "I'm seeing so much of America today," the postcard said. It was addressed to Mom and me. There was no signature.

4

BACK IN 1996, the airlines had returned my suitcase just a few days after I'd left for Christmas vacation. Todd was still in the apartment, since he rarely rushed home for the holidays, so he was able to ID it, take possession. "It's the real deal," he told me. "Your actual suitcase. I'd know it anywhere." He'd given the other back, which I hadn't anticipated happening in my absence and was distressed about.

Of course, it's always possible that while I was hitting the tarmac in Indiana, Harlow was sneaking into my room, as she so liked to do, and putting Madame Defarge safely back into her powder-blue sarcophagus. "Always possible" as in "No chance in hell."

I do feel terrible about that. I'm sure she was an expensive and irreplaceable antique. I'd meant to put a note inside the suitcase before it was returned, making my apologies. Let me do so here:

Dear jogging puppeteer,

Although I didn't steal Madame Defarge myself, she did disappear while under my care. I'm so sorry. I'm sure you valued her highly.

The only consolation I can offer is my belief that she's now living the life of ceaseless retribution for which she is so justly famous. She has, in short, returned to form as a political activist and dispenser of rough justice.

I still hope to get her home to you someday, intact in all her parts. I look for her on eBay at least once every month.

My sincerest apologies,
Rosemary Cooke

My own bulging suitcase had no such missing items. There was my blue sweater, there were my bedroom slippers, my pajamas, my underwear; there were our mother's journals, not as sprightly as when last seen—travel had frayed their corners, disheveled their covers, left the Christmas ribbon at a rakish angle. Everything a bit squashed, but essentially unharmed.

I didn't open the journals immediately. I was tired from the trip home and scraped raw from all the talking and thinking of Fern I'd done over the last weeks. I decided to put them away for a bit on the top shelf of my closet, pushed back so I wouldn't see them every time I slid the mirrored doors apart.

And then, having made that decision, I flipped open the cover on the top one.

There was a Polaroid of me, taken in the hospital in the early hours of my life. I'm red as a berry, shiny from the pickling of the womb, and squinting at the world through suspicious, slitted eyes. My hands are fists up by my face. I look ready to rumble. Under my picture, there is a poem.

dear, dear,
what a fat, happy face it has
this peony!

I went ahead and opened the cover of the second notebook. Fern also has a picture and a poem, or at least part of a poem. The photo was taken the first day she arrived at the farmhouse. She's almost three months old and wrapped like seaweed around someone's arm. It must be our mother's; I recognize the large, green weave of the shirt from other pictures.

The hair on Fern's head, including her side whiskers, is up. It springs from her bare face in an aggrieved and agitated halo. Her arms are twigs, her forehead creased, her eyes huge and startled.

A Mien to move a Queen—
Half Child—Half Heroine—

Mom's notebooks are not scientific journals. Although they do include a graph or two, some numbers and some measurements, they're not the dispassionate, careful observations from the field that I expected.

They appeared to be our baby books.

5

I'VE TOLD YOU the middle of my story now. I've told you the end of the beginning and I've told you the beginning of the end. As luck would have it, there is considerable overlap between the only two parts that remain.

Last fall, Mom and I spent many weeks looking through her journals together, preparing them for publication. In her late sixties now, Mom's taken to wearing overalls—"I haven't seen my waist since Aught One," she likes to say, but she's actually gotten skinnier as she's aged, ropier arms, bonier legs. She's still an attractive woman, but now you can see the skull beneath the face. These old photos reminded me of how happy she'd always looked back before we broke her.

"You were the prettiest baby anyone ever saw," she told me. The Polaroid provides no evidence of this. "Perfect ten on the Apgar." Six hours of labor, according to her journal. Weighing in at 7 pounds, 2 ounces. 19 inches tall. Quite a decent catch.

I was five months old when I first learned to sit up. There's a photo of me sitting, back straight as a knitting needle. Fern is leaning against me, her arms around my middle. She appears to be either just starting or just finishing a yawn.

At five months, Fern was already crawling on her knuckles and her little clenched feet. "She used to lose track of the floor," Mom said. "Her hands were fine. She could see them and where they ought to go. But she'd wave her feet around behind her, trying to find the ground up in the air or out to the side or anywhere else but down. It was just so cute."

I started to walk when I was ten months old. At ten months, Fern could make it all the way downstairs by herself, swinging on the railings. "You were very early with all your benchmarks, compared to other children," Mom said consolingly. "I think maybe Fern pushed you a little."

At ten months, I weighed 14 pounds, 7 ounces. I had four teeth, two on the top, two on the bottom. Fern weighed 10 pounds, 2 ounces. Mom's charts show both of us small for our age.

My first word was *bye-bye*. I signed it at eleven months, said it at thirteen. Fern's first sign was *cup*. She was ten months old.

I WAS BORN in a hospital in Bloomington, an unremarkable delivery. Fern was born in Africa, where, barely a month later, her mother was killed and sold as food.

Mom said:

We'd been talking about raising a chimpanzee for several years. All very theoretical. I'd always said I wouldn't have a chimp taken from its mother. I'd always said it had to be a chimp with nowhere else to go. I kind of thought that would be the end of that. I got pregnant with you and we stopped talking about it.

And then we heard about Fern. Some friends of some friends bought her from poachers at a market in Cameroon, because they hoped we'd want her. They said she was all but dead at the time, just as limp as a rag, and filthy, streaked with diarrhea and covered in fleas. They didn't expect her to live, but they couldn't bear to walk away and leave her.

And if she did make it, then she'd have proved herself one tough little nut. Resilient. Adaptable. Perfect for us.

She was still in quarantine when you were born. We couldn't take any chances on her bringing something into the house. So for one month, you were my only baby. You were such a happy little soul. And easy—you hardly ever cried. But I was having second thoughts. I'd forgotten how tiring it all was, the sleepless nights, the endless nursing. I would have said no to the study then, but what would happen to Fern? And every time I hesitated, I was promised all this help. A village. Of grad students.

It was a blustery day when Fern finally blew into town. So tiny and terrified. The wind slammed the door behind her and she just jumped from the arms of the guy who'd brought her over to me. That was that.

She used to grip me so tightly that the only way I could put her down was to pry her loose, one digit at a time. For two years, I had bruises from her fingers and toes all over my body. But that's how it works in the wild—the baby chimp clings to its mother for the whole of the first two years.

Her grip was so strong that this one time just after she arrived, I'd put her down and her little hands were flailing about in protest when they found each other by accident. They clamped together like clamshells. She couldn't get them apart. She started screaming and your father had to go in and unlock her hands for her.

For the first week, she mostly slept. She had a cradle, but I could put her into it only if she was already asleep. She'd curl up on my lap with her head on my arm, and yawn so I could see all the way down her throat, which would make me yawn, too. And then the light would slowly go out of her eyes. The lids would come down, flutter for a bit, then close.

She was listless and uninterested in things. Whenever I saw that she was awake, I'd talk to her, but she hardly seemed to notice. I worried that she wasn't healthy, after all. Or not very bright. Or so traumatized that she'd never recover.

Still, that was the week she took hold of my heart. She was so little and so alone in the world. So frightened and sad. And so much like a baby. So much like you, only with a lot of suffering added.

I told your dad I didn't see how the two of you could be compared when your world had been so gentle and hers so cruel. But there was no turning back by then. I was deeply in love with you both.

I'd read everything I could about the other home-raised chimps, especially the book by Catherine Hayes about Viki, and I thought it would work out. At the end of her book, Catherine says they plan to keep Viki with them always. She says that people keep asking if Viki might someday turn on them, and then she opens the morning newspaper and reads about some kid who's murdered his parents in their beds. We all take our chances, she said.

Of course, Viki died before she reached full size; they were never put to the test. But we'd thought that, too, your father and I, we truly did, that Fern would be with us forever. Your part of the study would end when you went off to school, but we'd keep working with Fern. Eventually you'd go to college, you and Lowell both, and she'd stay home with us. That's what I thought I was agreeing to.

A few years ago I found something on the Web that Viki's father had said. He was complaining about the way Viki is always held up as an example of a failed language experiment. Doomed to failure, because they tried to teach her to speak orally, which, of course, a chimp is physiologically incapable of doing. As we now know.

But Mr. Hayes said that the significant, the critical finding of their study, the finding everyone was choosing to ignore, was this: that language was the *only* way in which Viki differed much from a normal human child.

"WHERE YOU SUCCEED will never matter so much as where you fail," I said.

"Good Lord," Mom answered. "How debilitating. If I believed that, I'd just end my meal right here, right now with a chaser of hemlock."

We'd had this conversation one night when we were lingering at the table, finishing our wine. It had been a special dinner to celebrate the sale of our book. The advance had exceeded our expectations (though not met our needs). Candlelight bobbed and weaved in the drafty kitchen and we were using that part of the good china that had survived the Fern years. Mom seemed calm and not too sad.

She said, "I remember reading somewhere about some scientist who thought we could miniaturize chimps to control them, the way we've done with dachshunds and poodles."

I did not say that I'd read about Ilya Ivanovich Ivanov, who in the 1920s made several attempts to create a human-chimp hybrid, the elusive humanzee. He'd inseminated chimps with human sperm, though his first thought had been to go the other way— human mothers, chimp sperm. These are the dreams that make us human, Mother. Pass that hemlock over to me when you're done with it.

MOM SAID:

When Fern woke up, she woke up. Spun like a pinwheel. Burst like a sunburst. Swung through our house like a miniature Colossus. You remember how Dad used to call her our Mighty Whirlitzer? All the noise and color and excitement of Mardi Gras, and right in our very own home.

When you got just a little older, you and she were quite the team. She'd open the cupboards and you'd pull out every pot, every pan. She could work the childproof locks in a heartbeat, but she didn't have your stick-to-itiveness. Remember how obsessed she was with shoelaces? We were always tripping over our feet because Fern had untied our shoelaces without us noticing.

She'd climb up in the closets and pull the coats from the hangers, drop them down to you below. Fetch coins from my purse for you to suck on. Open the drawers and hand you the pins and the needles, the scissors and the knives.

"DID YOU WORRY about me and what the impact might be?" I asked. I poured myself another glass of wine to fortify me, since I couldn't think of an answer I was going to want to hear sober.

"Of course I did," she said. "I worried about that all the time. But you adored Fern. You were a happy, happy child."

"Was I? I don't remember."

"Absolutely. I worried about what being Fern's sister would do to you, but I wanted it for you, too." The candlelight was casting shadow puppets in the kitchen. The wine was red. Mom took another sip and turned her softly sagging face away from mine. "I wanted you to have an extraordinary life," she said.

MOM DUG OUT a video one of the grad students had made. There were a lot of these, which is why we still have an old VHS player long after the rest of you dumped yours. The opening shot is a long track up the farmhouse stairs. The sound track is from *Jaws*. My bedroom door swings open and there's a scream.

Shift to Fern and me. We're lounging side by side in my beanbag chair. Our postures are identical, our arms crooked behind our necks, our heads cupped in our hands. Our knees are bent, one leg crossing over the other so one foot is on the ground, the other in the air. A picture of complacent accomplishment.

The room about us has been trashed. We are Romans sitting amid the ruin of Carthage; Merry and Pippin in Isengard. Newspapers have been shredded, clothing and toys scattered, food discarded and stepped on. A peanut butter sandwich has been ground into the bedspread, the curtains bedazzled with Magic Markers. Around our contented little figures, grad students clean up the mess. On the screen, pages fall from the calendar as they work.

Someday, we'll be able to embed that video in a book. For this one, we used the photos from the baby books and tried to turn the lists of firsts—first steps, first teeth, first words, etc.—into something more like a story. We're using a picture of Fern in one of Grandma Donna's hats. Another, in which she's holding an apple to her mouth with her feet. Another, where she's looking at her teeth in the mirror.

In each notebook, there was a set of facial close-ups—mood

studies. We've paired them so that the embodiment of emotions in child and chimp can be contrasted. Here is me playful, all my teeth showing, and here is Fern, lip pulled over her top teeth. When I cry, my face clenches. My forehead is wrinkled, my mouth open wide; tears streak my cheeks. In Fern's crying picture, her mouth is also open, but she's thrown her head back, closed her eyes. Her face is dry.

I can't see much difference in the picture of me happy and the picture whose label says EXCITED. It's easier with Fern. Her lips are opened in the first, funneled in the second. Her happy forehead is smooth; her excited one deeply creased.

Fern snuck into most of my pictures. Here I'm in Grandma Fredericka's arms and Fern is down below, clutching her leg. Here I sit in a toddler's swing and Fern is dangling from the crossbar above me. Here we lean against our terrier, Tamara Press, all the small animals of the farmhouse in one concatenated row. Both of us have our hands plunged into Tamara's fur, gripping it in our fists. She gazes mildly at the camera as if we were not hurting her with all the love in our hearts.

Here we are hiking with Dad at Lemon Lake. I'm strapped into a BabyBjörn, my back against his chest, my face squished by the straps. Fern is in a backpack. She peeks over his shoulder, all wild hair and eyes.

The poetry in our baby books was written in our mother's hand, but the poets were Dad's two favorites, Kobayashi Issa and Emily Dickinson. When I first read these in the journals, back in my college bedroom in the winter of '97, it occurred to me that, for all his rigorous rejection of anthropomorphism, he could hardly have picked two who score more highly on Lowell's test of kinship. Bonus points for bugs.

ISSA

Look, don't kill that fly!
It is making a prayer to you
By rubbing its hands and feet.

DICKINSON

Bee! I'm expecting you!
Was saying Yesterday
To Somebody you know
That you were due—

The Frogs got Home last Week—
Are settled, and at work—
Birds, mostly back—
The Clover warm and thick—

You'll get my Letter by
The seventeenth; Reply
Or better, be with me—
Yours, Fly.

2012.

Year of the Water Dragon.

An election year in the U.S., as if you needed to be reminded, the vituperative tunes of the Ayn Rand Marching Band bleating from the airwaves.

And on the global level—Dämmerung of the Dinosaurs. Final Act: Revenge on the upstart mammals. Here is the scene where they cook us in our own stupidity. If stupid were fuel, we would never run out. Meanwhile, religious bullies at home and abroad are, in the short time remaining before the world ends, busily stomping out all hope of even ephemeral happiness.

My own life, though, is pretty good. Can't complain.

MOM AND I are living together these days in Vermillion, South Dakota. We are renting a nondescript townhouse, smaller even than the house of stone and air. I miss the mild winters of Bloomington and the milder ones of Northern California, but Vermillion's a university town and pleasant enough.

For the last seven years, I've been a kindergarten teacher at Addison Elementary, which is as close to living with a chimp troop as I've been able to get so far. And Kitch was right. More than right, prophetic. I'm good at it. I'm good at reading body language, especially that of small children. I watch them and I listen and then I know what they're feeling, what they're thinking, and, most important, what they're about to do.

My old kindergarten behaviors, so appalling when I was a kindergartner myself, are apparently quite acceptable in a teacher. Every week we try to learn a word we hope their parents don't know, a task they approach with enthusiasm. Last week's word was *frugivorous*. This week's is *verklempt*. I'm preparing them for the SATs.

I stand on my chair when I need to get their attention. When we sit on the rug, they climb all over my lap, comb through my hair with their fingers. When the birthday cupcakes come, we greet them with the traditional chimpanzee food-hoot.

We have a whole unit on proper chimp etiquette. When you visit a chimp family, I tell them, you must stoop over, make yourself smaller, so you're not intimidating. I show them how to sign *friend* with their hands. How to smile so that they cover their top teeth with their upper lips. When our class picture is taken, I ask the photographer for two—one to go home to their parents and one for the classroom. In the classroom picture, we are all making our friendly chimp faces.

After we've practiced our good manners, we take a field trip to the Uljevik Lab, now called the Center for Primate Communication. We file into the visitors' room, where there's a bulletproof wall of glass between the chimps and us.

Sometimes the chimps don't feel like having guests, and they show it by rushing the wall, body-slamming it with a loud crash, making the glass shiver in its frame. When this happens, we go away, come back another time. The center is their home. They get to decide who comes in.

But we also have a Skype connection in the classroom. I leave this open throughout the morning, so my students can check on the chimps anytime they like, and the chimps can do likewise. Only six chimps remain here now. Three are younger than Fern—Hazel, Bennie, and Sprout. Two are older, both males—Aban and Hanu. So Fern is not the largest, nor the oldest, nor the malest. And yet, by my observation, she is the highest-status chimp here. I've observed Hanu making the chimp gesture of supplication—arm extended, wrist limp—to Fern, and I've never seen Fern do that to anyone. So there, Dr. Sosa.

My kindergartners far prefer my niece Hazel to my sister. They like Sprout, the youngest at five years, best of all. Sprout is unrelated to Fern, but he brings back my memories of her more often than she herself does. We see fewer images of older chimps, more of the tractable babies. Fern has grown heavy and slow. Her life has worn on her.

My kindergartners say she's kind of mean, but to me she's just a good mother. She manages the social life at the center and doesn't tolerate nonsense. When there's a row, she's the one who stops it, forces the rowers to hug and make up.

Sometimes our own mother appears on the other end of the Skype connection, telling me to pick something up at the store on my way home or reminding me that I have a dentist appointment. She volunteers at the center daily. Her current job is to make sure Fern gets to eat the foods she likes.

The day our mother walked in for the first time, Fern refused to look at her. She sat with her back to the glass and wouldn't turn around even to see what Hazel and Mom were saying to each other. Mom had made peanut butter cookies, Fern's old favorites, and they were delivered, but she'd refused to eat them. "She doesn't know me," Mom said, but I thought the evidence was otherwise. Fern would not turn down a peanut butter cookie for no reason.

The first time Mom was the one to deliver lunch to the chimps—there is a small window for this, just large enough to slide a tray through—Fern was waiting for her. She reached out to grab Mom's hand. Her grip was tight enough to hurt and Mom asked her several times to ease up, but Fern never showed any sign of hearing. She remained impassive and imperious. Mom had to bite her before she'd let go.

In subsequent visits, she's softened. She signs with Mom now, and keeps a careful track of where Mom is, much more so than with anyone else. She follows her about as best she can, with her inside and Mom out. She eats her cookies. In Fern's baby book, there's a photo in the farmhouse kitchen of Fern and me at the table, each with a beater to lick. Fern is gnawing on hers like a chicken leg.

I used to wonder what I'd tell Fern when she asked about Lowell or Dad. We'd had to remind Grandpa Joe in his nursing home that Dad had died, over and over, and five minutes later he'd be asking us again, in an anguished voice, what he'd done so bad that his only son never came to see him. But Fern has never mentioned either one.

Sometimes my kindergartners and the chimps do a craft project together, either when we visit or over Skype. We finger-paint. We cover paper with paste and glitter. We make clay plates with our handprints impressed into them. The center holds fund-raisers, where they sell chimp artwork. We have several of Fern's paintings on the walls of the townhouse. My favorite is her rendition of a bird, a dark slash across a light sky, no cage for creature or artist in evidence anywhere.

The center has shelves and shelves of video still to be analyzed; the researchers are behind the data by decades. So the six chimps left in residence are all retired from the science game. Our intrusions are welcomed as a way to keep them stimulated and interested, and no one worries about us muddying the results.

These six chimps are cared for in the best way possible, and yet their lives are not enviable. They need more room inside and much more out. They need birds, trees, streams with frogs, the insect chorus, all of nature unorchestrated. They need more surprise in their lives.

I lie awake at night and, just as I once fantasized about a tree house where I'd live with Fern, now I'm designing a home for humans, like a guardhouse, but bigger—a four-bedroom, two-bathroom guardhouse. The front door is also the only entry to a large compound. The back wall is all bulletproof glass and looks out on twenty acres, maybe more, of dogwood, sumac, goldenrod, and poison ivy. In my fantasy, humans are confined to the house and chimps run free over the property, the six from the center but others as well, maybe even my nephews, Basil and Sage. This is the clue that it's all just a dream; introducing two full-grown males into our little community is a terrible and dangerous idea.

In the last several years, the news has carried reports of horrific chimp attacks. I'm not afraid of Fern. Still, I understand that she and I will never touch each other again, never sit with our arms around each other, never walk in tandem as if we were a single person. This dream sanctuary is the best solution I can imagine—an electrified fence around us, a bulletproof wall between.

IT WILL TAKE more than a kindergarten teacher's salary. Publishing her journals as a children's book was Mom's idea. She wrote the originals and did much of the work preparing the final version, but Fern and I are whimsically listed as coauthors on the cover. All profits will go directly to the center, to a fund for enlarging the chimps' outdoor enclosure. Cards for donations will also be slipped inside each book.

Our publisher is excited and optimistic. The pub date has been arranged around my summer vacation. The publicity department expects a number of media bookings. When I think too much about this, I panic, find myself hoping for print rather than radio, radio rather than television or, selfishly, no notice at all.

Some of this is my familiar fear of exposure. It terrifies me to think that, come summer, there will be no more hiding, no more passing. Everyone from the woman who cuts my hair to the queen in England might know who I am.

Not who I really am, of course, but an airbrushed version of me, more marketable, easier to love. The me that teaches kindergarten and not the me who will never have children. The me who loves my sister and not the me who got her sent away. I still haven't found that place where I can be my true self. But maybe you never get to be your true self, either.

I once thought of the monkey girl as a threat only to myself. Now I see how she could blow the whole caper. So, added to the old fear of exposure, is this other fear that I'll mess up, miscalculate just how much monkey girl to let out. There's no data to suggest that I can make you love me whatever I do. I could be headed back to middle school, no hallways and classrooms this time, but the tabloids and the blogs instead.

Pretend I'm on your television sets. I'll be on my best human behavior. I won't climb on the tables or jump on the couches even though humans have done those things on television shows before and not been rousted from the species for it. And still you'll be thinking to yourselves—it makes no sense, because she looks perfectly normal, even rather pretty in some lights, and yet. There's just something off about her. I can't put my finger on it . . .

I'll creep you out a little bit in that uncanny valley way I have. Or else I'll annoy you; I get that a lot. Just don't hold it against Fern. You would like Fern.

I wish Mom could do the media instead of me, but she can't be passed off as an innocent victim. The studio audience will shout at her.

So here we are. The human half of Bloomington's Sister Act, the phantasmagorical Rosemary Cooke, is about to take the show on the road. Every word I say out there will be on my sister's behalf. I'll be widely admired. Fern will be stealthily influential. That's the plan.

That was the plan.

6

AND IF YOU won't listen to *me* . . .

My sister's life, as performed by Madame Defarge:

Once upon a time, there was a happy family—a mother, a father, a son, and two daughters. The older daughter was smart and agile, covered in hair and very beautiful. The younger was ordinary. Still, their parents and their brother loved them both.

Mon Dieu! One day, the older daughter fell into the power of a wicked king. He threw her into a prison where no one would see her. He cast a spell to keep her there. Every day he told her how ugly she was. The wicked king died, but this did not break the spell.

The spell can only be broken by the people. They must come to see how beautiful she is. They must storm the prison and demand her release. The spell will be broken only when the people rise up.

So rise up already.

ON DECEMBER 15, 2011, *The New York Times* carried the news that the National Institutes of Health had suspended all new grants for biomedical and behavioral studies on chimpanzees. In the future, chimp studies will be funded only if the research is necessary for human health and there is absolutely no other way to accomplish it. Two possible exceptions to the ban were noted—the ongoing research involving immunology and also that on hepatitis C. But the report's basic conclusion was that most research on chimps is completely unnecessary.

Small victories. Fern and I celebrated the news with champagne. Our father used to give us one sip each on New Year's Eve. It always made Fern sneeze.

I wonder if she remembers that. I know she won't have confused our little celebration with New Year's. The holidays are observed at the center, and Fern has always been very clear about their order—first Mask Day, then Bird-Eating Day. First Sweet-Tree Day, and, only after that, No-Bedtime Day.

I wonder about Fern's memory a lot. Lowell said: She recognized me instantly. Mom: She doesn't know me.

Research at Kyoto University has demonstrated the superiority of chimps to humans at certain short-term memory tasks. A vast superiority. As in, We can't even play on the same field.

Long-term memory is more difficult to study. In 1972, Endel Tulving coined the phrase *episodic memory* to refer to the ability to remember incidents in one's individual life with detailed temporal and spatial information (the what, when, where) and then access them later as episodes through a conscious reexperiencing of them, a sort of mental time travel.

In 1983, he wrote: "Other members of the animal kingdom can learn, benefit from experience, acquire the ability to adjust and adapt, to solve problems and make decisions, but they cannot travel back into the past in their own minds." Episodic memory, he said, is a uniquely human gift.

How he knows this isn't clear. It seems to me that every time we humans announce that here is the thing that makes us unique—our featherless bipedality, our tool-using, our language—some other species comes along to snatch it away. If modesty were a human trait, we'd have learned to be more cautious over the years.

Episodic memory has certain subjective features. It comes with something called "a feeling of pastness," and also a feeling of confidence, however misplaced, in the accuracy of recollection. These interiorities can never be observed in another species. Doesn't mean they aren't there. Doesn't mean they are.

Other species do show evidence of functional episodic memory—the retention of the what, where, and when of individual experiences. The data has been particularly persuasive with regard to scrub jays.

Humans are actually not so good at remembering the when. Extremely good at remembering the who, though. I would guess chimps, social as they are, might be the same.

Does Fern remember us? Does she remember but not recognize us as the people she remembers? We certainly don't look the way we used to, and I don't know if Fern understands that children grow up, that humans grow old, same as chimps. I can find no studies that suggest what a chimp might remember over a period of twenty-two years.

Still, I believe Fern knows who we are. The evidence is compelling, if not conclusive. Only the exacting ghost of my father keeps me from insisting on it.

7

BACK IN FEBRUARY this year, my publicity agent called with the unwelcome and surprising news that she'd been getting requests for bookings all morning from major media markets. She rattled off a string of familiar names—Charlie Rose, Jon Stewart, Barbara Walters, *The View*. She said the publishing house was trying to see if it was possible to move the pub date up and what did I think? Could I make that work on my end? Her tone, while delivering this news, was strangely subdued. This is the way I learned that Lowell had been arrested at last.

He'd been picked up in Orlando, where, in addition to a list of charges roughly the size of *War and Peace*, the police contended he'd been in the final stages of planning an attack on SeaWorld. They'd only just prevented it.

An unidentified female accomplice was still at large.

FERN IS THE reason Mom and I decided to publish the notebooks. Taken together, Mom's two journals make for a sweet and cheerful children's book. "Fern and Rosemary are sisters. They live together in a big house in the country." No women are trussed up like roasted turkeys, no kittens are killed in the telling of that story. Everything in it is true—the truth and nothing but the truth—but not the whole truth. Only as much of the truth as we thought children would want and Fern would need.

That won't be enough truth for Lowell.

So this story here is for him. And for Fern, too, Fern again, always Fern.

My brother and my sister have led extraordinary lives, but I wasn't there, and I can't tell you that part. I've stuck here to the part I can tell, the part that's mine, and still everything I've said is all about them, a chalk outline around the space where they should have been. Three children, one story.

The only reason I'm the one telling it is that I'm the one not currently in a cage.

I've spent most of my life carefully not talking about Fern and Lowell and me. It will take some practice to be fluent in that. Think of everything I've said here as practice.

Because what this family needs now is a great talker.

I'M NOT GOING to argue here for Lowell's innocence. I know he'd think that the SeaWorld orca factory is a callous monstrosity. I know he'd think that SeaWorld has to be stopped before they kill again. I know he'd do more than think this.

So I expect the allegations are true, although an "attack on Sea-World" might mean a bomb, or it might mean graffiti and glitter and a cream pie in the face. The government doesn't always seem to distinguish between the two.

Which is not to suggest Lowell didn't intend serious damage.

Money is the language humans speak, Lowell told me once upon a time, long, long ago. If you want to communicate with humans, then you have to learn to speak it. I'm just reminding you that the ALF doesn't believe in hurting animals, human or otherwise.

I find myself wishing Lowell had been captured earlier. I wish I'd turned him in myself back in 1996, when the list of charges was smaller and the country more like a democracy. I expect he would still have gone to jail, but he'd be out and home by now. In 1996, even those citizens charged with terrorism had constitutional rights. Lowell's been in custody for three months and he still hasn't seen his attorney. His mental condition is not good.

Or so I hear. Mom and I haven't been allowed to see him, either. There are recent photos in the papers and on the Web. He looks every bit the terrorist. Startled hair, scraggled beard, sunken eyes. Unabomber stare. I've read that since his arrest he hasn't said a single word.

Everyone else is mystified by this silence, but his reasons couldn't be more obvious to me. He was halfway there when I last saw him sixteen years ago. Lowell has decided to be tried as an animal. The nonhuman kind.

Nonhuman animals have gone to court before. Arguably, the first ALF action in the United States was the release of two dolphins in 1977 from the University of Hawaii. The men responsible were charged with grand theft. Their original defense, that dolphins are persons (humans in dolphin suits, one defendant said), was quickly thrown out by the judge. I'm unclear on the definition of person the courts have been using. Something that sieves out dolphins but lets corporations slide on through.

A case was filed in Vienna in 2007 on behalf of Matthias Hiasl

Pan, a chimpanzee. It went to the Austrian Supreme Court, which ruled that he was a thing, not a person, though the court regretted the lack of some third legal category—neither person, nor thing—into which they could have slotted him.

A nonhuman animal had better have a good lawyer. In 1508, Bartholomé Chassenée earned fame and fortune for his eloquent representation of the rats of his French province. These rats had been charged with destroying the barley crop and also with ignoring the court order to appear and defend themselves. Bartholomé Chassenée argued successfully that the rats hadn't come because the court had failed to provide reasonable protection from the village cats along the route.

I've been talking with Todd's mother recently and I think she'll agree to represent Lowell. She's interested, but it's a complicated case, likely to last some time. Great quantities of money needed.

Always money.

There's no money in Thomas More's *Utopia*, nor private property, either—these things are too ugly for the Utopians, who must be protected from life's rougher aspects. The Zapolets, a nearby tribe, fight some of their wars for them. Slaves butcher their meat. Thomas More worries that the Utopians would lose their delicate affections and merciful sympathies if they did these deeds themselves. The Zapolets, we are assured, delight in slaughter and rapine, but there's no discussion of the impact of butchery on the slaves. No Utopia is Utopia for everyone.

Which brings us back to Lowell. He's worked for decades as a spy in the factory farms, the cosmetic and pharmaceutical labs. He's seen things we refuse to see, done things no one should have to do. He's sacrificed his family, his future, and now his freedom. He is not, as More would have wanted, the worst of men. Lowell's life has been the direct result of his very best qualities, of our very best qualities—empathy, compassion, loyalty, and love. That needs to be recognized.

It's true that, as my brother grew larger, he also grew danger-ous, same as my sister. But they're still ours and we want them back. They're needed here at home.

THE MIDDLE OF a story turns out to be a more arbitrary concept than I ever realized as a child. You can put it anywhere you like. So, too, the beginning and so, too, the end. Clearly, my story isn't finished yet, not the happening of it. It's just the telling that I'm done with here.

I'm going to end with something that happened quite some time ago. I'm going to end with the first time I saw my sister again after a separation of twenty-two years.

I can't tell you what I felt; no words are sufficient. You'd need to have been in my body to understand all that. But this is what we did.

Our mother had been visiting Fern for about two weeks by then. We'd decided not to overwhelm her with both of us at once, and so I'd waited. When Mom's reception was so chilly, I'd waited longer. A few days after Fern and our mother had begun to sign to each other, Mom told her I was coming.

I sent some items in ahead: my old penguin Dexter Poindexter, because she might remember him; a sweater I'd worn so often I thought it must smell of me; one red poker chip.

When I came in person, I brought a second red chip. I entered the visitors' room. Fern was sitting by the far wall, looking at a magazine. I knew her first only by her ears, higher on the head than most chimps' and rounder.

I stooped courteously over and walked to the glass between us. When I knew she was watching, I signed her name and then our sign for Rosemary. I pressed my palm, poker chip in the middle, against the bulletproof glass.

Fern stood heavily and came to me. She placed her own large hand opposite mine, fingers curling slightly, scratching, as if she could reach through and take the poker chip. I signed my name again with my free hand, and she signed it back with hers, though I couldn't tell if she'd remembered me or was simply being polite.

Then she rested her forehead on the glass. I did the same and we stood that way for a very long time, face-to-face. From that vantage point, I could see her only in teary, floating pieces—

her eyes

the flaring of her nostrils

the sparse hairs on her chin and rimming her ears

the tiny rise and fall of her rounded shoulders

the way her breath painted and unpainted the glass

I DIDN'T KNOW what she was thinking or feeling. Her body had become unfamiliar to me. And yet, at the very same time, I recognized everything about her. My sister, Fern. In the whole wide world, my only red poker chip. As if I were looking in a mirror.

ACKNOWLEDGMENTS

Many, many thanks are due here.

To Tatu, Dar, Loulis, and also the human animals at the Chimpanzee and Human Communication Institute in Ellensburg, Washington.

To the wonderful people at the Hedgebrook Retreat, the staff and also my fellow residents, all of whom gave me encouragement and space when I needed just those things, and most especially to the amazingly awesome Ruth Ozeki for her friendship and support.

To my beloved friends Pat Murphy and Ellen Klages, who showed me the way out of a corner into which I'd written myself.

To Megan Fitzgerald for some special Bloomingtonian research.

To the many readers who looked at bits and pieces for me— Alan Elms, Michael Blumlein, Richard Russo, Debbie Smith, Donald Kochis, Carter Scholz, Michael Berry, Sara Streich, Ben Orlove, Clinton Lawrence, Melissa Sanderself, Xander Cameron, Angus MacDonald.

To Micah Perks, Jill Wolfson, and Elizabeth McKenzie, who read the entire manuscript more than once and gave me much smart and helpful criticism.

ACKNOWLEDGMENTS

I am also very grateful to Dr. Carla Freccero for her readings and lectures on animal theory.

Heartfelt thanks to the late Wendy Weil and her associates at the Weil Agency, Emily Forland and Emma Patterson. And as always to the great Marian Wood.

But most of all, I owe this one to my daughter. She gave me the idea for this book one year as a New Year's gift and provided excellent feedback as I wrote it. She and my son both contributed useful information on what college in the mid-'90s had looked and sounded like to them, while my husband gave me his usual necessary and unstinting support.

KAREN JOY FOWLER ON WRITING
WE ARE ALL COMPLETELY BESIDE OURSELVES

IT SHAMES ME to admit that, at sixty-three years old, I still don't understand exactly what my father did for a living. He was a professor of psychology, but identified more strongly as a mathematician. His published work consisted mostly of equations strewn with bizarre symbols and, when actual words appeared, all too often, they looked something like this: "This case has an undampened oscillation of period 4 whose amplitude depends on the initial conditions" (from an essay on social interactions). I grew used to answering questions about what my father did thusly: "He's a psychologist," pause "not the way you're thinking." Every few years I pull out the book he co-wrote with Gustav Levine, *Mathematical Model Techniques of Learning Theories*, and every few years I put it away again, decide to take another run at *Finnegan's Wake* instead.

When I was a child, though, my father's professional life was clear to me. My father ran rats through mazes. I would visit him at work, walk through the aisles of cages, putting my fingers through the bars, and the rats would rush to them, noses and whiskers ticking from side to side. Sometimes a rat would come home, live in my bedroom for a while. I think that few people can get the nostalgic hit that I do off the smell of rat cages.

There was one corner of the lab I was told to stay out of and this corner was where the monkeys lived. The monkeys – I think they were rhesus monkeys – were kept one to a cage, and screamed if you headed in their direction. Get too close and they would grab and bite you. They were, or so it seemed to me, mad in both senses of that word – terribly angry and completely insane. To this day, I have no idea what was being done to them, but I remember being glad my father was not the one doing it. It was easier to pretend that the rats were contented. I've spent my life haunted by the misery of those monkeys.

So my experience with animals in my early years was confusing. I think it must be confusing for all children, all the little carnivores like me, reading *Charlotte's Web* and *Wind in the Willows* and other books in which animals wear clothes and have tender feelings and philosophical discussions and hope not to be eaten.

In my family, we had a house full of beloved pets and a lab full of research subjects. At dinner when we talked about rats, as we often did, the conversation was all about their intelligence, how they learned. My older brother planned (but never did) a science fair project in which he taught a rat to play basketball, because this was Indiana and basketball must be wedged in wherever it might fit. Yet our neighbor dealt with the rats in his basement by poisoning them all, killing my little dog Snippet and some of the neighborhood cats at the same time.

My father was an enthusiastic, if incompetent, hunter and a passionate and expert fly-fisherman. He could rhapsodize one day about the awe-inspiring navigational skills of the great migrating birds and a day later, get up at 4am to head to the woods with his rifle, try to pick off one on the wing. He was my unsentimental guide to the natural world. He taught me the names of plants and birds and star clusters. He taught me to see myself as one animal among many. He died when he was fifty-five years old and I was twenty-two.

Though none of his grandchildren ever met him, I see bits of him scattered all through them. My nephew has his love of the outdoors, my niece his mathematical gifts. My son has his tennis skills and his love of a good, dispassionate theoretical argument. And my daughter, also a great outdoorswoman, has a doctorate in marine biology and did her dissertation on the way Australian sea lion pups learn to dive.

For the millennial New Year, she and her boyfriend took me back to my childhood home in Indiana. My husband had to stay behind in California. He worked at the Sacramento utility company and had to be at his post at midnight in case the world ended. Y2K. You remember. So while he was there, keeping us safe, we were off in Indianapolis, celebrating Hoosier-style – a Pacers' game, a John Mellencamp concert, dancing until dawn at the Slippery Noodle blues club.

The next day we drove to Bloomington to visit my old next-door neighbors. We went to the university campus so that I could show my daughter the building where the rat lab had been. Afterwards I told her about the experiment done at I.U. by psychologist Winthrop Kellogg, a famous study in which he and his wife raised a chimpanzee alongside their infant son. I told the story the way it had always been told to me, with an emphasis on the findings – that chimps develop much more rapidly than children, but that at about sixteen months, the children begin to make up ground. My scientist daughter brushed that finding aside. "What would it be like," she asked me, "to have been the child in that experiment? You should write that book."

I may not have many good ideas myself, but I recognize one when I hear it. Initially I was very nervous about all the things I didn't know regarding chimpanzees. Fortunately, there are any number of books written by the people involved in these studies. I did my best to read them all. Meanwhile, I consoled myself that I knew exactly what it was like to be raised by psychologists. I wouldn't have to make that part up at all.

TOPICS FOR READING GROUP DISCUSSIONS

"Start in the middle," Rosemary's father says at the beginning of the book. How does the order that Rosemary tells her story affect how we get to know her?

It's not until page 77 that we discover Rosemary's sister Fern is a chimpanzee. Rosemary's keen to control the way the reader is introduced to certain ideas, in this case so that she can establish Fern as her sister and not an animal. Did that work for you? And how do these deliberate omissions relate to those things Rosemary can't bring herself to remember, such as the reason for Fern being sent away?

There are hints to Fern's true nature in the book before you're told: did you sense there was something different about her?

"An oft-told story is like a photograph in an album; eventually, it replaces the moment it was meant to capture." How we experience the past is central to the book. Rosemary's memories of her childhood are sometimes sharp, and sometimes cloudy. Many of her memories rely on her senses. And often we are aware that how she remembers experiencing something isn't necessarily the way it actually happened. How true to your own experience does the presentation of memory seem?

Rosemary combines being fiercely intellectually engaged and engaging with being – she says – a lazy scholar. She says, "To this day, the Socratic method makes me want to bite someone." How does Rosemary's intellect relate to the structured academic environment she was raised in?

"My father made a crude joke ... If the joke were witty, I'd include it, but it wasn't. You'd think less of him and thinking less of him is my job, not yours." How do these moments where Rosemary is talking straight to the reader affect our relationship to her and to her family?

Rosemary says more than once that unfairness bothers children and chimps greatly. Do you agree?

Many people will have known that Fern is a chimpanzee before beginning the book. Some people say this makes it more compelling, others wish they hadn't known. There is a study that suggests that knowing the end – or the middle – of a plot doesn't actually decrease our enjoyment of it. What do you think, does knowing a plot detail spoil the story or enhance it?

Does the ending mean Rosemary has atoned for her earlier sins? Did she need to?

"Maybe it was useful, when plotting books, to imagine that someone's life could be shaped by a single early trauma, maybe even one inaccessible in memory. But where were the blind studies, the control groups? The reproducible data?" To what extent does this book reject scientific ideas in favour of emotion and lived experience?

"This, then, is the me I know – the human half of the fabulous, the fascinating, the phantasmagorical Cooke sisters." To what extent does Rosemary still define herself against, and alongside, Fern? And what exactly is it that makes them different? Using tools and language have both been suggested as the line between being a human and an animal, but we now know that some animals use tools and language too. So what are the qualities that distinguish Fern and Rosemary?

"It's hard to overstate how lonely I was. Let me just repeat that I'd once gone, in a matter of days, from a childhood where I was never alone to this prolonged, silent only-ness." When Rosemary meets Harlow, she finds her fascinating, despite knowing intuitively that she's untrustworthy. What is it about Harlow that Rosemary finds so irresistible?

"It seemed to Lowell that psychological studies of non-human animals were mostly cumbersome, convoluted, and downright peculiar. They taught us little about the animals but lots about the researchers who designed and ran them ... 'We need a sort of reverse mirror text. Some way to identify those species smart enough to see themselves when they look at someone else.'" How does this idea relate to the characters in the book?

"I've tried so hard to rescue her. Years and years of trying and what does Fern have to show for it? What a miserable excuse for a brother I turned out to be." How do feelings of responsibility colour the Cooke family's interactions with each other?

"'The world runs,' Lowell said, 'on the fuel of this endless, fathomless misery. People know it, but they don't mind what they don't see. Make them look and they mind, but you're the one they hate, because you're the one that made them look.'" Has reading this book changed the way you feel about animals and humans? In what context?

The non-human rights movement, which seeks legal rights for great apes, cetaceans, and elephants, is rapidly expanding. In India, dolphins have been awarded non-human personhood status, and keeping them for entertainment is banned. Others argue they should be granted rights as "living property", thus protecting their best interests but not bestowing independent rights. What legal status do you believe animals should have? Should it vary according to the relative intelligence of a species? Should animals that are demonstrably self-aware, such as chimps, be granted the right to life and freedom from captivity?

"It's hard enough here to forgive myself for the things I did and felt when I was five, hopeless for the way I behaved at fifteen. Lowell heard that Fern was in a cage in South Dakota and he took off that very night. I heard the same thing and my response was to pretend I hadn't heard it." In the book, Lowell takes action and Rosemary finds herself paralysed. How does this relate to the themes of scientific experiment vs lived experience?

"The Davis primate center is today credited with significant advances in our understanding and treatment of SIV, Alzheimer's, autism, and Parkinson's. Nobody's arguing these issues are easy." If you draw a line between useful and not-useful animal experiment, where do you place it?

"So the studies don't back me up. There'll always be more studies. We'll change our minds and I'll have been right all along until we change our minds again, send me back to being wrong." Is this a fair description of the scientific process?

"Next time, I'll put things right between my father and me. Next time, I'll give Mom the fair share of blame for Fern ... Next time, I'll take the share that's mine, no more, no less." How does Rosemary's wish to relive and correct the past reflect her acceptance of what really happened?

Rosemary's mother says to her, "I wanted you to have an extraordinary life." To what extent is that a legitimate desire of a parent for a child? To what extent is it fair to a child to enact it? Is the choice that Rosemary's parents made for her, to give her a chimp sister, acceptable?

When Lowell is arrested, Rosemary says, "I've read that since his arrest he hasn't said a single word. Everyone else is mystified by this silence, but his reasons couldn't be more obvious to me. He was halfway there when I last saw him sixteen years ago. Lowell has decided to be tried as an animal. The non-human kind." Does this best serve Lowell's purpose and that of the animals he has always sought to defend?

"Lowell's life has been the direct result of his very best qualities, of our very best qualities – empathy, compassion, loyalty, and love." Bearing in mind that Lowell's organization promises not to harm humans or animals, though he is said to have set fire to property amongst other things, is this a fair description of his activity?

MORE INFORMATION AND FURTHER READING

PROJECT NIM

A book and film about Nim Chimpsky, a chimp at the centre of a research project that was mounted to determine whether a primate raised in close contact with humans could develop a limited "language" based on American Sign Language.

http://www.project-nim.com/

Nim Chimpsky, The Chimp Who Would Be Human by Elizabeth Hess

THE GREAT APE PROJECT

The Great Ape Project is an idea, a book, and an organization hoping to include the non-human great apes within the community of equals by granting them the basic moral and legal protection that only human beings currently enjoy.

http://www.greatapetrust.org/

IOWA PRIMATE LEARNING

Bonobo Hope at the Iowa Primate Learning Sanctuary is a non-invasive, interdisciplinary and interspecies scientific research facility in Iowa, with special focus directed to areas of language, the creation and implementation of tools, musical and artistic creativity, and intelligence, all of which help answer the foundational question, "What makes us human?"

http://www.iowaprimatelearning.org/

PRIMATE COGNITION LAB, COLUMBIA, HERBERT TERRACE

The Primate Cognition Laboratory researches the cognitive abilities of non-human primates: their ability to learn lists of pictures and numerical stimuli and to evaluate their own performance on various tasks. Most remarkable is that they can engage in these cognitive activities without the help of language.

http://www.columbia.edu/cu/psychology/primatecognitionlab/

WASHOE EXPERIMENT

Washoe (1965 –2007) was a female common chimpanzee who was the first non-human to learn to communicate using American Sign Language, as part of a research experiment on animal-language acquisition by Allen and Beatrix Gardner.

See also Friends of Washoe, a non-profit organization, dedicated to the welfare of chimpanzees and especially the chimpanzees at the Chimpanzee and Human Communication Institute.

http://en.wikipedia.org/wiki/Washoe_%28chimpanzee%29
http://www.friendsofwashoe.org/learn/about_fow_chci.html
http://www.cwu.edu/chci/

THE MIND OF AN APE BY DAVID AND ANN JAMES PREMACK
A 1983 account of the authors' work teaching chimpanzees to use a symbolic language – addresses questions of language, thought, intention, and understanding in chimps.

KANZI: AN APE OF GENIUS
The 1993 documentary, *Kanzi: An Ape of Genius* shows the research and life of Kanzi, a bonobo chimpanzee, and Dr Sue Savage-Rumbaugh at the Georgia State University Language Research Center in Atlanta, GA.
http://kanzi.bvu.edu/

KOKO, A TALKING GORILLA
Koko: A Talking Gorilla is a 1978 documentary directed by Barbet Schroeder that focuses on Dr Francine "Penny" Patterson and her work with Koko, the gorilla Patterson claims to have taught to communicate with humans using symbols taken from American Sign Language.
http://www.imdb.com/title/tt0076097/

MAX PLANCK INSTITUTE FOR EVOLUTIONARY ANTHROPOLOGY
The Max Planck Institute for Evolutionary Anthropology unites scientists with various backgrounds (natural sciences and humanities) whose aim is to investigate the history of humankind from an inter-disciplinary perspective with the help of comparative analyses of genes, cultures, cognitive abilities, languages and social systems of past and present human populations as well as those of primates closely related to human beings.
http://www.eva.mpg.de/

ON APES IN THE WILD

Richard Wrangham

Scientists have been bringing chimpanzees into their homes for at least a century. In 1913 the Kohts family of Moscow began a four-year experiment in which they treated an infant chimpanzee called Joni as if he was a brother of their same-aged son, Roody. Nadia Ladygina-Kohts was a psychologist, and her husband Alexander Kohts was Director of the State Darwin Museum.

In those days animals were generally assumed to have mental lives that shared nothing with humans, but Nadia Kohts came to think otherwise. Psychologist Frans de Waal edited an English translation of her book about Joni. He wrote that Nadia "opened her heart and eyes to every nuance of sensitivity, emotion, and intelligence in Joni. She didn't see him as a robot, devoid of thoughts and feelings, as the behaviorists would have wanted, but as a living being, not all that different from humans."*

Intimate appreciation of a chimpanzee's internal life was the great benefit of living together as a family, and it helped build the

---

* FBM de Waal (2002). *The Chronicle of Higher Education*, 49 (15): B11

idea of chimpanzees as a bridge between humans and other animals. Only after experiencing human culture have chimpanzees learned hundreds of word-symbols, used pointing as a regular way to communicate, or shown a frequent interest in helping non-relatives solve problems. But the costs were huge. The subjects of the home-rearing experiments were traumatized babies and young accommodating to the loss of their mothers by making do with human foster-parents. All died unhappily after being exiled from their human families as juveniles for being too dangerous. Only recently have sanctuaries been developed that allow captive chimpanzees to live with their peers without invasive experiments.

In 1960 Jane Goodall launched a different approach to understanding apes. Instead of taking an orphan chimpanzee into her home she entered softly into theirs. As she watched chimpanzees from dawn to dusk, their way of life came into focus for the first time. Personalities were as strong as Fern's. The network of wild adults and young was rife with evidence of mental complexity, and the apes had a powerful reporter. Goodall "opened her heart and eyes to every nuance of sensitivity, emotion, and intelligence" in the Gombe community. She portrayed their world like a painter filling an empty canvas.

Five decades later, our understanding of wild chimpanzees comes from a dozen or more research sites and grows richer and more complex all the time. The emotional tone of ordinary life is wildly unpredictable. Many days are quiet, structured by the simple needs of walking to the next food patch, eating and resting. These are the times when, on a warm afternoon, a Fern-aged juvenile might be found idly playing with her mother's foot, while her mother lies on the warm ground with her eyes closed, resting her full stomach, wriggling her toes just enough to amuse her daughter. While the cicadas buzz and a tinkerbird softly chirps in the distance, while other mothers snooze and males groom each other, and the wind intermittently rustles the canopy, two older juveniles might be gently disturbing the peace by chasing each other slowly through low bushes. The only member of the group still feeding has been pushing a grass stem into a hole in a termite-mound, and carefully removing it: soldiers cling to the stem with their jaws, until bitten off and chewed. A few yards away, if we are lucky, we might be surprised to see a young one toying with a rock, walking a few steps while she balances it uncertainly on her back, or takes it into her day nest and lies with the rock on her belly, like a doll. So the day can go on, glimpses of ingenuity and imagination occasionally punctuating the relaxing, moving, eating and relaxing.

On other days social tensions carve out obvious avoidances and nervous looks followed by repeated charges and chases, screams, and in the end, some making-up by careful approaches that can include hugs and kisses. Grudges can apparently be held for days: remembered slights seem to explain at least some of the conflicts that are unprovoked by any immediate competition. More often the reasons are obvious. A young one loses her temper when the play gets too rough, mothers intervene to help their children, and suddenly adults are chasing each other. Adult males vie endlessly for status. Those of higher rank who do not receive appropriate signals of subordinacy are quick to charge at their subordinates, just as those of lower rank try to exploit perceived weaknesses in their elders. Sometimes there is competition for choice foods, or over mating rights. Rambunctious days can end in hurt feelings, bleeding limbs and very occasionally worse: every community watched for a decade or more has been seen to have a death caused by other chimpanzees.

The wild is not easy. Chimpanzees experience the hostile forces of nature as much as any other species. Disease, hunger and miserable, cold rainy seasons can be so harsh that one might wonder if it would be preferable to live in captivity. But chimpanzees are social beings; they are not domesticated animals and they are not humans. In the least disturbed sites adults can expect to live almost forty years. They can be alone when they want but mostly they spend their time with close relatives and long-term friends. They might have tantrums when their mother denies them the comfort of nursing or a friend refuses a request for meat, but eventually they patch up after conflicts. They can console each other after fights, come to the aid of allies, and give rumbling belly laughs as, with deliberate slowness, they chase each other around tree trunks, trying to swat each other's behinds. They have their own triumphs and joys, and no one tells them what to do or where to sleep or what they are allowed to eat.

Nadia Kohts was a sympathetic pioneer who understood that Joni had a thoughtful mind and deep emotions. But when he died young, the Kohts had his body stuffed. In the end, he was not sufficiently human-like to be treated like a human. He was an experiment. But if Joni was an experiment he was also a chimpanzee, and it was his misfortune that, like thousands of others, he spent his short life in a human environment.

That was Joni's tragedy. It represents a past when science had ethical standards lower than we like them to be today. Alas, it might also represent the future for all apes. The tropical forests are falling so fast that human environments may soon be the only places left for chimpanzees, bonobos, gorillas and orangutans.

Our wild, wonderful relatives are still out there for now, in their own environments. That is where they should be.

Richard Wrangham is Ruth B. Moore Professor of Biological Anthropology at Harvard University.